Veronica Stallwood was born in London, educated abroad and now lives near Oxford. In the past she has worked at the Bodleian Library and in New College library. Her first crime novel, *Deathspell*, was published to great critical acclaim, as were the ten Oxford novels which followed, all of which feature Kate Ivory, and her atmospheric suspense novel, *The Rainbow Sign*.

When she is not writing, Veronica Stallwood enjoys going for long walks, talking and eating with friends, and gazing out at the peaceful Oxfordshire countryside from the windows of her cottage.

Praise for Veronica Stallwood:

'Stallwood's speciality is adroit plotting set in a vividly realised Oxford locale, and this is vintage stuff' *The Times*

'One of the cleverest of the year's crop [with] a flesh-and-brains heroine' *Observer*

'Some Rendell-like skewed psychology . . . an evident gift for characterisation' William Weaver, *Financial Times*

'Not only plausible but in my view, absolutely compelling' Gerald Kaufman, *Scotsman*

'Dreaming spires updated, a fetching, formidably erudite heroine matching minds with an egomaniac? Sayers would give it the nod' *Good Book Guide*

'Stallwood is in the top rank of crime writers, and can produce shivers even in a heatwave' *Daily Telegraph*

'A deceptive and atmospheric tale' *Time Out*

'The author has produced another cracking read, packed with plausible charac‌‍   ‍dark undertones' *South*

'A cleverly draw   ‍ies'
Coventry Evening

D1316862

Also by Veronica Stallwood

Deathspell
The Rainbow Sign

Kate Ivory Mysteries

Death and the Oxford Box
Oxford Exit
Oxford Mourning
Oxford Knot
Oxford Blue
Oxford Shift
Oxford Shadows
Oxford Double
Oxford Proof
Oxford Remains

Oxford Fall

Veronica Stallwood

headline

Copyright © 1996 Veronica Stallwood

The right of Veronica Stallwood to be identified as the Author of
the Work has been asserted by her in accordance with
the Copyright, Designs and Patents Act 1988.

First published in 1996
by Macmillan London Limited

First published in paperback in 1996
by HEADLINE BOOK PUBLISHING

This paperback edition published in 2005
by HEADLINE BOOK PUBLISHING

6

Apart from any use permitted under UK copyright law,
this publication may only be reproduced, stored, or transmitted,
in any form, or by any means, with prior permission in writing
of the publishers or, in the case of reprographic production,
in accordance with the terms of licences issued by the
Copyright Licensing Agency.

All characters in this publication are fictitious and any resemblance
to real persons, living or dead, is purely coincidental.

ISBN 978-0-7472-5513-0

Typeset in Times by Avon DataSet Ltd,
Bidford-on-Avon, Warwickshire

Printed and bound in Great Britain by
Clays Ltd, St Ives plc

Headline's policy is to use papers that are natural, renewable and
recyclable products and made from wood grown in sustainable
forests. The logging and manufacturing processes are expected to
conform to the environmental regulations of the country of origin.

HEADLINE BOOK PUBLISHING
A division of Hodder Headline
338 Euston Road
London NW1 3BH

www.headline.co.uk
www.hodderheadline.com

For Carlo, with love
For all the years of friendship

ACKNOWLEDGEMENTS

With thanks for their encouragement and help to Kate Charles, Bill Clennell, Glenys Davies, Hugh Griffith, Robert McNeil, Susan Moody, Annabel Stogdon, Cathy and Peter Wilcox, and Jeremy Wilson.

Chapter One

Cut is the branch that might have grown full straight,
And burned is Apollo's laurel bough,
That sometime grew within this learnèd man.
                    Christopher Marlowe, *Doctor Faustus*

'Theology.'

'Hello, is that the Theology Section of the Bodleian Library?'

'Yes, that's what I said. Theology.' The voice had a hollow ring to it, as though speaking from the depths of a hall with a high, painted ceiling and a floor glossy with beeswax, where one might expect to hear monkish voices chanting a *Veni Creator* in the background. But then, the librarian would long since have asked singers, whether monachal or profane, to desist or leave.

'Could I speak to Andrew Grove, please?'

'I'm sorry, but Mr Grove is in California for the next ten days.'

'Bother.' There was something about a voice announcing itself as Theology that prevented Kate Ivory from expressing herself in her usual forthright terms.

'May I ask who is speaking?' continued Theology.

'Kate Ivory. I'm a friend of his. I'm the one who writes novels.'

'Ah. Yes. I believe I've heard of you. You're also the one who drinks pinot blanc in the wine bar, aren't you? Perhaps I could help you instead.' In the background,

1

sober shoes clacked across floorboards, and a bell chimed for attention.

'I doubt it,' said Kate. 'Unless you've got a simple, well-paid job that I could do for the next few weeks. A nice safe job, with no possibility of danger.'

'I know of no openings in the Theology department for a historical novelist at present, I'm afraid. But I'm sure the Library's Assistant Secretary could be of greater help to you in the matter of employment than I. And I do believe that most of the Library's posts are as safe as the Health and Safety Regulations can make them.'

'That's all you know,' said Kate Ivory, whose experience of library work had been full of unexpected, and sometimes life-threatening, incident. She did not, however, feel like explaining any of this to anyone as pompous as the Theology librarian.

'Why don't I give you the extension number of the Assistant Secretary?' And having done so, the Voice of Theology replaced its receiver, doubtless to turn its attention to a more deserving object.

Kate dutifully wrote down the number, frowned at it for a moment as she mulled over her previous temporary assignments in Oxford's libraries, then crushed the paper into a ball and lobbed it into her wastepaper basket.

How thoughtless of her librarian friend Andrew to be abroad when she needed him! Of course she should have known that he was going to be away. But somehow, when he got on to the subject of conferences, she found herself nodding and saying, 'Yes, Andrew,' occasionally, and pouring herself another glass of pinot blanc, and mentally rewriting the opening of her next chapter, while Andrew monologued on about co-operative cataloguing schemes. She had heard rumours that there was much tiptoeing along hotel corridors after midnight, but could not believe that such respectable people as librarians would ever behave like that.

But meanwhile here she was, with a book due to be published in a month's time and every penny of her advance already accounted for. Her latest manuscript was sitting on her agent's desk waiting for his opinion, and four long months remained until her next royalty cheque turned up. She needed money. Not a lot. Just the sort of money that meant that she could eat, and keep her car on the road, and sometimes fill its tank with petrol. Her workroom could do with a coat of paint, and there was a chair upstairs that needed re-covering, but those could wait; food couldn't. She turned back to her address book and looked through the pages. She dialled again, twice, but struck a couple of blanks. She dialled a third number.

'Hello.' The voice at the other end of the phone sounded engrossed in its own concerns.

'Emma? Kate here.' There was no response, so Kate added, 'Kate Ivory. The writer. The one who took over your creative writing class for you last year while you were having the baby.'

'Yes, I know which Kate. How could I forget! And just look what happened to my class while you were in charge! It's never been the same again. The friendly spirit, the camaraderie, have quite gone.'

'Well, it was hardly my fault, was it?'

'I'm not sure about that. Wherever you go disaster seems to follow. What is it you want, by the way?'

'You know you're on the committee of this conference thing.'

'Yes, I do know. And it's not a conference thing, it's a study fortnight on "The Effect of Gender on Genre", to be held at Bartlemas College, and which has attracted large numbers of highly educated Americans, all willing to pay enormous sums of money to live in elegant discomfort and hear what I and my fellow tutors have to tell them about crime fiction, and romantic novels and SF and so on.'

There was a pause at Kate's end of the phone while she digested this. Then she tried another tack. 'How are the children, Emma? Little . . . er . . . must be quite a handful by now. Not to mention all the others.' She realized that she should have taken more notice when Emma mentioned the names of her children, especially the latest addition. How many had she got? Four? Five? Some extraordinary number, anyway. She aimed for a more sympathetic tone. 'It must be quite tricky for you, running a house, bringing up your children, writing your books, and organizing a study fortnight as well.' She pushed from her mind the picture of the tip that was Emma's house, the tottering pile of dog-eared folders that she called a filing system, and her unruly rabble of cheerful but neglected children.

'Do I gather that you're looking for work?'

'Well . . .'

'If you wanted to take part in the study fortnight you should have registered when I first told you about it. All the tutors have already been engaged, and the panels are full. College is providing the administrative back-up, and the committee gets expenses only. I can't even offer you any typing. I'm sorry, Kate, really I am, but if it's money you need I'm afraid I can't help you this time.'

'Oh, well, I expect I'll find something soon.' Very soon, if she was to continue to eat regularly.

'Why don't you try your friend at the Bodleian? He's always helped you out in the past, hasn't he?'

'He's away at the moment, but I'll ask him when he gets back.'

'Good luck,' said Emma, then, as though regretting her unhelpfulness, she added, 'Why don't you come round to supper one evening next week? I'm sure Sam and the children would love to see you.'

Soup kitchen, thought Kate. I'm being offered nourishing meals in place of gainful employment. 'Sorry, Emma,' she said. 'I'm really booked up at the moment.'

'Oh well, if you change your mind just give me another ring.'

Most of Bartlemas College, in the University of Oxford, was built in the eighteenth century, when insanitary medieval buildings were razed to the ground on the orders of a progressive Governing Body and replaced by airy, well-proportioned quadrangles, open on their fourth side. Only the Hall, the kitchens, a rather austere seventeenth-century chapel and its fifteenth-century tower remained of the original buildings. By the standards of the people who would be arriving for Emma's study fortnight, it was indeed inconvenient as to bathrooms, and uncomfortable as to beds. But it was considered to be one of the most beautiful of the newer colleges, and its Fellows' Garden, redesigned by a follower of Gertrude Jekyll, was much admired. And what was more relevant to the needs of the visitors, the Bartlemas chef had been poached from one of the best London hotels, and his desserts were the envy of High Tables throughout the university.

One afternoon in spring, some months before Kate's conversation with Emma, in a room whose tall windows overlooked Pesant Quad, two people were talking.

'How much do you get in during an average morning?' The enquiry sounded casual, but its recipient was not deceived.

'We'd consider it an unlucky session if we made less than thirty or forty.'

'Pounds?' The questioner sounded disappointed.

'Thousands. Of pounds, that is.'

'Ah.'

The questioner turned away from the room and looked out of the window, feigning indifference to the subject. The glass was old and had distorted over the centuries so that the view outside wavered as though seen through the green water of a brook. Behind the glass, a group of undergraduates undulated across the central lawn. Opposite, at the junction of two sides of the quadrangle, the eighteenth-century architect (James Gibbs, some said, but without foundation) had incorporated an earlier tower, tall and square, surmounted by crocketed pinnacles, and built in a soft golden stone that soaked up the afternoon sunlight. Two or three people stood on its roof, pointing at the surrounding landmarks, their voices sounding at this distance like the twittering of birds.

'The Tower of Grace,' said the second speaker, who had moved to look over the other's shoulder. 'It ruins the symmetry of Pesant Quad, which must have hurt the builders' classical sensibilities, but I'm glad they left it standing for us to enjoy.'

'Why "Grace", do you suppose? Was it named after a woman? Surely not!'

'We imagine, in our modern way, that people in past ages must have cared less for their wives and children than we do. With death and demons around every corner, surely they held life cheap? And how could you love a small baby, or even its mother, knowing that they could be taken from you at any moment, by disease, or accident, or the ignorance of your physician?'

'But you're going to tell me that it wasn't so?'

'The evidence is in letters in the college archive, stored in a dull grey box in the muniments room.'

The first speaker sighed, wishing to move on to a more modern subject. 'And?'

'The letters tell of a wealthy merchant whose sons came to study at Bartlemas College, or rather its predecessor on this site, St Anselm's Hall. His first wife having died, this merchant had married a second, much younger woman. But she was slight of build and fragile of constitution, and when she was expecting his child the doctors feared for her survival, and that of the baby.'

'So he promised to build the tower in exchange for their safety?'

'Not quite. He asked the Brothers to pray for his wife and unborn child, certainly, and we know from the records that this was done. But the young woman died anyway, and her baby with her. And he grieved so much for them that he gave all his fortune to build the tower, and named it after his dead wife.'

'Grace?'

'Her name was Gráinne, but they translated it as Grace.'

'And he died of a broken heart as the last stone was placed in position?'

'I believe not. There is evidence that he married again – a more robust woman this time, it appears – had four more children, and remade the fortune that he had given away.'

'I'm not sure that I understand the moral of your story.'

'Were we talking of morals?' The speaker was smiling now. 'I thought the subject was money.'

'Which brings us back to the grateful old members of College who are providing the substantial sums of money that are needed today.'

'Why? Do you have a project in mind that you want the Development Fund to finance for you?'

'Perhaps. I have an idea I'd like to discuss with you, certainly.'

'I'll need something in writing, and five copies, so that the committee can take a look at it.'

'I was thinking of an informal approach. Just between the two of us.'

'You make it sound like a conspiracy.'

'Oh, I think a plan needs more than two people involved to qualify as a conspiracy, don't you?'

'Shall I pour you some more coffee?'

'Thank you.'

'Those windows have Gibbs surrounds, you notice.'

'But, like so many others, were probably not designed by Gibbs himself. So many things are called one thing but are in fact something quite other. And as you have no doubt remarked, not everything in this college is what it seems.'

The undergraduates had left the quad; the visitors were descending from the roof of the tower. It was so silent that the two speakers might have been alone in the college.

'Perhaps you'd better tell me what this is all about.'

It had been one of those rare English summers where the sun shines down relentlessly from a blue sky, day after day, the humidity builds up every evening, and people long for a thunderstorm to clear the air. Hosepipe and sprinkler bans had turned green lawns to brown stubble. In the parched gardens flowers bloomed, blossomed and faded, then formed their seedheads, all faster than normal. The harvest was in a fortnight early, and now, in the second half of August, the countryside had a golden, autumnal look to it. In such conditions, even the most placid of natures can snarl and snap, and shout abuse at their partners and loved ones, as can be heard in the following telephone conversation:

'What do you mean, you want to get out?'

'Just what I say, Chris. I've had enough of it.'

8

'You can't. I won't let you.' There is the sound of a fist thudding on to a desk.

'I'm not arguing with you on the phone.'

'Where, then?' This is delivered in a near shout.

'I'll see you at lunchtime, as we arranged. We can talk then.'

'Goodbye.' The receiver crashes back into its holder.

'Goodbye, Chris.'

After her conversation with Emma, Kate Ivory decided to work off her disappointment by walking into the centre of Oxford to look for a new notebook. There was something soothing to the spirit, she found, in spending money on things that were not entirely necessary. And she had been a stationery junkie since childhood. While other children had whined at their mothers for lollipops, she had coveted coloured pencils and brand-new notebooks.

It was still oppressively hot, and she dressed in a short sleeveless dress with a scooped neck, which had been dip-dyed in shades from aqua to peacock. She fluffed up her newly blonded hair, hooked a pair of light-catching titanium ear-rings into her ears, and pushed her bare brown feet into Italian leather sandals.

If no one would employ her she would get on with making notes for her next book, and for that she needed a new notebook. It was her superstition, her lucky mascot. And it couldn't be any old notebook from a cut-price stationer's; no, she had to tour the shops that sold decorative objects to rich tourists and find something that appealed to her imagination. Then she could start writing, in longhand, using a proper fountain pen, amassing notes on her chosen theme until the glimmerings of a novel emerged. When she was feeling well off, she bought herself a new fountain pen as well. But she had to admit today that her collection of five matt black, gold-nibbed pens was probably extensive enough for even the most prolific writer. But then, she argued, some women spent their lives looking for the perfect scarlet lipstick. Why shouldn't she continue her search for the ultimate fantasy writing instrument, the one that would mould to her grip and produce saleable words by the thousand, with no effort on her own part?

Outside her house she saw Harley, stubble-haired eldest of her neighbours' children, sitting on the low wall outside number 12, kicking his feet against the brickwork with no thought for the finish on his expensive trainers. She had managed to keep on reasonable terms with her neighbours, in spite of the noise they made and the fact that they owned an unprepossessing toddler that she could think of only as Toadface.

'What's up, Harley?' she asked. Harley had helped her out the previous year, improving her rotten driving skills with some tricks he had picked up from his joy-riding mates.

'Nothing,' he answered. Maybe it was just that the end of the school holidays were approaching. She didn't think Harley had much enthusiasm for academic work.

Before walking down the street towards the city centre, she asked him: 'By the way, Harley, I've often wondered, what's your surname?'

'You what? You've lived next door for four years, you must know our name.'

She couldn't tell him that she thought of them always as the Toadface family. She shook her head.

'It's Venn,' he said. 'Like the diagram.'

Not Toadface, then. She felt she had taken a step forward in their relationship.

'See you,' she said, and set off down the street, wondering briefly what diagram he was referring to. Harley's head drooped down towards his chest, and his heels kicked listlessly at the wall.

In the sultry August weather tempers are still fraying. All over Oxford the telephone wires are quivering as repressed emotions are let loose by the high temperatures and oppressive humidity.

'But listen to me, Chris! Don't you understand how trapped I've become? You must know how I feel. I'm walking down a narrow path, fenced in on both sides, and it's leading straight towards a cliff edge.'

'No. That's just ridiculous.'

'Can't we talk it over? Work something out?'

'You think it's my fault?'

'I'm not blaming you, Chris.'

'Oh, but I think you are.'

'Don't sigh at me like that. I know you, you're going to put the phone down on me, aren't you? You've got to listen. We've got to do something. We have to make some changes. It can't go on like this.'

'Oh, really! You exaggerate everything. You're just being hysterical.'

'I'm warning you, I can't take it any more.'

'Just calm down, won't you? Go and make yourself a nice cup of coffee or something.'

'Don't patronize me! I'll meet you for lunch and we'll talk things over then.'

'Sorry, I can't make lunch. I've got an appointment, I'm afraid.'

'Who with? Why can't I come too?'

'I'm meeting the surveyor. It will be horribly dull. You'd hate it. And we have to talk business, there'll be no time for any personal stuff, believe me.'

'This evening, then?'

'Yes, sure. Of course.'

'I'll see you.'

'See you. Goodbye.'

He feels quite happy about the way he has handled it. Another problem put off for another day, he thinks.

Unfortunately, he is wrong. After this one, there will be no more days for him, ever.

Kate walked through the Covered Market, stopping to buy a pound of apples from a fruit stall, then sauntered down the Turl, turning heads as she passed. She paused to inspect every hardbacked notebook in the city. She found one that was pretty enough, but the wrong size; one that was the right size, with thick shiny paper, but no lines. She went on down the High, towards Magdalen Bridge. Still nothing that caught her fancy. You're wasting a perfectly good working day, she told herself, but the sky was blue, the sun was warm, and it felt good to be idling her time away for a change.

Just before she reached Magdalen Bridge, she crossed the road. On the south side of the High she stopped outside the window of another stationer's shop. The pavement here was narrow and she was continually jostled by people waiting to cross the road, or pushing past her towards the city centre.

Tourists, festooned with cameras, intent on capturing a famous Oxford view, trod all over her feet. Kate ignored them, for she had spotted a blue notebook with golden suns and moons on the cover. Teenagers shouted in her ears and thumped into her with backpacks. Behind her, a frustrated motorist blared his horn at a cluster of cyclists. An aggressive young woman in combat boots strode between her and the plate glass window. 'Sorry,' said Kate, ear-rings jangling as she moved. She wondered if she didn't prefer the notebook with scarlet poppies and a black cat. A couple of middle-aged men in tweed jackets and black gowns, deep in conversation, threaded their way expertly past, avoiding the throng of noisy Italian teenagers. Diesel fumes hung in blue clouds over them all.

'Sorry,' said Kate again, as yet another passer-by stepped on her foot.

'My fault,' came the unexpected reply.

Kate looked up from the window, where she was inspecting an unusually beautiful matt black fountain pen with a gold wraparound nib. For a moment she was distracted from the display by the man who had paused next to her and seemed concerned about the condition of her foot. 'Greek god' was the phrase that dropped into her mind when she looked at him. Really, he was extraordinarily good-looking. A long, thin face with high cheekbones and black eyebrows. Intelligent, but not an intellectual, she judged. Slate-blue shirt, darker green tie, grey linen jacket. He would look just right sitting on her velvet sofa, but at such short notice she could invent no excuse to transport him there.

'I'm fine, I think,' she said, gazing into his dark blue eyes and wishing she had told him a large fib about how she was nearly crippled with the pain and needed an urgent whisky to cure it. 'There's no damage at all,' she said, rubbing her left ankle against her right foot and taking in his thick brown hair, firm jawline and healthy tan. 'And I don't think it will hurt for long,' she said in response to his heartwarming smile. 'But it was kind of you to notice,' she said, regretfully, to his broad shoulders and straight back as they retreated up the High. She watched him walk towards Carfax for a few dozen yards before he turned left into a cobbled side street and disappeared from her view. Bartlemas Row, thought Kate. I wonder if he's from the College. I wonder whether Emma knows him. Maybe he's unattached and maybe she could introduce us. Then she sighed, acknowledging that life was rarely that obliging, and went into the shop and asked to try the pen in the window. 'Yes, that's the one, with a fine nib, and in matt black, please.'

'Hello, Emma Dolby speaking.'

'Yah, Emma, Senta Norris here.'

'What can I do for you, Senta?' Emma is trying to sound warm and helpful, but is not quite succeeding. Senta Norris is a bright new talent in historical sagas, and fighting her way to the top of the bestseller lists. The sole of Senta's narrow-fitting size five shoe is imprinted on Emma's forehead in Senta's hurry to reach the top.

'Look, Emma, at one of our, like, committee meetings, we talked anthology, right? Like, short pieces of fiction from the attendees.'

'True,' said Emma. 'And I don't believe that we agreed on an editor. Have you any ideas on the subject?'

'Well, as a matter of fact, I think I could see my way to taking on the job myself, Emma,' gushes Senta. 'Free of charge to the committee, of course.'

'And you think you could get this anthology published?' asks Emma, who has some idea of the character she is dealing with.

'Well, as a matter of fact . . .' Senta pauses, aware for once that she is repeating herself and wondering whether Emma is as naïve as she is making out. 'I think my publishers might be interested, if we got something sexy enough together.'

' "Gender and Genre"? Is that sexy enough for them?' asks Emma.

'Well, I'm sure a good title will occur to us,' says Senta. Her eyes rest on a letter from her editor saying that a volume entitled 'Sex on the Page', edited by Senta Norris, will be published by them within twelve months and that Senta, as editor, will earn five thousand pounds and a ten per cent royalty, copyright in each contribution to be awarded to the publishers for a one-off fee of fifty pounds.

'What do you mean, *betrayal*?'

'You heard, Chris. You know what I'm talking about.'

'Look, you've got it all wrong. Really, it's just a silly misunderstanding.'

'Oh, but I understand everything perfectly. Now I can see it all.'

'Just calm down, will you?'

But the other will not calm down and in fact advances in a fury, hands outstretched, eyes wide, teeth bared. 'Why did you do it? What did you gain?'

'No, really, let me explain.'

'Are you scared at last, Chris? Do you know what it feels like? Fear? Despair?'

'Yes, OK. Just stop for a minute, will you? I can put it all right again, I promise.'

I don't believe this. What are you doing? Stop! What's happening?

'You are an evil little boy. You have told lies. You will come to a bad end.'

'And what about me? Have you forgotten me, too, after all these years?'

'Go away! Get away from me!'

A loud cry. Sky and clouds swing past, then a blur of trees and stone, and, finally, earth. A splintering crash. A long silence.

Pain. Pain everywhere.

What's happening? Where am I?

Hello? Is anybody there?

He doesn't hear the feet running away from the parapet and descending the narrow spiral staircase, then fleeing from the tower. He will never hear anything in this world again.

Hello?

Later, as Kate Ivory left the shop with her purchases (she had bought a bottle of dark brown ink and the ideal A5 notebook, its cover decorated with a design of leaves and flowers, as well as the new fountain pen), she heard the wail of an ambulance siren crossing Magdalen Bridge and racing up the High Street. She noticed, idly, that it appeared to turn left into Bartlemas Row, but thought no more about it as she made her way home.

She did not notice the figure who passed her on the pavement, who stared at her as though memorizing all the details of her appearance, from her short bright hair and swinging, shining ear-rings, to the peacock hem of her dress and her bare brown legs.

Kate didn't hear anything or notice anyone, for an idea was coming to her about her new story. All she needed now was a plot and some interesting characters.

Chapter Two

> For the serpent was *wiser* than any of the animals
> that were in Paradise. But the creator cursed the
> serpent, and called him devil.
>
> *The Testimony of Truth*

Hello?

Where am I?

*He would like to ask who he is, but this is too important
a question to ask lightly, calling up too many other disturbing questions in its wake. And anyway, who would hear?
Who, if anyone, would answer?*

*He sits in the unending darkness, hardly daring to
wonder.*

Kate saw the newspaper three days later when she was
in Mrs Clack's shop, buying postage stamps. First she
saw the headline, then she recognized the man in the
photograph printed alongside it. Unmistakable. It was
her Greek god, the man who had trodden on her foot
and then apologized. She paid for her stamps and picked
up the paper.

'Have you seen it? Dreadful, isn't it?' said Mrs Clack.

Kate handed over her forty pence, said, 'Yes, dreadful,' and went outside so that she could read the rest of
the report while standing on the pavement, without Mrs
Clack's inquisitive face peering at her.

College fund-raising expert dives to death
from Oxford's historic tower

FALL FROM GRACE

A college fund-raiser 'had been drinking' when he
climbed to the roof of the historic Tower of Grace
in Bartlemas College, Oxford, colleagues have
revealed. Mr Christopher Townsend slipped over
the balustrade and fell to his death on the flagstones of the quadrangle below.

The Head Porter of Bartlemas College, Jim
Morrison, found 37-year-old Mr Townsend's body
in the quadrangle at 3 p.m. on Monday. Mr Morrison said: 'I called an ambulance from my mobile
phone, and stayed with the body until they arrived.
The paramedics did everything they could, but I
could see it was hopeless all along, in spite of the
efforts they were making.'

The police have launched an enquiry, but say
they are not looking for anyone else in connection
with the death. An inquest was opened at Oxford
Coroner's Court yesterday and adjourned.

Christopher Mark Townsend, of Eynsham
Close, Botley, worked at Bartlemas College as
Development Officer, raising money from wealthy
former students of the college for projects such
as student accommodation. 'He was a respected
member of staff and will be greatly missed,' said
Aidan Flint, the Master of Bartlemas. The College
Bursar, Robert Grailing, said: 'The Tower of Grace
is a favourite attraction for tourists to Oxford.
They can get a panoramic view of the city from
the roof. Thousands come here every year, and
there has never been a fatal accident associated
with the tower before, but I will, of course, be

reviewing the safety of the roof, and its accessibility to members of the college.' He added: 'Chris Townsend was a very popular man, and had probably been enjoying a convivial lunch with friends or colleagues at one of the local pubs.'

Mr Townsend's wife, Briony, was being comforted by friends and was unable to speak to us. A neighbour, Mrs Lisa Batten, said: 'They were a lovely couple, both of them so good-looking, and so happy together. Briony had made that beautiful garden, and the house was lovely, too. Everything seemed to be perfect for them, and I can't believe it's all ended. I saw him leave for work that morning, just like normal, and it's really weird to think he's never coming home.'

Monday afternoon. That was when she'd bought her new pen and notebook and it must have happened soon after she saw him. If only she had stopped him for longer outside the pen shop, broken the chain of events that had led to his fall. Why hadn't she made more of a fuss about her bruised foot? Offered him one of her apples? On the other hand, if he was married to Briony he would probably have ignored her and carried on to whatever rendezvous he had on the roof of the Tower of Grace.

And why? What had happened in the interval between bumping into her in the High, and falling from the tower? She remembered a face full of life, a smile that invited her to share in the joke. Perhaps hindsight was adding to her memory of him, but he had seemed so good-looking, such a vital person, that it was difficult to think of all that energy and enjoyment of life being extinguished in a few moments.

'You all right, dear?' Mrs Clack was shouting. 'Another of your men friends, was he? You don't have much luck with them, do you, dear?'

At last Kate turned round and faced Mrs Clack through her open door.

'No, I didn't know him. I may have met him, briefly, once. But I didn't even know his name, and he wasn't one of my men friends.'

That ought to silence the gossiping tongue, but it probably wouldn't. It took more than a few facts to stop Mrs Clack from spreading juicy rumours.

'Yes, very well, Sadie,' Emma Dolby was saying, leaning away from the telephone and attempting to reach a blue folder on a nearby table. 'I have the schedule here and I'll have to rejig the classes to fit in with the new circumstances.' Her fingers touched the folder, scrabbled with the cover, unbalanced the heap of files it rested on, and brought the whole lot to the floor in a shower of loose papers. 'Just a moment,' she said, putting down the phone and scraping up papers and folders from the floor.

'Are you still there?' came the voice from the receiver. 'Emma? Are you all right?'

'Fine,' said Emma, a little out of breath. 'Everything's under control, Sadie. But perhaps it would be better if we had some extra assistance. Someone who could help out with the admin work, and nursemaid the students when they needed it, and even contribute to the classes.'

'Have you someone in mind?'

'I'll give it some thought, see if anyone suitable occurs to me.'

Emma replaced her receiver and then set about putting papers in their correct folders. After five minutes she gave up and went to make herself a cup of sweet coffee, which she drank while eating half a packet of chocolate biscuits. The baby woke up while she was doing this, so she shared the last biscuit with him and then put a load of washing in the machine. In fifteen minutes she would have to collect the older children from their Activity Programme.

Faith Beeton sat on the pristine green-and-white sofa in her sitting room and looked about her. Six months after moving in, she had all the basic furniture: she had curtains at her windows, rugs on the floor, and the place was starting to look like home. She still had two boxes of books to unpack, and had run out of empty bookshelves, but she recognized that she would never have quite enough bookshelves, however many she acquired. Faith, whose singing voice would have deeply offended a musical person, nevertheless sang to herself with pleasure. 'Home Sweet Home'. Home. The first that she had owned, and a far, far cry from the place where she had spent her childhood.

She looked around for the book she had been reading, Sidney's *Arcadia*. She would make a few more notes on the work, with its interesting mixture of genres, and its influence on Shakespeare's tragedies, then she would study a few more paint charts. She went upstairs and into her bedroom. She had decorated it in the colours of a stormy sunset, with warm greys, dark smoky blues and streaks of coral and flame. The lighting pleased her, illuminating without revealing too much, which suited her well. She twisted a vermilion silk scarf around her neck and knotted it loosely, then checked in the mirror. True enough, it improved the sallowness of her complexion. She picked up the *Arcadia* from her bedside table and twitched the quilt precisely into place. All was as it should be again now. She had nearly made a bad mistake, but it had been corrected in time.

She went into the next room. This was what the estate agent had described as the second bedroom, but which she had known immediately would be her study:

desk by the window, computer and printer on the desk, telephone on the windowsill, small filing cabinet, overflowing bookshelves against every spare foot of wall. She had made it. Older than average, maybe, but then she had been what they described as a mature student, struggling at first to keep up with the eighteen-year-olds, and then finding to her delight that she could outstrip them. And now a three-year fellowship at an Oxford college.

She needed pictures on the walls but she would acquire them gradually, as she discovered what was expected of her. She might even find out, slowly, what her own taste was. After all the years of ruthlessly suppressing her personality, she might allow it to put forth a small shoot or even a modest flower. Reproductions or originals? she wondered.

The phone rang, breaking into the fantasy.

'Hello.'

'Emma Dolby here. I need your help, Dr Beeton.'

The tone was too sweet to trust. 'Really? How?' said Faith, curbing the impulse to invite Emma to call her by her first name.

'I'm sure you know about the study fortnight we're running on "Gender and Genre",' began Emma, tentatively.

'I've heard about it. And how clever of you to pronounce it so beautifully,' said Faith.

'Yes. Well, I'm afraid that one of our tutors, Dr Happle, has faxed me a message to say that he'll be unavoidably delayed in Turkey and unable to take his classes after all.'

'Dear Timothy,' said Faith. 'How astute of him to know that some unexpected event will occur while he's away. And don't you wonder what this year's unavoidable delay looks like? Some naughty young lad, dark and svelte, with doe eyes, do you suppose?'

'Er,' said Emma. 'Um. The thing is, Dr Beeton, do you think you could take over his classes?'

'Not really,' said Faith.

'Are you going to be away? Is that the problem?'

'No.' She thought of adding that she had intended to paint her bathroom walls. She was considering painting them an apricot colour, to cover up the chilly grey that the previous owner had favoured. Or even, she thought suddenly, render them a sharp acid green that she could set off with navy blue and white. Oh yes. Father would have hated it! But she wasn't going to explain any of this to Emma Dolby.

'It is very important to the college,' Emma was saying, her voice gaining confidence. 'The study fortnight does bring in a lot of money.'

'No,' said Faith. She had observed the bad effect on a woman's life of saying 'yes' in circumstances such as these and had therefore practised assiduously the skill of saying 'no'.

'Oh,' said Emma, apparently defeated. 'Very well, then, Dr Beeton. We'll leave it for now.'

'You can leave it, full stop,' said Faith, and disconnected. Oh! the joy of being rude after all the years of terrible politeness.

She spent the next ten minutes looking through paint samples until she found the particular shade of acid green that she was searching for. The phone rang again.

'Faith? Timothy Happle here.'

'I thought you were in Turkey, exploring unavoidable delays.'

'I leave at dawn tomorrow.'

'I do hope you have a pleasant holiday.' She hoped her tone was as dismissive as she had intended.

'Look, Faith, I know it's a bit of an imposition at this short notice, but we need you to take over some of the teaching for the "Gender and Genre" study fortnight.'

23

'I thought I'd already turned it down.'

'But I don't believe you've really thought about what it means. To college, that is. To you personally. And to your career.'

Faith could recognize a threat when she heard one. Her father had been an expert on the veiled threat, and her mother had given in every time. Just at this moment she could sympathize with her mother. Timothy Happle could indeed influence her career for good or evil. It was a three-year fellowship that she had at Bartlemas, and she didn't want to leave in two years' time with a less than enthusiastic reference. As a matter of fact, she had no intention of leaving at all.

'What particular genre do you expect me to teach? I warn you now that I refuse to open any book that describes itself as romantic.'

There was a pause and the sound of papers rustling. 'How about crime fiction?' he said. 'I believe that some of the works on the reading list are quite well written. Well, their authors are often Oxford people, I believe, taking time off from their serious pursuits.'

Faith sighed. In a few weeks' time the academic year began and she would be teaching undergraduates. Good, she looked forward to it. Last year, being her first, had been hard work, but she was getting the hang of it, was more familiar with the material. The last thing she needed now was to get herself landed with tutoring a summer school.

'Very well,' she said, recognizing defeat. 'You'd better give me the reading list and the range of topics over the phone so that I can get on with researching them. When do you get back from Turkey, by the way?'

'In two and a half weeks. I'll be able to oversee your lectures and seminars, and help you with anything you're having problems with.'

'How kind,' said Faith, knowing that this too was a hint that she should make sure that no problems arose.

'I'll tell Emma Dolby that you're taking over, then,' he said, sounding as though he was about to close his last suitcase and telephone a taxi to take him to the airport. 'She'll fill you in on all the details.'

'I'll look forward to it,' lied Faith. Just you wait, Timothy Happle, she thought. One of these days I'm going to trample all over your face on my way to the top, and how I shall enjoy it!

Some while later she went downstairs again to pick through the boxes of books. An hour on *Arcadia*, then she would have to start making notes on Dorothy L. Sayers. At least Emma hadn't asked her how her cookery book was going. That was a joke of which she was growing very tired.

Kate Ivory was lying under an English heaven, as she put it to herself, her bare legs crushing the grass on her small square of lawn. Her eyes were shut, and she was kidding herself that she was working out the plot of the new book. Susannah, her gawky marmalade cat, was lying across her stomach. Inside the house the phone was ringing. She thought about answering it. This would involve opening her eyes, disturbing Susannah, standing up, walking. If she was going to be poor, she might as well be irresponsible and happy as well. There were few advantages to the insecure life of a professional writer, but lying in the sun on a summer's day while everyone else was working was definitely one of them.

On the other hand, old habits are hard to kick, and she caught the phone on its seventh ring.

'Kate? It's Emma.'

The hour of immobility in bright sunshine, not to

25

mention the glass of white wine she had drunk, had left her feeling stupid.

'Hello, Emma.' Oh yes, it must be Emma Dolby, who produced offspring by the dozen and then wrote stories to keep other people's children quiet. She was sounding a lot friendlier than when Kate had asked her for work.

'Are you all right, Kate? You sound a bit odd.'

'I'm fine. I was working on the new book.'

'I thought you'd be lying in the sun, drinking white wine.'

'I'd just got to a really tricky bit of the plot outline. And anyway, I can't afford white wine these days, remember.'

'Well, put the book to one side. I've got a useful bit of self-promotion for you.'

'You don't want me to take over your writing class again, do you?'

'Oh no. I've told you, never again. Not after last time.'

Kate had brought her wine glass in with her, and she stretched the phone cord out to its fullest extent and shuffled across to the wine bottle. Emma's reminder about the unpleasantness in the writing class could only be blotted out by another glass of wine.

'I'm talking about the study fortnight,' said Emma.

'The one you're organizing at Bartlemas? The one I didn't register for and to which I can usefully contribute precisely zilch?'

'Gender and Genre,' said Emma. 'And I'm sure you have an immensely important contribution to make.'

'Tell me more,' said Kate, gleefully. Something must have gone seriously wrong with the arrangements for Emma to have come back to her like this.

'There's a place free on the organizing committee and we wondered whether you could fill it.'

'That's the unpaid committee, with mean expenses, is it?'

'And there's some admin work to do,' said Emma, as though she had not heard Kate's comment, 'and then you could look after the students when they arrive – point them in the direction of the Bodleian, show them where to buy postcards and stamps, and how to use an English telephone, that sort of thing.'

'Sounds within my capabilities. How's the pay?'

'Moderate, but it will last for four weeks, and you'll get plenty of free meals.'

'I'll think about it. When do you need to know by?'

Emma sighed. 'Oh all right. I suppose I could fit you into a panel on historical fiction, if you like, and give you a workshop on creative writing to run.'

'Would I get paid for both of them?'

'Yes.'

'Fine,' said Kate. 'I'll do it. When do I start?'

'This afternoon?' asked Emma, hopefully.

'Monday morning,' said Kate, who had heard the weather forecast: hot and sunny for the next three days. 'And by the way, Emma, why this sudden need for my services? Why do you need a new committee and panel member at such short notice?'

'Not so much new. More a replacement. Didn't you read about Chris Townsend?'

For a moment the name meant nothing to her, then Kate said, 'The one who fell off the Tower of Grace?'

'Yes. Wasn't it awful? A dreadful accident. He was the Development Officer at Bartlemas, and this study fortnight was his idea. He'd been talking the Bursar round to the idea of using the college throughout the year for income-generating projects. The Bursar and the Steward are supposed to be looking after the accommodation and catering side, but the Steward is somewhere in the Greek islands for the next three weeks and we really need another pair of hands, now that Chris is no longer Organizer.'

Kate imagined Emma herself taking over the organization of a fifteen-day jamboree for some two hundred people and shuddered.

'You're quite sure it was an accident?'

'Of course. What else would it be? Chris had no reason to commit suicide, if that's what you're thinking.'

'I just don't want to get mixed up with any more suspicious deaths.'

'Really, Kate, there was nothing suspicious about it. I keep telling you, it was an accident. He was checking over the route of the tour we're going to give the students, and he must have slipped or something. Tragic, but just one of those things. He was a wonderful person, and very popular, and everyone is very upset.'

And you are being just a little too persuasive, a little too emphatic, thought Kate. But then the job was what she was looking for, and if the weather was good it might even include some sessions sitting on the grass, drinking cold white wine, in the company of attractive people.

'I'll see you at nine on Monday morning at Bartlemas, then,' she said.

'I have to take the children to their Activity Groups first,' said Emma. 'You'd better make that nine-thirty.'

'Fine. I'll see you then. 'Bye.'

Kate went to retrieve the book she had been pretending to read in the garden, and the cushions on which she had been reclining. A head appeared over the fence between her garden and the muddy field that was number 12's.

'Hello, Kate,' said Harley.

Kate recognized a desperate cry for help. Harley, after all, was as eloquent at expressing his emotions as she was herself.

'I expect I've got some Coke in the fridge,' she said, by way of invitation. 'And a box of white Magnums in the freezer. Do you want to come over?'

28

'Don't mind,' said Harley.

'What's up?' she ventured, when Harley was installed at her kitchen table with a can of Coke, a Magnum, and a packet of hedgehog-flavoured crisps that she had found at the back of her cupboard.

'It's Dave,' he said.

Which of Harley's law-breaking friends was that? she wondered, before remembering that Dave was the name of Harley's dog, called, like Harley himself, after his father's favourite motorbike.

'He's OK, isn't he?' she asked. Come to think of it, she hadn't seen Dave around for a while.

'Jace don't like dogs,' said Harley.

'Jace?'

'Mum's new friend.'

Since Trevor, Harley's father, had moved out, after some wall-shuddering rows, Harley's mother, Tracey, had had two or three new 'friends' staying with her. The tenancy must be in her name, Kate reckoned, so that when she and her husband split up it was Tracey who stayed in the marital home.

'It's difficult not to like Dave, though.'

'Jace says he's dangerous.'

From his long pointed nose through his barrel-shaped body covered in thick foxy-red fur, fluffy as a teddy bear's, to his plumed, ever-waving tail, Dave was a softie.

'How? Why?'

'They told us when we got him he was a German shepherd cross,' said Dave.

'Maybe he is, but crossed with a particularly docile sheep,' said Kate.

'He's not that bad!' exclaimed Harley. 'He can be fierce if he wants. He just don't want.'

'The nearest thing he does to fierce is bay at the full moon,' said Kate. 'This Jace must be a real fool to be taken in by him.'

'Yeah,' said Harley. 'But Mum says he's got to go.'

He got up to leave, then picked up the half-empty can of Coke to take back to number 12 with him.

'I'll let you know if I think of something,' said Kate. But what could she do to help? She didn't like dogs much herself, even if Dave was an exception. She wasn't about to offer him a home at number 10.

Chapter Three

Poor painters oft with silly poets join
To fill the world with strange but vain conceits:
One brings the stuff, the other stamps the coin,
Which brings naught else but glosses of deceits.
                    Philip Sidney, *The Old Arcadia*

Hello?

Nothing.

Some long time later, he locates two yielding ovoids, remembers what they are, and opens them. Organs of sight. Eyes.

Here you are, someone said once. Look at all these things, all these warm, moving, winged and legged things that I will show to you. If you give them names, that is how they will be known hereafter and you will have dominion over them.

But if indeed he once owned this power over words and the things they stood for, it is one he has since lost. For now he can remember none of them, neither their appearance nor the words he might have used to describe them. He has to discover and label anew.

He will start with himself. Me. I. Myself. He uses his new-found eyes and looks at himself. Two pink feelies, two small jointed rods, two larger jointed supports. Names come creeping back: these are arms and legs; not feelies, but hands and fingers. He uses his hands to explore further, and finds a large sphere with soft, stranded topping. Head? Yes. The discovery resembles an act of creation.

What is he, then? Human? Man. Whatever that might mean.

He pushes with his hands against the ground and slowly rises to his feet. He stands, swaying, for his legs and feet have forgotten their functions. Gradually he inches forward with first one foot and then the other, into the dark countryside.

Above him, the sky is an inverted ultramarine bowl. Shouldn't there be stars? Here, there are no stars, only the pale glimmering of his own white limbs in the blueness. He keeps walking. Beneath his feet the earth is hard, with small stones over which he stumbles. There is no vegetation. He sees no other living beings. He walks for a long time.

Ahead, now, he sees a towering gate, made of some dark metal, pierced and moulded into fantastic shapes. Metallic birds and beasts with horns and talons and wings peer at him from brazen foliage. He cannot make out what lies behind the gate, for the spaces between the metal uprights are too narrow to gain more than glimpses and slight impressions.

Light. He has been able to see because there is light. A light that soars and flickers, like a pillar of flame, and behind it a figure standing, silent, before the gate. Two hands, two arms, two legs, one head, with a smaller flame burning on its forehead. Human? Not exactly. Two huge feathered growths spring outwards from its shoulders and shimmer blue and gold in the light from the flames: wings.

What?

No, not exactly human, therefore.

Does it have a name?

Hello?

'This is the Fellows' Garden,' said Emma Dolby, leading the way through a rustic gate, along a path bordered by shrubs and herbaceous plants that looked as though they had grown there for centuries.

'Very nice,' said Kate Ivory, admiring some grey-green foliage, and wishing that it wasn't all in such frightfully good taste. What it really needed to brighten the place up was a bed of colourful, vulgar flowers. Marigolds, say, or poppies.

'The Master's wife is a very keen gardener and is bringing the Fellows' Garden back to its original design.'

'The Garden of Eden?'

'It was originally laid out by one of the great garden designers in the early years of the century,' said Emma. 'Nancy Lancaster, I think.'

Although they were only a hundred yards or so from the traffic-congested High Street, here on their green island Kate could smell aromatic leaves and a hint of lavender flowers instead of the familiar diesel fumes. Birds chirruped their low-key autumnal songs. Out of sight, small animals and multi-legged insects doubtless lived out their appointed lives. Leaves, not yet turned to gold, whispered in the morning breeze.

'This is classy. Do we let the punters in here?' asked Kate.

'Punters! Do you think you could make an enormous effort and learn to call them students?'

'Sorry. I'll try,' said Kate, mindful of her essential pay cheque. 'So, are the students allowed into the Fellows' Garden?'

'Not in general, but they may come in when accompanied by one of their tutors.'

Emma's short round figure in its over-sized green t-shirt and gathered beige skirt strode sturdily ahead in sensible flat sandals. Her hair, cut by a friend of hers for free, was curly and brown and untouched by artificial colourings. Kate hoped that her own jeans, white lawn shirt and exuberant red plastic ear-rings would be considered suitable attire by the organizers of Gender and Genre. She removed a strand of some healthy climbing plant from her neatly cropped hair before asking tentatively, 'And do I count as a tutor?'

'I suppose so.' Their path led through a small grove of trees, and sunlight glinted through shapely leaves. 'If we continue past the bridge and turn right, we come out by the chapel. There's a very pretty little Temptation you should see.'

Kate was luckily diverted from making a flippant comment on pretty temptations by the sound of a voice rising from the other side of a nearby hedge.

'We need something pale, with feathery leaves just here, don't you think, Mr Evans?' The voice was female and its enunciation was excellent. 'What would you suggest?'

'I like a nice bit of lawn and some annuals, myself,' came the reply. This voice was male, and older. 'Foliage plants are all very well, but people want a bit of colour in the spring and summer. Flowers, like. If God hadn't wanted us to grow annuals he wouldn't have given us seed trays, would he?'

'What do you think, Briony?' asked the bossy female voice. 'You agree with me, don't you?'

'Do I? Really, I don't know what I think any more.'

'Why can't we have some petunias?' The male voice had cut in again.

'Marigolds, nemesia, poppies,' chimed in the voice called Briony.

'I can grow them from seed, bring them along in the greenhouse and plant them out next April,' went on Mr Evans. 'I could do you a bed along here in the college colours. People would like that.'

'What do you think, Briony?'

'I really don't care one way or the other.'

A young man with a wheelbarrow laden with small plastic pots of green plants and bulging black sacks crossed in front of Emma and Kate and disappeared around a screen of plants.

'Mr Evans! Where is that boy going? What is he doing?'

'Barry!' called Dave Evans. 'What you doing with that lot?'

'I'm doing what you told me, Mr Evans. I'm off down the m—'

'Yes, that's good. Just carry on.'

'Well?' demanded the woman's voice.

'He's taking them down to the greenhouse,' said Dave Evans. 'I've taken cuttings of the tender plants, in case we have a hard winter, and bagged up some leafmould for mulching later on.'

'Does it matter?' asked Briony.

'You've just got to snap out of it, Briony! Make an effort! It's no good being apathetic like this.'

'Come on!' Emma was hissing. 'We don't want to be caught eavesdropping.'

Kate, who thought nothing of listening in to other people's conversations, was craning her left ear towards the argument.

'Who were they?' she asked when Emma had dragged her on some yards and they were passing through a second rustic gate. Behind them the gardener, still invisible behind the screen of shrubs, continued with his litany of cheerful flowers: 'Geraniums. Lobelia. Or we could have a nice herbaceous border. Hollyhocks. Delphiniums. Stocks.'

'The younger woman is Briony Townsend, Chris's widow. She doesn't know what she's saying, poor woman. The other is Honor Flint, the Master's wife,' replied Emma. 'A wonderful character. The man is the gardener,

35

Dave Evans. The younger man is his assistant, Barry. Poor Mrs Flint has a terrible time trying to explain her ideas to Mr Evans. His last job was looking after one of the big municipal parks. I don't believe he's ever heard of Gertrude Jekyll.'

'Gertrude who?' asked Kate, following Emma through an archway. In front of them rose one side of Pesant Quad, with the tall grey shape of the Tower of Grace on their left.

'Do we really have to go inside?' They were out of the sun, and the air was cold on Kate's skin. And there was something about towers, maybe their height, maybe their air of indifference to the mortal lives around them, that made her uneasy.

'Oh yes, you can't miss it. It's the quickest way into the chapel from here. And you must see our Adam and Eve. So thin and innocent, and decorously shaded by fig leaves, even before the Fall made them aware of their nakedness.'

It was dark inside the tower, and for a moment Kate could see nothing, while her lungs inhaled ancient dust and the damp air that clings to stone buildings.

Emma's footsteps were loud on the flagstones. 'Light!' she commanded, finding the switch.

But not a lot of it, thought Kate. The glimmer lost itself in the high, shaded ceiling, and her eyes were consequently drawn towards a source of mild brilliance: a small painting, discreetly lit from above so that it glowed against the dark wall.

As they walked across to stand in front of it, Emma said, 'This is the Temptation I was telling you about.'

Thin, white-skinned Eve, a sly expression on her little heart-shaped face, handed a perfect apple to a perplexed Adam. With her other hand, Eve pulled down a branch of the tree, while above her a sinuous serpent hung down, approving her action. Around them stood and crouched the motley selection of animals that Adam, presumably, had named and over which he had been given dominion.

Kate said, 'Adam looks puzzled, as though he doesn't know what's going on. But then, he doesn't look too bright, poor man, does he?'

'No, not next to Eve, certainly.'

'Not even next to that tame reindeer. And why does the apple resemble Eve's breast, and the curves of her body echo the coils of the serpent? Is the artist trying to tell us something about the evil, fallen nature of woman, and her affinity with Sin, do you suppose? Could he possibly be reflecting the misogynistic ideas of some past age?'

'Stop trying to sound naïve, Kate. You can't expect a sixteenth-century German to paint with the eyes of a twentieth-century woman.'

'The interesting questions are to do with the nature of the temptation and the role of the woman in the whole affair,' said a voice from the gloom behind them. Emma and Kate turned to see where it was coming from.

'Oh,' said Emma. 'It's Dr Beeton.'

Kate could see that Dr Beeton was female, slightly built and dark-haired, but could make out no further details of her appearance.

'Have you read the Gnostics?' Dr Beeton asked.

'Not recently,' said Kate, hoping that she wouldn't be asked a supplementary question that would show up her ignorance.

'You should try Pagels on the subject.'

'I will,' promised Kate, mystified.

She turned her back on the politically incorrect painting, preparing to make her way across the tower and into the chapel, when her eye was caught by another picture, less well lit but gaudier in its colours, which was hanging on the opposite wall.

A tall figure, blue of wing and golden of face, stood in the centre of the composition, holding in front of him – her? it? – a sword from which flames curled upwards. What's the white feathery excrescence on its forehead? wondered Kate. To its left stood two small, insignificant human figures, modestly decorated with fig leaf kilts; on its right swayed a larger, more ferocious serpent than the one in the Temptation scene. Colourful flowering plants, which would have won the approval of Dave Evans, twined themselves around the figures, while little, intricate leaves and grasses sprang beneath their feet.

'After the Fall,' explained Emma. 'Adam and Eve expelled from the Garden of Eden.'

'And who's the lad with the shining face and the flaming sword?'

'God set a cherubim to guard the eastern gate of Eden, so that man could never return,' replied Dr Beeton, who was apparently still with them. 'You can tell he's a cherubim by the blue of his wings.'

'Oh, I don't know,' said Kate. 'I don't think the Garden of Eden was lost to us for ever. If they planted a few more jolly flowers it would look remarkably like the Fellows' Garden that we've just walked through, though I'm not sure I'd cast Honor Flint and Dave Evans as Adam and Eve.' The cherubim glared out of the frame in disapproval.

'I wonder what Eve really thought about being expelled,' put in Dr Beeton. 'Was she secretly pleased to leave God and his Garden behind, do you think, so that she and Adam could set up on their own?'

'I hadn't thought of it like that before,' answered Kate. 'She looks a manipulative little piece, doesn't she?'

'Perhaps I should introduce you,' said Emma, belatedly. 'Dr Beeton, this is Kate Ivory, who is also involved in our study fortnight, on the admin side.'

'I thought I was leading a couple of seminars,' hissed Kate. 'And giving a writing workshop.'

'Oh, that study fortnight. Well, I expect we'll meet again, then,' said Dr Beeton without enthusiasm, and she faded back into the gloom from which she had emerged.

'Do you think we could leave now?' asked Kate.

'Leave? But we've only just got here. You haven't seen the painted glass in the chapel yet.'

'I know I should be grateful for the guided tour, Emma, but this place makes me feel uneasy.' She hitched up her right shoulder, as though trying to brush off the cold, stuffy air, and turned away from the second painting.

'What do you mean?'

'The fall. The death.'

'Fall? What's wrong with it? Oh, *that* one. Chris Townsend, you mean. Don't be ridiculous. There's nothing to get goosepimples over. It was a simple accident. The man had had too much to drink and was larking around. It's tragic, but these things happen every day. Now, we must go up the tower. There's a wonderful view from the roof.'

Emma had taken out a key and opened a heavy wooden door. Behind her, Kate could see narrow stone stairs, spiralling upwards into the darkness, their treads worn down in the middle by generations of academic feet. Emma was right. Why should she be concerned with a death that had to be accidental? Dark blue eyes and a neatly sculptured jawline, she remembered.

'I'm not very good at heights, I think I'll stay down here.'

'Rubbish. You'll be expected to accompany a group of students around the college, and a visit to the top of the tower is the highlight of the tour. You can see all over Oxford. Come on!'

Emma was not someone to whom one could confide

one's terror of heights. Her own children were not allowed to show any nervousness of the dark, or when threatened by ferocious dogs, or drill-wielding dentists, so Kate knew that she was unlikely to win her sympathy for her own lesser misgivings. She followed Emma up the staircase, keeping closely behind her, and with one hand firmly on the tower wall. It was just as well that Emma was not very fit, and Kate had no trouble keeping up with her.

They went through a room where the bell ropes hung down and scrolls around the wall announced complicated sets of changes that had been rung in the past. After this brief respite they were climbing upwards again, until at last they reached a small door, and emerged on to the roof.

'Look!' said Emma. 'There's Christ Church. And Merton tower.'

Kate still had her back to the view and was studying the nearest stone pinnacle.

'The University church,' said Emma, pointing enthusiastically. 'The Radcliffe Camera.' She turned to assure herself that Kate was following her. Kate shifted her gaze a foot or so outwards and allowed it to rest on a gargoyle.

'All Souls?' added Emma, coaxing now. 'The Bodleian?'

Kate inched round until she could see the tops of the trees in the Fellows' Garden, and the three sides of Pesant Quad. The breeze that she hadn't noticed at ground level tugged at her hair and pushed her towards the edge. She felt the first autumn chill in its touch. Autumn, Fall, dying fall: the words chased themselves through her mind. She closed her eyes again. 'Very nice,' she said, her hands clenched on the balustrade in front of her. As she felt the grainy stone, the roughness of the lichened surface, she thought suddenly 'Balustrade!' and opened her eyes again: this was where the accident had happened. She forgot her fear for a moment and examined it. It was a couple of feet wide and reached to her waist. The columns were too close together to permit the smallest person to pass between them, so he must have gone over the top. How much taller was Christopher Townsend? How easy would it have been for him to fall over, accidentally? The thought made her feel giddy again. She should concentrate on the view and try to forget the fact that someone had fallen to their death from this very place.

She edged over to stand next to Emma. Ahead and beneath them the traffic flowed up the High Street like a metallic snake, and they could look down on the roofs of the shops, and across to colleges and libraries. Just below them and to their right, Kate could see the patch of pavement where she had stood and admired pens and notebooks while people had trampled all over her feet. She could also see Barry, the gardener's assistant, pushing his wheelbarrow, empty now, back across the High Street, towards the college. She wondered for a moment where Dave Evans kept his greenhouse. It seemed to be a long way from the garden, but presumably he knew what he was doing.

Up here, with the clouds wheeling past her head, she had the impression of being marooned on an island, cut off from the real life of the city. An island with a ghost, she thought. Which side of the tower had he fallen from? She saw a figure sliding, diving, turning in the air, before . . . She closed her eyes to rid herself of the image.

Emma twisted over the edge to point. 'Magdalen College tower,' she said. 'Lean over here. You need to see it at this angle, Kate. And you'll see it better if you open your eyes,' she added.

'Yes, lovely,' said Kate, shading her eyes and pretending.

'Are you going to manage to bring your party up here?' asked Emma, doubtfully. 'You need to be able to tell them what they're looking at, you know.'

'Oh yes, I'll get used to it quite soon, I'm sure.' It was true that she was determined to conquer her fear. She wondered how good Christopher Townsend had been at heights. Was she the only one whose head swam at altitudes above ten feet? Perhaps if she practised tower-climbing regularly she would begin to enjoy it. Perhaps not.

'Can we go down now? I'll study the map and make sure I know what all the landmarks are, I promise,' she said, as they turned and made their way back through the door and down the winding staircase. 'I'll be able to lead them blindfold,' or with her eyes closed.

'Oh, very well. I'll show you the seminar rooms next. We can walk through Pesant Quad to get to the new block.'

Of course Emma was right: Christopher Townsend's death had been a drunken accident. She didn't want to believe the truth of it because he had charmed her with his looks and his smile, and she had to admit it wouldn't be the first time she had been wrong about an attractive man. But a voice whispered in her head that he hadn't been drunk when he had bumped into her in the High Street – preoccupied, perhaps, but not drunk – so how had it happened so quickly? She had heard the ambulance siren just after she left the pen shop, which couldn't have been more than fifteen or twenty minutes later. But then, it might have been a different ambulance. Perhaps he had gone into college, met up with some friends, drunk half a bottle of whisky, climbed up the tower, probably wearing new leather shoes with slippery soles, and then fallen over the edge, first slithering over three feet of balustrade.

But there was no mystery for her to solve, and so

she must stop thinking like this. She pushed the unlikely
sequence of events to the back of her mind and tuned
in to what Emma was saying.

'I'll take you up to the Development Office in a
minute. You need to meet the Bursary staff as well, since
you'll be working with them. And I'll get Sadie to hand
you over Chris's files so that you can see what he was
doing.'

'Who claimed he was drunk?' asked Kate, without
thinking.

'What? What on earth are you talking about?'

'Nothing,' said Kate. 'I'm sorry, my mind drifted off
for a moment. Let's go and meet the people in the
Bursary.'

Early September is not the best time of year for pruning,
but Briony Townsend was out in her garden, secateurs
in hand, attacking roses and clematis, viburnum and
ceanothus. She worked with wild, jerky movements,
pausing from time to time to push her hair back out of
her face and wipe her damp hands down the front of her
jeans. She had already reduced the grass to half a centimetre of stubble, but seemed unable to stop herself from
destroying the vegetation that still grew in lush profusion
around her. A heap of twigs and small leafy branches
lay at her feet and trailed back along the path, hinting
at more devastation further out of sight. In the garden
next door, hidden by a trellis of climbing plants, a dog
howled, as though in sympathy with Briony's distress.

'Oh no, Briony! Stop it, please, dear!'

She hadn't heard Honor Flint enter from the side
gate.

'You wanted me to take an interest in gardening
again, didn't you? Well, I have.'

'Here, give me the secateurs. You'll ruin that poor

clematis if you do that to it. And the roses haven't stopped blooming yet, so you shouldn't clip them about like that. It's taken years for your plants to reach maturity, and now you're chopping them down.'

Briony looked at Honor Flint and stamped her foot, crushing a plant with small green leaves. The air filled with the scent of thyme.

She had originally planned the garden as a succession of individual compartments, each with its own character, each hidden from the others, so that at no time could you see the whole. Luxuriant plants, trained over pillars and arches, screened off each section while leading the eye through to the next vista. But now Briony hacked and slashed so that the overall design was blurred and would soon disappear entirely if she carried on like this.

She picked up a strand of some trailing plant and cut it away with the secateurs.

'What's the point of it all now?' she cried. 'I made it for us. For the two of us. Every day I worked in this garden. I drew the plans, I learned how to lay bricks, I dug and I composted. I begged for cuttings from strangers, I sowed seeds in trays. And what was it all for?' She slashed at a bush with the flat of her hand and the scent of rosemary joined itself to the thyme.

'Now, why don't we go back into the house and make ourselves a pot of tea?'

Briony shook her head impatiently. 'It was my whole life,' she said. 'And now it's all gone. It's been shattered. Why shouldn't I add to the destruction?' She looked around her with hatred, and, jaw clenched, attacked another plant.

'You'll feel much better if you sit down and talk to me about it instead of taking it out on your lovely garden,' said Honor, finally succeeding in seizing the secateurs and guiding her firmly into the house. 'And what arrangements are you making about the funeral? Have you informed all the relatives?'

Honor was the kind of tall, well-built Englishwoman, with greying hair and weathered skin, who finds it quite natural to boss other people about. She had probably been captain of hockey at school, and had scorned those who, like Briony, had preferred a warm corner and a good book to standing in a bracing English gale and acquiring the team spirit. Honor surely never opened a book, unless it was a gardening manual.

Briony went into the kitchen, made the pot of Earl Grey tea that was expected of her, and handed a bone china cup and saucer to Honor, whose strong brown hands looked as though they would crush them to powder.

'Now, what's brought all this on?' asked Honor, with what she thought was tact. 'It's not just Chris's death, is it?' She prided herself on her perceptiveness.

'Oh no,' said Briony, with heavy sarcasm, which was quite wasted on Honor. 'Losing one's husband through a stupid, drunken accident wouldn't bother one at all, would it? Who could imagine such a thing?' She picked another couple of tissues from the open box on the table, scrubbed her face with them and then blew her nose loudly.

'But there was talk, wasn't there?' hinted Honor. 'Not necessarily based on anything concrete, of course, but still upsetting for you. That sort of thing can prey on your mind if you let it. You can talk to me about it if you like.'

'About my husband and that woman, you mean?' Briony crushed the tissues into a sodden ball which she flung in the direction of the wastepaper basket.

'Do put some sugar in your tea and drink it up, dear. It will make you feel better.'

'I suppose they're all feeling sorry for me? Poor little

Briony, doesn't know that her husband was screwing another woman!'

'That's a very horrid word for a woman to use. And I'm sure Sadie wouldn't misbehave like that, or Chris himself, if it comes to that.'

'Sadie!'

'You mustn't think like that,' said Honor, looking uncomfortable.

'That's the trouble,' said Briony. 'People don't like it when you tell them what you really think.'

'Why don't you go and change out of those dirty jeans?' Honor wished to change the subject.

'No, I don't want to. And anyway, I haven't finished in the garden.'

'Don't be silly, dear. You'll be sorry in a few days when you see what you've done. Now, I've got my notebook here, so let's just plan the funeral service, shall we? What do you think Christopher's favourite hymns were?'

It was impossible to descend noisily into a nervous breakdown when someone like Honor Flint took command of your life, and so Briony allowed herself to be taken in hand, and organized, and only showed her grief in seemly, acceptable ways in front of the Master's wife.

After she had left, Briony reflected that Honor Flint might have confiscated the secateurs, but the pruning saw and small axe, well maintained, sharpened and free from rust, were still hanging on their hooks in the garden shed. She could cut an avenue of destruction from one end of the garden to the other, and no one could stop her.

Chapter Four

[Angels] vary the forms of their own bodies, and
sometimes contract into a smaller mass and
again extend themselves in a longer, as we see
happen in the earthworm, only they do it in a
better substance more easily ductible.

Michael Psellus, *De Daemonibus*

'Hello?'

*A very long time has passed. Weary beyond belief after
his walk, he has been sitting on the stony ground, regain-
ing his strength. He has tried several times to move nearer
to the gate and to whatever it is that stands before it, but it
is as though they retreat away from him the harder he tries
to approach them. He concludes that it is not up to him to
reach the gate and its guardian, but for them to come to him.*

*While he has been waiting, he has been pulling mem-
ories from his mind, slowly and painfully. He sits with his
head in his hands, hoping for assistance in his perplexity.
And an end to silence.*

He tries again. 'Hello?'

'Yes?'

At last, a response to his call. 'Can you tell me where I
am?'

'Yes.'

*The voice is low, and difficult to place as to gender. He
raises his head. The gate has come quite close, its guardian
only some twenty feet away from where he sits.*

47

'Well?'

'You are outside the eastern gate of the Garden of Eden.'

Silence for a while as he thinks about it, matching it with the facts that are now sitting in his head.

'Why?' he asks.

'Because my colleagues and I were set here, with our flaming swords, to make sure that you and your kind could never return to the Garden.'

'I'm not sure that's the answer I was looking for.'

'Answers rarely are, in my experience, and usually because people ask the wrong questions.'

He returns to a subject that has been worrying him. 'Can you tell me what, or who, you are?'

'Yes.'

'Well?' It is tedious dealing with something that takes every question so literally.

'I am your attendant or, if you like a plainer term, your gaoler. I stand here at the threshold to prevent your entry into the Garden. I am an angel, or, to be more specific, a cherub.'

'Well, that's all right by me. I have no wish to enter your garden. I have had enough of them to last me for a lifetime.' He pauses, realizing how inappropriate the phrase is. 'I am quite happy to remain outside and never pass through its gate, for a very long time, if not for ever.'

'Your wishes are not my concern. I am, as I said, merely the guardian of this place.'

'Have you a name?'

'I have.'

Impatiently, 'So what is it?'

'Zophiel. I am the swiftest of God's cherubim.' His wings beat once with a strong muscular action and he rises into the air for some few inches before subsiding back on to the ground.

'And this may seem obvious, but can you tell me who I am?' And then he adds, quickly, before the cherub can give

one of his irritating answers, 'And if you know who I am,
will you please tell me.'

'Very well. Your name is Christopher Mark Townsend,
and you were thirty-seven years old when you came here.'

'Thank you.'

He has made a start, but a start in what, he is not yet
clear.

'The Bursary,' said Emma, reaching the top of a flight of
stairs and opening a door. Kate followed her into a large,
high-ceilinged room, whose excellent proportions were
ruined by the partitions and paraphernalia of a modern
office.

'Sadie,' said Emma, addressing a tall woman standing
at a desk near the door. 'This is Kate Ivory. The one I
told you about, who's taking on some of the admin work
for the study fortnight. I'm sure she'll get the hang of
things if you show her around.' I wish she sounded more
confident in my abilities, thought Kate, but before she
could argue Emma looked at her watch, said, 'Oh dear,
I'm late,' smiled vaguely all round the room, added, 'I
was supposed to be in Headington five minutes ago,'
and then exited through the door, closing it behind her.
Sensible shoes could be heard clattering their way down
the staircase in the silence that followed her departure.

'She reminds me of the White Rabbit,' said Sadie.

'The ears and whiskers character?' asked Kate, grin-
ning. 'Always late. Never quite in control of the situation.'
She felt a sense of relief: now she could communicate
directly with people, instead of having herself interpreted to them by Emma.

The other woman smiled and shook her head, as
though she too was relieved that Emma had left, and
said, 'I'm Sadie James.' Emma had probably left a trail
of disorder in her wake, the way she did in her own

chaotic house. 'I'm the Acting Development Officer,' Sadie added. 'So I'm in overall charge of the study fortnight. But you, of course, will be in charge of the day-to-day smooth running of it.' She paused for a second or two before adding, 'Under Emma's direction.'

Kate nodded. There wasn't much to say, except to hope that Emma didn't appear too often, and she didn't think she could express that wish aloud to Sadie James until she knew her a lot better. She was about twenty-six, she thought, looking at the other woman as she led her through, towards the far door. She had an amazing amount of curly chestnut hair. Was it all real? Probably, she conceded, and the colour owed more to nature than did her own. Dark greenish-grey eyes, well-marked eyebrows, a small, straight nose and a large mouth, made to look even larger by a liberal application of scarlet lipstick. Tall, slim, stunning. Half a head taller than Kate. But the smile was friendly.

'Right,' said Kate. 'I'd better start catching up on what's been happening. You're the one who knows all about the study fortnight and you're going to fill me in on my part in it, aren't you?'

'I'll start by introducing you to everyone, since you'll be working with me in the room next door.'

Behind them a phone was ringing. 'John!' someone shouted. 'I'm tied up for a couple of minutes. Can you get that for me?'

'I don't answer the telephone,' said a man's voice. 'I'm Assistant Bursar, not someone's secretary.'

Sadie made a face at Kate, said, 'Sorry about this,' and answered the phone herself, which gave Kate a chance to look around.

The man called John was still talking, though he seemed to have lost his audience. He caught Kate's eye and addressed his remarks to her. 'I'm only in this room while they're redecorating my office,' he said. 'I don't belong in here, you see. None of this comes into my job description.'

Oh, One of Those, Kate thought, and nodded. Every office seemed to have a member of staff who had very clear ideas about what their job was, and how it didn't include any of the helpful little touches that kept an atmosphere sweet. He was leaning forward in his chair, staring at her in a rude way. A thin man with sparse brown hair, a prominent nose and light greenish eyes. Flecks of dandruff stood out on his dark jacket, and bony wrists and hands with reddish hair on the back stuck out from the sleeves. Kate hoped that she could get away from him soon, because she didn't like the way he was staring at her legs, but Sadie was still on the phone so there was no rescue for her from that quarter.

'Are you taking over from Chris?' went on John. 'Have you done much of this work before?' And without giving her a chance to answer, he continued, 'Where have you been working? It's funny that they could find someone competent at such short notice, isn't it?'

'I'm Kate Ivory,' she said. 'And I'm taking over the routine duties to do with the study fortnight. I'm here temporarily.'

'Kate Ivory? Not the famous author?' There was a snide note in his voice that Kate didn't at all like. 'Perhaps you'll get on so well that you'll never want to leave!'

'I don't think I'd want to work here permanently, thank you. And I have a book to get back to when I've finished here.'

'I'm surprised that you can drag yourself away from it for a routine job like this,' said John.

'What do you do?' asked Kate, to change the subject.

'I'm John Clay. Not that I expect you to have heard of me. I look after all the room bookings and housekeeping arrangements, as it were, while the Steward is away, so I expect we'll have a lot to talk about. I can see that we're going to be great pals. I like to get involved in the Development Office's little schemes. When they let me, of course.' He pulled a face.

'Did you know Christopher Townsend well?' asked Kate, nosy as ever.

'We were great friends!' said John, unconvincingly. 'We all miss him tremendously, especially our Sadie. She's missing him more than anybody. The two of them were *so* close.'

Kate wouldn't have been surprised by a wink after that. I'll have to steer clear of him, she thought. He's definitely not my type, with all those snide remarks about people I haven't had a chance to get to know for myself. But he was well dressed, she acknowledged: expensive shirt, very nice silk tie, and a sharp suit, only slightly marred by the flakes of dandruff on the shoulders. College employees must be better paid than she had thought.

He looked at his watch. 'Time for my coffee break,' he said. 'I mustn't hang around here. Would you like to join me? You might as well mix with the élite!' He laughed, to indicate that it was a joke, but Kate felt that he did in fact believe himself to be above the others in the room.

'I'm in the middle of the induction course,' she improvised.

'Pity. Maybe another time, then.'

As he left the room the telephone on his desk started to ring. He ignored it.

'Answer that for me, will you, Annette?' he said.

'Answer it yourself,' she replied.

Obviously a happy and co-operative work force.

'These three rooms form the Bursary,' said Sadie, who had finished her own telephone call and was frowning at the phone on John Clay's desk, as though willing it into silence. 'The Bursar, Rob Grailing, lives in the room behind that door over there. He's a nice man. You're bound to get on all right with him. That's his secretary, Annette Paige, at the desk by his office door.' A fair-haired woman looked up and gave a tight-lipped smile at the sound of her name. 'She's not so easy to get on with,' said Sadie in a low voice. 'You'll have to tread carefully if you need anything from her. She's inclined to consider herself hard done by and put upon.'

Kate smiled brightly across at Annette, who glared stonily back at her.

'There's a part-time clerk, Becky, who sits at the other desk when she's here. A nice girl, but not desperately bright. And through the door on the other side there is the Development Office. Chris Townsend was our Development Officer, but I expect you've heard that he died recently in an accident.'

'Yes,' said Kate, and left it at that.

'Are you taking over from Chris?' interrupted Annette, leaving her chair and joining them by the door. 'I didn't think the college had even advertised his job yet.'

'Kate is just helping out for a month with the study fortnight,' Sadie explained. 'She's here temporarily.'

'That's all right, then,' said Annette, going back to her desk. 'You wouldn't want someone unqualified running the Development Office.'

'Of course not,' said Kate, and tried to look suitably humble. She should get herself a badge with 'Unambitious Bimbo' printed on it, perhaps.

Sadie led the way into the Development Office. 'Don't worry if you haven't sorted everyone out yet, I can always remind you who people are until you get the hang of the place.' She closed the door. 'And if you need to get away from that poisonous crowd, just keep this door firmly shut.

By the window, Sadie said, 'This is Chris's desk. Was,

I suppose. You might as well use it while you're here. I'll show you where he kept his files.'

'People won't mind? I don't want them to think this is a bid for his job.'

'Take no notice of Annette,' said Sadie. 'She's the possessive kind and doesn't like the idea of newcomers. I think she hoped to be asked to take on the admin side herself, but really she has a hard enough task getting her own work done, let alone any more. And she couldn't take workshops and seminars like you.'

Kate tried to look as though she ran workshops and seminars every week of the year, while Sadie opened the drawers of Chris Townsend's desk.

'Pens and pencils, stationery. And here in the bottom drawer are the files on his current projects. It's probably simplest if I leave you to go through them and see what's relevant. Read through the correspondence, take a look at the programme for the fortnight. I'll leave you with them, shall I?'

'Fine,' said Kate. 'And what about the computer? Won't most of his side of the correspondence be on that?'

'Good thinking. I suppose you know how to work one of these things?'

'Yes,' said Kate, mentally thanking the university for standardizing on a single word-processing package.

'Thank goodness one of us can. I hate them. I'd rather use a pencil and notebook any day. Why don't we go and get a cup of coffee now, and then I'll leave you here to get on with your reading for the rest of the morning?'

Through the main office they found a small room with an electric kettle and a few chairs. Coffee was of the instant variety, but Kate felt she needed a shot of caffeine, from whatever source. The Bursar's secretary was already there, drinking coffee. Ah, Annette, thought

Kate. Possessive about Chris and not very friendly to outsiders.

'Have you seen our nice young policeman yet, Sadie?' asked Annette. 'He's really nice. Sandy hair, lovely blue eyes, and a proper pair of shoulders. He's been taking statements from everyone. Really nice.'

Sadie didn't seem anxious to join in this conversation, Kate noticed, but Annette persevered.

'He's been asking about Chris. About what went on the afternoon he died. Whether we'd seen him just before it happened. Why he went up the tower. How he was in himself. Had he been drinking? Was he depressed? Well, I told him, wouldn't you be if you worked here?' She laughed.

'What did he say to that?' asked Kate.

'Oh, he had no sense of humour,' said Annette. 'He made me tell him what I meant by it. Asked if Chris was really depressed over his work, all that sort of thing.'

'And was he?' asked Kate.

'No more than anyone else,' said Annette. 'And you don't see us diving off the top of Grace, do you?'

'Really, Annette!' said Sadie. 'Do you have to talk about it like that? You are the most insensitive person I've ever met!' Sadie's full scarlet lips were pulled into a thin line.

'All right, keep your hair on.' Annette seemed incapable of speaking in anything other than clichés. 'You have to laugh if you're not going to cry, don't you? And we all know why *you're* so upset.' She turned to Kate. 'Our Sadie had a bit of a crush on Chris,' she confided.

'Shut up!' said Sadie. 'You just love spreading gossip. You should make sure you've got it right before you put these stories around.'

Anyone with a modicum of sensitivity would have done so, but Annette carried on. 'It's no use trying to hide it. We all saw how you looked at him, and the way the two of you used to go into your office and close the door on the rest of us.'

'Perhaps that was to get away from the vicious sound of your voice in the outer office,' said Sadie.

'There's no need to be rude,' said Annette, putting her cup and saucer back on the tray in a pointed manner. 'I was only having a bit of fun. You should learn to take a joke.'

'Did your policeman have a name?' asked Kate as she left the room.

'I didn't notice. Well, you don't think of policemen having names, do you? And what are you interested in it for, anyway? None of it is anything to do with you.' And she returned to the main office.

'Sorry about that,' said Sadie.

'It must still be upsetting for you all,' said Kate, noticing the patch of bright colour that still stained Sadie's cheeks, and the way she had clenched her hands on her knees. Seeing Kate's eyes on her, Sadie released the tension in her body and attempted a relaxed smile.

'For some of us, anyway,' she said, lightly. 'I shouldn't let Annette get on my nerves like that, but it's a tense time and I have to keep raising money for the Development Fund, and without Chris's back-up it isn't easy. He was so optimistic and confident that he made it all seem such fun.'

They sat silently drinking their coffee, while Kate thought about a tall handsome man with an attractive smile, and a stunning young woman with chestnut hair and scarlet lips. You couldn't help wondering just what they did once they had closed their door, though, could you?

Kate spent the rest of the day reading through folders and logging on to Chris's computer to read what seemed to be relevant in his WordPerfect files. Two hundred and fourteen students would be arriving, she learned, and staying in the college for two weeks. Bartlemas had a connection with a university on the eastern seaboard of the States, which organized the American side of things. Kate saw that a large number of American librarians and teachers wished to gain further qualifications, on top of the impressive degrees that they already held. Most of them seemed to be between the ages of forty and sixty. Maybe they were also hoping for dreamy autumnal afternoons in punts, and rendezvous with exciting lovers beneath gothic arches, but she had the feeling that she was about to get submerged in crowds of earnest middle-aged people who wished to know all that Oxford could teach them about genre fiction, and who might find Kate's approach to life and gender woefully frivolous.

Oh dear, she thought, as she read a folder of correspondence from prospective students: one or two of them sounded like trouble. All those questions about the availability of showers and baths. And was Bartlemas capable of catering to their diet? Was there a fitness room available? What about jogging routes? Kate was not about to volunteer her personal jogging routes: she preferred her own company to that of a bunch of students, however mature and even if they were interested in the sort of genre fiction that she wrote herself. She picked up another letter, written in green ink. More trouble. She had observed that people who wrote in green ink were all weird. The person – Curtis Skinner, she saw, glancing to the end of the page – also said that he found it difficult to make friends and was looking forward to meeting a whole new social experience during his time here at Bartlemas. She closed the file and put it back in the desk drawer. It was time to turn to something more serious.

She should check what was happening at the

printers: she needed maps and leaflets before she could make up the welcome packs. She took the bright blue document wallet out of the drawer and pulled the contents out on to her desk, looking for the letters with the quotes and the delivery dates. It seemed as though Chris had changed his mind over the wording, which would have delayed the production of the leaflet.

Funny, she thought, as she picked up an invoice with a query in red Biro in Chris's handwriting. It seemed to have nothing to do with the rest of the correspondence in the folder. And then there was the note stuck to one corner, written in green felt-tipped pen:

CURIOSITY KILLED THE CAT

She felt as though someone had put a mild electric shock through her arms and hands. They tingled as she looked at it. This was a warning, she could tell, or perhaps even a threat. Something was very wrong here, she thought. The atmosphere in the Bursary office, the way Sadie was hiding her real feelings, and the fatal accident on the tower. She believed that they must all be connected. It was no use telling herself that her novelist's curiosity had got her into trouble in the past and should be severely kept in its place, she couldn't change her nature now. She pulled off the note and put it into her bag.

The interesting question was, who was it intended for? How long had it been in the file? Was the warning for Christopher Townsend or for herself? And what was the invoice about? It had nothing to do with the printers, as far as she could see, since it appeared to deal with building materials.

'Any idea what this is?' she asked Sadie, who arrived shortly afterwards. She handed her the invoice, but said nothing about the note.

'What? Oh, that shouldn't be in there!' and she

snatched it away. 'What are you doing looking at invoices?' she snapped. 'They're nothing to do with you!'

'Really, I was checking on what was happening about the printing,' protested Kate. 'And as I was reading through the story so far, I found this. I have no idea what an invoice was doing in a file of correspondence.'

Sadie had folded up the paper so that its contents were invisible. 'Maybe it isn't your fault,' she conceded. 'Chris had a habit of answering the phone with an open file in front of him. He would pick up whatever document he needed for the conversation, and place it on top of the correspondence in the file. Then when he had finished the phone call he would close the file and place it back in the filing cabinet. The misfiled paper would be lost for weeks, sometimes. I expect that's what happened here.'

'Of course,' said Kate, wondering why Sadie was making such a meal of the explanation. 'Well, you've found your paper now, anyway. I'll keep my eyes open for any more misfiled gems, shall I?'

'I hope there won't be too many,' said Sadie briskly. 'You'd better get on and check the stuff at the printers. We need it back in time to get the welcome packs together.'

And Sadie smiled too brightly and left the room, taking the invoice with her.

Still odd, thought Kate, and jotted down what she could remember of the details of the invoice in her notebook. And where had Sadie taken it? She kept getting the impression that the real business of the Bartlemas Bursary was carried on out of sight, in some underground room full of conspirators.

CURIOSITY KILLED THE CAT. With Sadie out of the room, she took the note from her bag and looked at it more carefully. It could just be an unpleasant joke from anyone in the office, a hint not to listen in to other people's conversations, for example. But it was Chris's file that she had found it in. And something had killed Chris, even if it wasn't yet clear what it was. Which thought gave her a nasty feeling along her spine.

Emma was on the phone. One of her brood had come out in a rash and the leader of the Activity Programme had refused to let him stay for the morning session. Emma had argued that the rash was probably a result of the heat, or something he ate, but the woman had been adamant, and so Emma had to stay at home and look after him until the spots subsided. She sounded frazzled. Kate could hear the baby wailing in the background, and a constant undertone of the whining noise a child makes when it is bored.

'I'll fill you in on what will be happening, and what your part in it is,' Emma was saying.

'That would be useful,' said Kate. Emma often sounded efficient like this, but Kate knew from past experience that when it came down to it important pieces of paper would be missing, and Kate would find herself frantically improvising as arrangements fell apart.

'The students turn up in a couple of weeks' time, so you'd better get on with familiarizing yourself with the programme. Then you can prepare the welcome packs they'll receive on registration. Oh, and make sure that the card index file of participants is up to date.'

'Yes, Emma,' said Kate, as the tide of instructions washed over her.

'And I think you should check on the printers,' said Emma. 'They didn't seem to understand my instructions for some reason.'

'Yes, Emma,' said Kate. She would ring them up and find out what was happening.

'The students arrive during the Friday afternoon, register, and are shown to their rooms. At registration they will be given their welcome packs, with copies of the programme, and lists of tutors, and details of other amusements that are available. Then at six-thirty we all meet for a glass of wine. At seven-fifteen we go into dinner, and please wear something suitable, Kate. A skirt or dress, preferably well below your knees, not that dip-dyed thing of yours.'

'Yeah, yeah,' said Kate. 'Stop sounding like my mother.'

'I didn't know you had one,' said Emma tartly. 'Did I tell you I've got you down to lead the trip to Birmingham?'

'Oh, great. Thanks, Emma. The others get to go to the theatre in Stratford, or to stare at the opulence of Blenheim Palace, or go on a tour of picturesque Cotswold villages. Me, I get landed with bloody Birmingham? Why?'

'You're taking them to a concert at the Symphony Hall. A celebrity concert. Some world-famous soprano, I forget her name. You should be pleased.'

'I should?'

'Well, you're interested in music, aren't you? You were always going to concerts last year. You haven't gone off it, have you?'

'No.' She wasn't going to explain to Emma that her enthusiasm had been for a musician, rather than for the music itself. At the time she had tried very hard, read some books, listened to some difficult CDs, tuned her radio to Classic FM, all to try to please him. But then she had found out that the bastard was two-timing her and she had given the books back to the library, donated the CDs to the jumble sale, and had re-tuned her radio to GLR. It was all a great relief and, given a few more months, she might even stop dreaming about the man,

and waking in the middle of the night to find she missed
him.

When she had put the receiver down Emma went back
to read another story to her cross, feverish child. While
she was looking for the book he wanted, she wondered
whether she should have told Kate about the enquiries
she had received about her. But she had been so irritated
at Kate's reaction to the news about Birmingham that it
had slipped her mind for the moment. Really, the woman
should be grateful that she was going to a marvellous
concert in that brilliant concert hall. She wasn't going to
ring her back to give her all the details. If she remembered, she would mention it next time she saw her.

It had been a bit odd, though, now she came to think
about it. The caller had asked who Kate was, and what
she was doing at Bartlemas, and what she had done
previously. Emma had made a really amusing story out
of it, the way Kate had got herself involved in all those
silly mysteries, like some sleuth in a crime novel. 'She
just seems to fall over dead bodies wherever she goes!'
she had said, then had wondered whether it wasn't in
rather bad taste, given the recent nasty accident at Bartlemas. 'And she likes to think that she can go round asking
questions, and pushing her nose into other people's business, and find out who was responsible. It's ridiculous,
really. We all know that the police are quite capable of
finding out for themselves, without any help from our
Kate. But it's no good trying to tell her that!' She hadn't
got time to ring Kate back, even if she thought she
deserved such consideration, and it probably didn't
matter at all. She hadn't given the caller Kate's address
or phone number. 'Really, you must understand that I
have to respect her privacy,' she had said. But she had

suggested that these details might be found in the Oxford telephone directory.

She settled down on the sofa with her son. 'Green slime lay all over the forest floor . . .' she read.

Chapter Five

The good angels do not look into all the secret things of God ... some things indeed they know by revelation, and others by means of the excellent intelligence with which they are gifted; there is much, however, of which they are ignorant.

John Milton, *The Christian Doctrine*

'Hello?'

Silence. The light from the sword does not waver, but the answering flame amid the cherub's golden locks shimmies from left to right.

Nod for yes, shake for no, thinks Christopher. He tries again. 'Now that we've established my name, can we move on to what I'm doing here?'

A small flicker from the light. 'You are waiting.'

'Well, Zophiel, how do you suggest we spend our section of Eternity? Card games? Scrabble?'

'I don't think it is appropriate for me to suggest any lighthearted pastimes.'

'Is there nothing we could do to shorten the waiting time?'

'Time is not a concept with which I am familiar, except in a theoretical sense.'

'But if we could find some common interest, it would make life – or rather death – less tedious.'

'There is a possibility. It might be useful if you could tell me what brought you here. While I have been under-

taking his rather wearisome guard duty, I have been study-
ing the psychology of the victim, and it would be useful if
you could give me the details of your own case for my notes.'

'But I'm not a victim!'

'What else would you call someone who is the subject of
a successful murderous attack?'

'Well . . .'

'We call him a victim,' says Zophiel in his customary
flat tones.

'But we all know what a victim is like. A cringing fellow
who creeps around and whose very posture invites the world
to hit him and take advantage of him. You couldn't accuse
me of being anything like that.'

'In the course of my studies I have found that the typical
victim is not necessarily anything like the person you have
described. But I have found that his whole life exhibits a
pattern which culminates in the sort of incident which happened during your own last few minutes on Earth.'

'So you want the story of my life?'

'And in the telling you might come to understanding.
You might try to understand the small, wayward steps that
led you to this place, and thus bring enlightenment both to
yourself and to me.'

'A vindication of the rights of the victim?'

'The victim's point of view is rarely heard. Perhaps it is
time to redress the balance.'

'I've always enjoyed talking about myself. This is going
to be most rewarding for both of us, I feel.'

'You may not find, as we progress, that the exercise is
as simple and as painless as you think.'

'I'll risk it. Where shall I begin?'

'You should begin at the beginning.'

The beginning. Childhood? Birth?

Birth normal, I believe. Childhood less so.

My mother died when I was small, some time
between my second and third birthdays. I don't

remember it. I imagine that in the manner of the time it was kept from me and eventually someone told me some pious fiction. 'Mummy has gone to join the angels,' or some such garbage.

'What was that you said?' The wings are quivering. The golden eye is flashing. Behind him the brazen fanged beasts set up a low growling. A sudden wind rises and moans in the treetops.

'I'm sorry, Zophiel. Nothing personal, you understand. No disrespect intended. Just a way of speaking.'

No, what I remember is a childhood spent with my father. A good man, Mark Townsend. A social worker. He provided child minders and sent me to congenial schools and made time – what they now call quality time – for his son. Since I didn't remember my mother, I hardly missed her. How should I? It wasn't until I reached school that I realized that something was lacking in my life. And even then, although it was not as usual as it is now, it was hardly uncommon to be a child from a single-parent home.

I forget the boy's name, but he was the urchin in the seat behind me, a lad with black hair and little brown button eyes, sharp pinching fingers and a way of stepping on my feet, who started the teasing.

'You've got no mum,' he said.

It took me a few minutes to understand what he was saying, but he persisted, and eventually I got there.

'Your mum's dead,' he said. And by this time he had raised interest from the surrounding children. One of them made a jeering noise that sounded like 'Nyeah', and several others joined in. At this point the teacher noticed the row and told us all off.

'I've got a mum, and so's the rest of us,' hissed my tormentor through greenish teeth. 'You haven't, so we're going to get you at break.' They did, too. And that was the first and only time I regretted not having a mother.

For on my way to and from school, I started to observe these mothers of theirs, and I was not impressed. They shouted, they smacked small bare legs with ferocity. Their faces were marked by lines of irritation, and if I had been aware of such things at that time I would have noticed that their figures had lost their firm contours, and their clothes were old, ill assorted and frequently spattered with the detritus of minced food spat out by the younger siblings of my schoolmates.

Of course, soon after my mother died I had someone to look after me while my father worked. A sensible, but rather stupid woman, I remember: a neighbour with children of her own, who found that the extra money came in useful for foreign holidays and paying for the goods she ordered from a catalogue. She, or one of the other women from the neighbourhood, still sometimes gave me my tea once I started school, but increasingly I liked to be at home on my own. I could do simple shopping on the Parade, and set the plastic-covered kitchen table with the two sets of cutlery, and the blue-ringed plates, that were all we needed for our meal. Afterwards, my father and I shared the chore of clearing the table, wiping down the plastic, and doing our scant washing-up.

We did very well together. He was not too fussy about tidiness, or dust, or old grey socks and coffee mugs festering under the bed. He would try to get home in time to give us both our tea, and this was often fish and chips, eaten at the kitchen table, out of the newspaper. I can still remember the look of that greasy grey paper, and the smell of the vinegar and the dark brown oil. We ate with our fingers, licking them afterwards and racing each other for the crispy bits of batter left on the paper.

'Strawberry ice cream for pud,' he would say when we had finished. And then he would make us both mugs of tea to wash it down.

Now, don't go imagining that I was a neglected child, or had a deprived childhood. Far from it. My father would make me eat raw carrots and apples when he remembered about the need for vitamins. There were a hundred times more books in our house than in the homes of my schoolmates. Sundays disappeared under a rustling tide of newspapers. We visited castles and museums at the weekend, and took a picnic with us. We rode down country lanes on our bicycles, and ate our ham sandwiches on the lawn of some stately home or other. And we talked. All the time we talked. No subject was taboo. I think my father enjoyed my company, or perhaps it was that he enjoyed the conversation of someone whose views had been formed entirely by himself.

So you will understand that I was not best pleased when Dianne Kemp entered my life.

When she first came to tea, one Saturday, there was something about the way my father didn't quite meet my eye that made me think that she had been kept a secret from me, and I didn't like it. They seemed too familiar with one another, left too many things unsaid, for their acquaintance to have been a recent one.

We spent that Friday evening and Saturday morning tidying and hoovering the house, though I couldn't see the necessity, myself. Looking back on it, mind you, I can see that Dad and I lived in a tip. Nothing sordid, you understand, but still a tip.

When we had finished our cleaning, Dad stood next to me and looked around.

'I suppose it's all right,' he said, doubtfully.

'Course it is,' I answered. There was nothing wrong with the place that I could see.

When Dianne arrived and was introduced to me I remember that she laughed a lot. A tinkly, happy, 'I'm going to be your new Mummy' kind of a laugh. She had the habit of looking at something, wrinkling her nose at it in disapproval, and then attempting to cancel the effect by letting out the laugh. I came to think of it as The Laugh, like that, with initial capitals.

'Well, I can see you two have been on your own for too long,' she said, standing in the middle of the sitting room. And she wrinkled up her nose, and then she laughed. Dad smiled, a nervous smile, and I just stared down at the polished toes of my black lace-up shoes.

'You two aren't very good at looking after yourselves, are you?' she said, as she opened the fridge door and looked inside. And she laughed again, touching Dad's hand and looking at him with a silly expression on her round, bland face. 'You're going to need some help, I can see that.'

Her eye lighted on the open washing machine and its rainbow mixture of wet clothes. More nose-wrinkle. 'You need a woman's touch about this place.' More laughter.

'Didn't you learn that an obsessively tidy house was a negative indicator of parental competence?' Dad said. This must have been a social worker's joke, and therefore not expected to be funny. And although he smiled, I didn't see the pockets bulge under his eyes, the way they did when he laughed at one of my jokes. Then he put his arm round her shoulders, and kissed her ear, until I had to tug at the sleeve of his cardigan to make him stop and pay attention to me.

'Well, what happened after that?'

'I thought you would know. I thought you knew everything.'

'No. There are many things in your world that are unknown to us.' He sounded a bit huffy, as though he did not like being reminded of the truth of this.

'So?' asks Zophiel, after a long silence. 'Which of you won the battle?'

'Battle? What battle?'

'The battle for your father's attention. For his love.'
'I'm tired. I'll tell you the rest tomorrow.'
'Tomorrow is not a concept that I understand.'
'Tough.'

I've been here before, thought Kate, looking up at the ceiling of Bartlemas chapel and catching the eye of an angel playing a strange bulbous instrument. In the background the organ hummed something religious and Bachian. Last time it all ended in tears, she thought. I came to a concert here with Andrew, and found myself involved in an argument with Liam. Two-faced, two-timing Liam. She shut her mind to thoughts of tall, skinny, beautiful Liam. That relationship was over, and she had even heard a whisper that he was leaving Oxford for a post at an American university. She concentrated on the present: Christopher Mark Townsend's memorial service.

Fifteen minutes ago, in the Bursary, it had taken a terse argument to get herself here.

'But you didn't even know him!' Annette Paige had exclaimed, when she saw Kate with her exuberant dip-dyed dress covered by a long navy jacket, a jade green hat pulled down low on her forehead, and her shining titanium ear-rings dangling nearly to her shoulders.

'I met him,' Kate had replied defiantly. 'Once. Briefly, perhaps. But it was only minutes before his death.'

'It's only her second day here!' Annette had cried to an uncaring Bursary.

'I should like to say my farewells,' said Kate, and cast down her eyes in simulated grief. As Annette was still making huffing noises, she added meekly, 'I'll sit right at the back.'

'You'll be lucky to find a place at all,' said Sadie, who was dressed in black, complete with black tights and high-heeled black ankle boots. Her exuberant hair was uncovered, but she had moderated the colour of her lipstick from scarlet to a shiny russet. 'The chapel isn't very big.'

'Then we'd better get over there,' said Kate, briskly, and ran down the stairs and across the quadrangle, with Sadie at her heels. Behind them, in the office, Annette was still combing her hair and dabbing at her nose with a pad of cotton wool.

'You don't mind making enemies, do you?' said Sadie, as they galloped their way across grass and flagstones.

'What? Oh, I can do much better than that when I'm really trying!' cried Kate, pushing through the chapel door into the cool gloom.

What would Briony think about holding the memorial service so close to the spot where her husband had died, she wondered, as they walked past the door to the tower. She glanced briefly at the two pictures of Adam and Eve, but today they were just dim brown shapes against the grey wall.

Kate slipped into a seat in the back row, just inside the door, while Sadie marched boldly down towards the front. She's behaving like the chief mourner, thought Kate.

Kate was in the last of three raked rows of pews, facing an identical set of three across the aisle. She had to crane to her right to see the altar and pulpit, but she could see the people in the seats opposite her with no difficulty at all. Sadie was near the front of the chapel, but facing Kate, so that she could study her expression.

Was she really heartbroken? Was this a woman whose lover had just died? Or was the college gossip way off beam? A couple of places to the right of Sadie, at the end of the row nearest to the altar rails, was another woman in black. Long fair hair, round face, small features: it had to be the widow, Briony. She was accompanied by an older, solid woman with grey hair and a weatherbeaten face, who was wearing an uncompromisingly ugly hat and a costume that looked as though it had been to many generations of funerals. Was this the widow's mother, perhaps? But no, the woman looked vaguely familiar. Kate had seen her around college. Ah yes, the Master's wife and gardening enthusiast, Honor Flint.

After studying these two thoroughly from her unobtrusive position, Kate stared around at the rest of the people in the chapel. Sadie was right, the place was filling up fast, and at this rate the late-comers would be forced to stand by the door to the tower. The Master had entered now, and was sitting next to his wife. Aidan Flint was a mousy man, pale-skinned and light-haired, and he looked as though he rarely stood up to his wife. But then, she reflected, who could know what really went on inside a marriage? In the pews opposite Kate, the Bursary staff had arrived: Annette Paige, still pink and damp around the nose and with her fair hair straggling from a light blue beret. To her left sat John Clay, in a raspberry pink linen jacket, his malicious eyes taking in as much as Kate's. At this moment their eyes met, and he sent her a mock salute and then turned to Annette, said something and smiled spitefully. Snake, thought Kate.

There was a slight disturbance on her left, and a small figure climbed into the pew beside her. Dark hair, dark eyes, skinny figure and a little monkey face, observed Kate, gazing in what she hoped was a surreptitious and discreet manner. Dark red trousers with a matching silk t-shirt and a cream linen jacket over the top. No make-up, but a very pleasant and expensive-smelling scent, which seemed vaguely familiar to Kate. The stranger sat with her lips pursed, her hands clasped tightly in her lap, and with no apparent interest in her surroundings. It was her scent that prodded Kate's memory into coming up with her name: Dr Beeton, according to Emma Dolby. She hadn't seen her properly before, when they were discussing the Temptation, but her nose was sure that it was the same person.

More people climbed into their obscure pew, so that its occupants were pressed closely together. Kate was jammed between a solid oak panel on one side and Dr Beeton on the other. All over the little chapel people were cramming into the narrow spaces. Sadie was being urged to make room by a man in ginger tweed with receding white hair and a boiled complexion.

'Who's that?' she whispered to Dr Beeton, pointing in an unladylike way.

'Steven Charleston, College Accountant,' came the reply.

As she watched, Charleston was then forced in turn to cede to a man of about forty, whose sun-streaked brown hair and sun-tanned complexion were at odds with his dark office suit and tie.

'Robert Grailing, Bursar,' came the unsolicited information from her left. Kate nodded her thanks and continued her observation. Sadie was whispering intently to the second man, presumably telling him that there was not enough room for them both, since the man frowned, then she glanced across at Kate, caught her eye, and looked away again immediately. But somehow room was found at last for the whole congregation, and the service started.

Kate's neighbour enjoyed singing hymns, Kate found. She had a loud and clear voice, with excellent projection. Unfortunately, she sang flat, and got flatter as each verse progressed. Perhaps she realized that Kate was listening to her, for she turned slightly to her right and smiled at Kate, as if she knew just how out of tune she was. She doesn't care, thought Kate. She probably doesn't care at all about the impression she makes on people. She warmed to Dr Beeton: a woman after her own heart, in spite of her academic manner.

The hymn ended and the Master, Aidan Flint, addressed them, talking about the Christopher Townsend he had known. Although Kate was prepared to believe that anyone as attractive as Christopher was also a wonderful person, even she couldn't quite accept that he was as totally perfect as the Master made him out to be. He also skated over any possible reason for Christopher's untimely dive from the Tower of Grace, so that Kate was left feeling dissatisfied. She knew she was being unreasonable: who expected naked truth at a memorial service, after all? But as she looked at the other characters she knew – Sadie, and Briony Townsend, Annette Paige, even Honor Flint and Rob Grailing – she felt that they were all playing parts and that behind the decorous exteriors there was a lot more that they knew about Christopher Townsend. The only person who seemed to be behaving naturally was Dr Beeton, who leaned back against the pew and whistled quietly and tunelessly through her teeth.

At the end of the service, while they were all making their way across to the Lamb Room, where they would be served with indifferent wine and supermarket snacks, Kate thought again about the invoice that Sadie had whipped out of sight so quickly. It had been a very nondescript letterheading, with a forgettable name. Something to do with buildings. Exteriors. Ardington Exteriors. Or something similar. And the invoice had been for some sort of cladding, and the sum? Five figures, she thought. Fourteen thousand pounds? Or was it twenty-four? She concentrated on calling up the sheet of white A4 with the query in red Biro in the bottom right hand corner.

Anderson Exteriors, then a word in brackets: (Denton). OK so far. She mentally moved down to the narrative, but that was a couple of lines of items that meant nothing to her. But the total at the bottom of the right-hand column was twenty-four thousand, three hundred and twenty-seven pounds. She couldn't recall the pence.

That was quite a sum to query. Especially if it was true that curiosity did kill the cat.

Kate had removed her jacket and hat and run her fingers through her hair until it stood on end in the way that she preferred. Her ear-rings flashed in the light streaming in through the long windows, and in her bright blue dress she no longer looked as though she was attending a funeral. The wine wasn't too bad, once you had drunk a glass or two of it, and the snacks, though dull, would save her from buying her own lunch.

'Hello.'

She hadn't noticed his approach. He stood now at her left elbow and smiled down at her. Not tall, but tall enough, brown hair, hazel eyes, well-chosen tie, pleasant smile. Robert Grailing. This was the man who had squeezed in beside Sadie James at the memorial service. Not really nondescript at all, but rather nice-looking, in a pleasant, dependable way. His clothes were dark and unremarkable, and he had brown hair, lightened to marmalade colour on top, where the sun had caught it. Regular features. Just the sort of man one saw in Sainsbury's on a Saturday morning, pushing a trolley with an equally pleasant-looking wife. *Married*, Kate told herself. *Probably*. She smiled in a more interested way.

'I've found some rolled-up things with smoked salmon inside,' he said, helpfully. 'Small, but quite good.' And he produced a plate of snacks which he held so that Kate could help herself to a greedy quantity.

'Thanks,' she said, with her mouth full.

'I thought it was time we met,' he said. 'I'm the Bursar, Rob Grailing.'

Kate tried to say, 'I know,' and 'How do you do,' but was defeated by another mouthful of smoked salmon rolled-up thing.

'Officially, I'm your boss,' he said. 'But your appointment was so rapid that we never got to meet.'

'Oh, right,' said Kate, unoriginally. 'It's nice to meet you, Mr Grailing.' Oh hell, that should probably have been Doctor. How was one supposed to tell?

'Call me Rob. Everybody does.' Which at least solved that difficulty. 'Is everything going all right?'

Kate, having taken another smoked salmon snack, now swallowed vigorously. 'It's fine. Everything Chris did was documented and clear. I can follow everything quite easily.'

'Good,' said Rob Grailing. 'I wonder whether we could—'

But Kate didn't learn what it was he wanted, for at this moment they were interrupted by the arrival of the Master. He was towed into their small group by his wife, who dominated him by a couple of inches in height and several hundredweight in personality. In their wake came a pale and rather sulky Briony. It must be galling to be upstaged at your late husband's memorial service by the boss's wife, thought Kate.

'Oh, so it was you who found the smoked salmon spirals,' said Honor Flint, accusingly, to Kate.

'Delicious, aren't they?' said Kate, offering a plate on which only one remained. Honor Flint took it and ate it in one rapid swallow.

'I wonder if we could have a word,' said Aidan Flint to Rob Grailing in the brief pause. Kate gathered that she was expected to lose herself in the mob, but refrained from doing so. A writer, she told herself, is always on the look-out for material. She omitted to remind herself that it was historical novels that she wrote, rather than the crime fiction that seemed more appropriate for this particular gathering.

'We've heard on the grapevine that you might need some help over this study fortnight of yours,' the Master began.

'Of course you do!' interrupted Honor who, having disposed of the last of the smoked salmon, was ready for speech again. 'And dear Briony needs something to occupy her during this difficult time.'

'Do I?' Briony asked nobody in particular.

'She mustn't be allowed to brood,' insisted Honor. 'I thought she would be happiest in the gardens, helping Dave Evans,' she informed them. 'She could have helped me keep the man under control. I really am not at all sure what he is doing some of the time. But she seems to have lost all her interest in growing things, and Dave Evans was really quite unpleasant at the idea of having Briony as his assistant. He said that Barry was learning his ways very nicely and he didn't want to have to train up anyone else.'

'What had you in mind for her?' asked Rob Grailing.

'Some simple tasks,' said Honor. 'There must be plenty of things she could do in the Bursary.'

'There's certainly a lot of talk about how over-worked the staff there are,' said Aidan.

Kate was bouncing up and down on the balls of her feet, longing to put her word in. She could see that Briony would be brought in – probably without a salary – and she would be out if she didn't stand up for herself.

'The work is quite specialized!' she cried at last. 'You need qualifications and experience and things.'

'What is it to do with you?' asked Honor, bluntly. Kate wondered what it was about an Oxford college that made people think they had the right to be so rude to others.

'Don't worry, Kate,' said Rob Grailing, his hand resting on Kate's arm in a reassuring, or perhaps restraining, way. 'Your job is quite safe. And I'm sure we can find something useful for Briony to do. There are all those leaflets to sort out, and envelopes to stuff for our next mailing for the Appeal.'

Kate breathed again. She didn't mind if they found Briony dreary chores like that to do.

'Yes,' she said. 'Or perhaps she could run the library. You don't need much by way of qualifications or experience to do that, do you?'

'What a naughty girl you are,' said Rob Grailing, quietly. 'Now why don't you go and find us some more food while the Master and I work out the details for dear Briony?'

Smoked salmon seemed in short supply, but Kate went roaming around the tables and windowsills looking for something edible. She found a plate of biscuits spread with cream cheese and topped with a mean sliver of olive. (Who on earth had done the catering? Surely not Bartlemas's excellent chef.) But just as she put out a hand to pull the plate expertly from the table without disturbing the people around her, someone else beat her to it. She looked up and admitted defeat. The man was about six foot six tall and nearly the same across the middle, with a face as plain as a garden spade. He had sparse grey hair and wore a grey cardigan instead of a jacket.

'Harry Bickerstaff,' he said, not offering her one of the biscuits which he had appropriated, but shovelling them all into his own mouth. 'We're both involved in this study fortnight, I believe.'

'I've read your books,' she said, and nearly added, 'a long time ago,' but thought better of it. 'And enjoyed them, very much.' Well, it was true that she had enjoyed his thud and blunder stories when she was about twelve. She doubted whether they sold very well to today's sophisticated young, who apparently spent their time surfing the Internet in search of interactive pornography.

'How kind of you to say so,' he said. 'I don't believe I've come across any of yours. Do you write under your own name?'

'Yes,' said Kate, tersely.

'Really? Well, I don't get on with this modern stuff. But then, you probably think I'm hopelessly old fashioned.'

'Of course not,' she said automatically. 'I expect I'll be seeing you in the Bursary,' and she started to edge her way out of the corner where he had trapped her with his bulk.

'Oh, good! I'm glad I've caught you both here.' It was Annette Paige, pink of nose and wearing her pale blue beret at a more rakish angle.

'I wanted to see you about some important matters, too,' Harry said to Annette. 'About this anthology, for instance.' He appealed to Kate: 'Do you know what's happening about the anthology?'

'Sorry,' said Kate. 'What was it you wanted us for, Annette?'

'Committee meeting. Tomorrow, ten-thirty, Seminar Room Four, Pesant Quad,' she said. 'I've put copies of the agenda in your pigeonholes, so please go through it before tomorrow,' and she left them as they both scrambled for diaries to write down the details.

'I suggested that I might edit the anthology,' Harry was saying, as he put his diary and pencil away. 'But I was told that this had already been taken care of. Don't you know about it? Aren't you in charge of that sort of thing?'

'I don't seem to be in charge of much except complaints and the organization of a trip to Birmingham,' said Kate, starting to edge past half an acre of woollen cardigan. 'But I'm sure that everything can be sorted out at the committee meeting tomorrow.' And she grabbed a bowl of prawn-flavoured crisps and escaped.

She was negotiating a clump of people with her loot when she caught a waft of the expensive scent that had been next to her in the chapel.

'Can I share some of your crisps?' said a voice behind her. She turned and offered the plate. Sure enough, the figure was wearing the wine-red trousers and cream jacket that she remembered from the service: Faith Beeton. She had a pleasant speaking voice, and it was odd to think that she sang so badly. Small dark eyes stared at Kate as she helped herself to a handful of crisps and crunched them down.

'We've met before, haven't we?' she said, eventually. 'More wine?' and she expertly lifted a half-full bottle from a nearby table and refilled their glasses. 'Where would it have been?'

'Yes, you're right: in the Tower of Grace,' said Kate.

'Of course. You were looking at the Temptation and wondering who or what the Gnostics were.'

'Oh, right. We were introduced at the time. I'm Kate Ivory.'

'I'm Faith Beeton,' said the other. 'I teach here. You're taking over Chris Townsend's duties for the study fortnight, aren't you?'

'Yes. And leading a couple of seminars. And giving a writing workshop,' added Kate.

'So you know something about this genre fiction?'

'I write it,' said Kate. 'Historical romances.'

'Oh.' Faith's comment did not invite Kate to expand on the subject. 'I've been told to cover the crime fiction section.'

'Well, some of it's quite good, or so I'm told,' said Kate, generously. 'It's not my thing, but there must be people who like it, I suppose.'

'Are there any of the biscuits left?'

'I'm afraid not. I can see only empty plates around the room. Perhaps it's a hint that we should leave.'

'I shall have to make myself some lunch, then. I was hoping to get away with living off the funeral meats. Do you want to join me? I live five minutes away.'

'Thanks,' said Kate, mildly surprised. She watched Faith Beeton swipe a full bottle of wine just before it was whisked away by a waiter, and gave a wistful look towards Rob Grailing's group. He and the Master still seemed to be in earnest conversation, while Honor harangued a listless Briony. Poor woman, thought Kate. She's probably longing to get home, take those shoes off, and allow herself to be thoroughly miserable in peace.

In one of those sudden silences that falls on large groups of disparate people, she heard Annette's voice saying, 'Well, I think it would be a very good idea if we had Briony working in the Bursary. There's no need for that Kate person at all. She's much too—'

But general conversation had started up again and Kate didn't hear the no-doubt unflattering comment that Annette was making about her. She wondered who she was talking to, and hoped that it wasn't anyone who had any power to hire or fire.

'Well, well,' Faith said. 'You have made yourself unpopular in a short time, haven't you? What have you been doing to upset the Bursary staff like that?'

Before Kate could stand up for herself she spotted someone else approaching them. A man with white hair, boiled ham for a face, dressed in a ginger suit.

'Who did you say that was?' she asked Faith.

'Steven Charleston, College Accountant.'

'Oh yes. Now I remember.'

'Not that I'd trust him with my piggy bank,' said Faith.

'Really? Why not?'

'Forget that I said it,' said Faith. 'Come on, let's go.' And she made for the door before Steven Charleston could corner them.

Chapter Six

Now the serpent was more subtle than any beast
of the field which the Lord God had made.

Genesis, 3,1

'There's something different about you today.'

'You noticed!' Zophiel sounds pleased.

*'It's your wings,' says Christopher. 'They're blue with gold
spangles. Almost like a peacock's tail. Very pretty.'*

*'We are issued with three pairs. And this is my favourite.'
He turns from side to side, making delicate movements with
the iridescent feathers.*

*Zophiel looks prettier altogether today, certainly. And
softer and more rounded. Christopher finds it unsettling. He
thinks he knows Zophiel better than that by now: does not
believe that there are any facets of his character that will
surprise him. He has found him a pleasant companion, that
is, a male companion. But now Zophiel starts to remind him
of Dianne, of Viola, of Honor and of Briony.*

*'I'd like to hear the rest of the story about your father. If
you wouldn't mind sharing it with me, that is.'*

*'As long as you stop sounding like Dianne. Where had
we got to?'*

*'The part where she turned up in your life and looked
set to change it, radically and permanently.'*

Ah yes, Dianne.

Round and plump and bouncy. Motherly, you might
call her.

83

She was another social worker, though junior to my father. She had more of the shine left on her, I think. She had not been working in the department for long enough to get the hard veneer of cynicism that the older staff acquired in order to survive. But she had gained that irritating habit that people in what they now call the caring professions all have, of looking at the rest of us as potential cases, or clients, as they say. I was an obvious candidate for her professional expertise: motherless, unpopular with his peer group, interested in subjects that were too old for his supposed stage of development, living with a father who spent most of his time engrossed in his work.

She missed the simple fact that I was happy the way I was.

If she had been cleverer, she would have noticed that my father, too, was happy with our life. Of course, he wanted a woman. He was presumably missing female companionship, and sex, and someone to shop and cook his meals for him. But he wasn't missing an elegant house and garden, or smart clothes, or sociable evenings in the company of 'friends'. Dianne couldn't understand this, but I knew him better than she did.

'*So you set yourself to oppose the intrusion by this Dianne woman?*'

'*I did no such thing. I was an intelligent child, and my observation of people over the years had taught me more effective methods.*'

I smiled at her. I allowed her to smooth my unruly hair with her soft, capable hand. At bedtime I let her read me stories suitable for my age and gender. For her I ate green vegetables and shepherd's pie. I drank cocoa. And by such sly, underhand means I gained her confidence. I believe she grew to love me, but then she didn't know me, and ignorance of the beloved makes loving so very much easier, don't you think?

While we were cosily ensconced in my bedroom, now cleaner and tidier than before (or Before Dianne, as I thought of it), she confided her plans to me for the improvement of my father, and of his clothes, and his house, and his garden. I encouraged her. I even suggested small details that I knew my father would hate. These confidences were supposed to be our secret, for Dianne understood that she would have to go carefully and discreetly if she was to join our little family. One of her projected improvements involved the bathroom.

There was nothing wrong with our bathroom. It had a bath, a basin, a lavatory, all in lime-encrusted white, and it boasted cold and hottish running water. The floor was covered with green lino. There was a cupboard on the wall, with a spotted mirror; there was a towel rail, there was a mug for our toothbrushes. More often than not there were toothpaste and soap. Once a month or so our two towels joined our sheets in the twin-tub washing machine. Once a year we boiled up our face flannels.

Dianne wished to introduce us to the bathroom beautiful. But she didn't tell my father about her fantasy.

'How marvellous!' she cried, when she first saw it. 'I don't suppose it's been altered since the house was built.'

She ran her fingers over the bubbles in the gloss-painted walls. She peered into the spidery darkness under the bath. 'Amazing!' And she laughed The Laugh. Then she shut up. She retired to the kitchen and made us our lunch: shepherd's pie. Again.

But that evening, while she was tucking me up in bed, I encouraged her to tell me her ideas for transforming the bathroom. 'An avocado bath and basin,' she said. Then, in case I hadn't understood, she said, 'A pale greyish green. Very smart. Very sophisticated.'

'Avocado is nice, but Dad loves that bright greeny-blue,' I said.

'Turquoise? Peacock?' she said, surprised.

'Peacock,' I agreed, imagining something bright and shining, in iridescent green and blue, with gold highlights.

'I'm not sure how that would look.' Her face drooped, as much as a fresh round face can. And she went on to tell me about thick, fluffy towels, and candlewick seat covers, and a brass holder to enclose the loo paper and hide it from the vulgar gaze. Eventually she went home, and I lay in bed making plans.

Next morning at breakfast I passed the information on to Dad. 'Dianne wants to change our bath and basin,' I confided. 'She wants to buy us peacock blue ones.'

'Oh?' I could tell he didn't like the idea.

'And a peacock blue loo.'

'Oh.'

'And paint the cupboard, and change the towels.'

I continued to chatter, repeating Dianne's ideas, embroidering where I thought necessary. 'Carpet for the floor,' I said. 'Plastic wallpaper instead of the blue paint. Bubble bath in coloured glass jars. Smelly soap. *Dental floss.*'

After that morning I didn't bother to let Dianne initiate the new schemes, I simply poured out my own fantasies, preceding each one with the words, 'Dianne says,' and ending it with, 'Its our secret, she says.'

I don't know which displeased my father more: Dianne's ideas for him, as interpreted by me, or the fact that I was parroting them out every morning over the cornflakes. He had, after all, been used to hearing only his own views and tastes repeated back to him.

He started to develop quiet moods, where he said little but stared down into his plate a lot. I found that these times were the best for planting my 'Dianne says' gems. Dianne continued to keep her plans for him to herself, and was unaware that they, and many more fanciful ones, were being passed on behind her back. I think, now, that she intended to marry him, and then change his lifestyle to something that more nearly approached her own desires.

She failed.

Did you ever doubt it?

One evening my father came home and spoke to me in that mumbling, embarrassed way that meant he was going to talk about feelings. He explained that Dianne would not be coming to the house any more. He knew that I had been fond of her, that perhaps I had even started to think of her as a second mother, but then these things just happened, and I would have to get used to the fact that she had left our lives for ever.

I nodded and looked brave. Within a week we were back in our old ways, and happy in one another's company. I noticed, but ignored, the fact that Dad's quiet moods became more frequent. Sometimes I would catch him sitting in his armchair, a book on his knee, staring into the distance. He started to look crumpled and middle-aged. But then, he wasn't getting any younger. And in just a few years' time I entered adolescence and lost interest in my father's love life: after all, there was my own to concentrate on.

It's odd, now that I look back on those days, for I remember him as looking very much as I do now. A few years older, and a bit saggier, I suppose. And of course the old man didn't know how to dress decently. But I suppose he wasn't bad looking for his generation. He could have made quite a hit with the women if he'd put his mind to it. I suppose he wasn't really bothered.

'So your father never remarried?'

'No, it wouldn't have worked.'

'But you and he remained close?'

'Of course we did, in spite of the fact that he developed an upsetting senility problem in his late sixties. But I found a very pleasant nursing home for him.'

'And you visited him regularly?'

'I saw him only last Christmas.'

'But that must have been eight months before your own demise.'

'Was it? Well, it's tricky fitting these things into a life as full as mine.'

'Full, possibly. Life, definitely over, I fear.'

'Well, you can get used to anything if you try, don't you think?'

'The one thing that surprises me about your story is that someone as determined as Dianne should give up so easily.'

'Well, there was a small repercussion, I have to admit.'

'What happened?'

For some reason, Dianne did blame me for the break-up of her relationship with my father. I believe she had no actual evidence, but she thought that I was in some way responsible. She came to the house one afternoon of the week following their farewell scene, while I was still at school and my father was at work. She must have 'borrowed' a key to the front door, I suppose. And then she demonstrated what a mean and vindictive woman she really was. No more of The Laugh, no more the sweet understanding of the motherless child. The bitch took all my comics from under my bed – there was nothing more exciting to find in my room at that time than Batman – and she cut them into narrow strips with a pair of scissors. Then she decorated my room with festoons of ripped comics. They hung with mocking celebration from the corner of every door and drawer; they dangled from the central light; they looped in bows and curls across my pillow. I have to admit that I cried when I saw them, but the relief I felt at the disappearance of Dianne soon cheered me again. My father had a narrow escape with that one, I can tell you.

'How can you be so sure that it was Dianne?'

She left a note on my bedside table. It was written in

*capital letters and unsigned, but I recognized her handiwork.
It said:* **YOU ARE A NASTY, EVIL BOY. YOU HAVE TOLD
LIES. YOU WILL COME TO A BAD END.**

'Quite mild in the circumstances, I would have thought.'

'Poor old Dianne, it was the rudest she could manage. I
can imagine the terrible row they had when he told her he
didn't want to see her any more, the accusations that flew
from one to the other. Very upsetting for both of them, I
imagine. I don't suppose she ever got it together after she
and Dad split up.'

'But she did get it right.'

'How do you mean?'

'The end that you came to could accurately be described
as bad, don't you think?'

'You're probably wondering why I invited you,' said Faith,
who seemed to have the same facility as Kate herself for
saying what was in her mind.

'I was too busy admiring the slick way you liberated
that bottle of wine for any such thing,' said Kate. 'But I'll
ask if you like.'

'You see, you didn't comment on my name,'
explained Faith.

'Why should I comment on a name like Faith?'

'Beeton. Most people ask me how the cookery book's
coming along. And all of them expect me to be a wonderful cook.'

'Aren't you?'

'No, I'm awful. I had years of dreary invalid cooking
for my father, who liked his vegetables well boiled and
his meat finely minced. Anything adventurous played
hell with his digestion, or so he claimed. And it's like
green fingers – or the lack of them – I just don't seem
to have the knack.'

'In which case, you'd better leave the lunch to me.'

'It's an odd coincidence, but my lunch guests usually cook for both of us, I find.'

Kate looked at her quickly: yes, it was intended as a joke against herself.

They were walking east over Magdalen Bridge, and soon after they had crossed the Plain, Faith turned left into a narrow street of small terraced houses.

'Mine!' she exclaimed as she stopped by a front door and inserted a key in the lock.

'I know the feeling,' said Kate. 'I pay my mortgage by the skin of my teeth, but it's great to feel that something belongs to you.'

Faith led the way through to the kitchen at the back and indicated the fridge. 'I'm taking you at your word. See what you can do with anything you find in there. There's more food in the cupboard over there, so help yourself to that, too. I'll pour us a drink.'

Kate found some eggs, hoped they hadn't been in the fridge for too long, and broke them gingerly into a bowl. OK so far. Cheese? It looked like a bar of carbolic soap, but it would grate. Omelette, then. Herbs? Obviously not. Pepper and salt: difficult but not impossible to find in a wall cupboard. A few tomatoes. Two faded, wrinkled courgettes. Bread that would cheer up if she sprinkled it with water and heated it through. A tub of margarine. Cans of lager, which she ignored. A tiny bottle of olive oil that had darkened but was still edible, she found, when she licked a drop off a finger. Half a carton of cream that had gone sour, but would add flavour to the omelette. She found a large frying pan that needed a good scrub, scrubbed it accordingly, and put it on to heat with a spoonful of the olive oil. Then, recklessly, she chopped up the courgette and let it sauter for a few minutes. Surely wrinkled courgettes wouldn't do you any harm?

'Thanks,' she said, as Faith, who took no apparent

interest in her preparations, handed her a generous glass of wine. It certainly cheered up the cooking process.

'This is much better than I'd have managed,' said Faith.

She probably says that to all her guests, thought Kate. 'No problem,' she said.

'What's that you've got frying in there?'

'Courgettes.'

'Chuck them, out, will you? I hate them.'

'But I found them in your fridge.'

'I've had them far too long. They were a mistake,' said Faith, and finished her glass of wine in a single gulp. 'A mistake I have since corrected,' she added, to Kate's bewilderment. They were only talking about a couple of ageing vegetables, weren't they?

They sat in the September sun on the patio behind Faith's house. The omelette and tomato salad, with warm bread accompaniment, didn't seem too bad when washed down with a further glass of the Bartlemas wine.

'I love this,' said Faith, leaning back in her chair, with the sun warm on her eyelids. 'What gives it an added spice is the thought that my father would have hated it.'

'You didn't get on?' asked Kate.

'Oh, we got on all right, for the simple reason that my mother and I gave in to his every whim. Life was simple if he was happy. Though I'm not sure that "happy" is quite the right term. He lay in bed in his room, waiting like a spider until one of us did something wrong, or rather, something of which he disapproved. And then he'd scurry out with his poisonous darts ready to stun us back into submission. But now I like to enjoy all the things that would have brought him out in a rash of fury. Bliss.'

An odd definition of bliss, thought Kate. 'What was wrong with him?'

'Nothing, probably. He swore that it was his nerves.

And almost anything that my mother or I enjoyed doing made his problem worse, or so he said. "Don't cross your father," was what my mother always said, so we cowered in corners, not doing much at all.'

'How did you escape? At least, I imagine from what you've said that you did escape.'

'Not really. First my mother died. After all the tiptoeing around after the old bugger, she was the one who was really ill. Of course, she wasn't allowed to mention it, or do anything about it. She just felt ill and went to bed one day, and died the following weekend.'

'What did you do then?'

'Took over where she left off. Ran the house, looked after the old man. Dreamed my dreams and seethed quietly. He died too, luckily before I grew too old to make something of my life. I upped and went off to college once he'd popped his clogs. I went to the local College of Further Education and took my A-Levels, got into university, then took a degree. Finally the doctorate. I loved it all.'

'Yes,' said Kate, slowly. She had the awful thought that Faith was quite capable of putting a pillow over an inconvenient paternal face if he lingered on too long for her ambitions. There was a silence as they both thought their own thoughts.

'Now,' said Faith, as Kate had begun to wonder again what she was doing there, 'tell me about this genre fiction we're supposed to be teaching.'

'I'm not sure I know much about the theory of it,' said Kate. 'I've always concentrated on the practice.'

Faith raised her eyebrows as though theory was all that existed. She must think that this literature she studies just happens, thought Kate. She can analyse and dissect, while I deal with the blank screen on my word processor. I think about writing a story that will keep the reader interested for a few hundred pages, while

Faith and her friends contemplate some entity which they have labelled *genre*. What a strange world they live in.

'It must be an odd life making up stories as you go along,' said Faith.

'Well, I do go in for a minimum of planning as well. I have been known to write a synopsis, though not, I fear, to stick to it.'

'And do you think about the structure of your work at all?'

'Structure? You mean the order I tell the story in?'

'I suppose so.'

'I just get on and tell it, and try to miss out as many of the boring bits as I can.'

'Extraordinary.'

'No, just a way of earning a living that doesn't involve working for other people.'

'And what do you know about Dorothy Sayers?'

'Nothing much. I don't often read crime fiction. It's too contrived for my taste. Every element of the story is supposed to have a meaning, they say. I'd find that too constricting. I like to put in a scene – like this lunch of ours, say – that is totally spontaneous and without any significance whatsoever to the plot.'

'And have you decided whether there really is a plot?'

'How do you mean?'

'I thought we might be characters in a post-modernist novel. Don't you feel like that sometimes?'

'No, I can't say that I do. More tomato salad, by the way?'

'Thanks. How ever did you manage to make this meal out of my unpromising ingredients?'

'It's a gift I have.'

'You must show me how to do it some time.'

'Perhaps in chapter twelve.'

'I'm sorry?'

'In our novel.'

'Oh yes, of course.'

'Though it sometimes seems as though I've strayed into the most heavily traditional of whodunits,' said Kate.

'And what would you say are its prime characteristics?'

'An inability to understand the meaning of what is happening at any given time, and what its significance may be to the whole. If it has a significance. If indeed there is a whole.'

'Have another glass of wine and all may become clear to you.'

'Thank you.'

'I'm interested in the idea that you feel yourself to have strayed into a whodunit,' said Faith, looking reflectively past Kate's shoulder. 'Do you feel, too, that a crime has been committed? And if so, what sort of crime would it be?'

There was a silence so complete that they must both have been holding their breath, waiting for Kate's reply. Unfortunately, she was getting a little fuzzy after drinking so much wine, and she couldn't think clearly about her reply. 'Murder?' she said, recklessly. 'Embezzlement, theft?' The word embezzlement was a mistake, she found.

'I can understand that you might suspect that a murder was committed,' said Faith, who seemed to have a remarkably good head for drink. 'But what's this you tell me about embezzlement?' She pronounced the word perfectly, and tipped a little more wine into Kate's glass as she did so.

'Is that what I said? Oh, it was just a wild idea. Nothing concrete.'

'Nothing new to report, then?' Faith sounded disappointed, as though Kate had let her down in some way.

'Only a threatening note!' exclaimed Kate. 'Something I found in a file on leaflets. It was attached to an invoice.'

'Very interesting,' said Faith. 'Can you remember anything about the invoice?'

'Not much,' said Kate, who if truth were told could not remember anything at all clearly at that moment.

'And what did the threatening note say?' Why was Faith Beeton starting to sound like a policeman?

'Something about "Curiosity killed the cat". It could have meant anything, couldn't it?'

'Possibly,' said Faith. 'Or it might have referred to something quite specific.'

'You don't think it was aimed at me?'

'Oh, I'm sure it wasn't.'

'That's a relief.'

Even in her fuzzy state it seemed to Kate that the atmosphere on the patio had changed again, lightened.

'I have a powerful dislike for the idea of "genre",' said Faith, leaning back in her chair and gazing into the depths of her wineglass. She spoke as though they had never left the subject of literature. And perhaps they hadn't, thought Kate. 'One should write about literature in general, or about a single work. To lump several works together and deal with them as a group is to devalue them.'

'I'm sure you're right,' said Kate, who had no idea what she was talking about. 'Why don't we finish the wine and then go back to College? I imagine they'd like us to do an hour or two's work this afternoon before we pack up for the day.'

Perhaps they hadn't expected her back, after all. She tried to sneak into her office without being seen, but when she opened the door she saw a broad ginger tweed back view bending over the open drawers of her desk.

Sadie was not in the office, and the intruder was alone in the room. Kate was still feeling fuzzy after all the wine she had been persuaded to drink, but this didn't seem right to her.

She closed the door. The click it made caused the ginger tweed figure to stand upright. He turned, and she saw that it was Steven Charleston, his face a rosier shade of pink than ever. Sandy eyebrows jutted from his carmine brow ridges, and his pale blue eyes popped at her.

'Yes?' she said, working hard to keep in charge of the situation, in spite of her somewhat inebriated state. She stayed near the door, hoping that he wouldn't catch too many of the wine fumes. And then again, if he attacked her, near the door was a good place to be.

'Kate Ivory?'

'Yes. A good guess, since this is my office, and *that* is my desk.' She stood, looking enquiringly at him.

'I'm Steven Charleston, the College Accountant.'

'Yes.' It was best if she didn't use too many words, and kept her mouth shut while saying them.

'I was just wondering whether you'd found any oddments, anything that doesn't quite fit in with any of Chris's files. Something that seems to have a quite different subject matter.'

'No.'

'He wasn't the tidiest of people, I'm afraid, and sometimes other people's papers found their way in with his correspondence.'

'You might have asked before . . .' She waved a hand towards her desk, indicating the still-open drawer.

'You weren't here,' he said. 'And the desk is Chris's really, isn't it?'

Kate scowled at him and wished that she could sit down.

'So, Kate, if you will allow me to call you that, you

haven't found anything ... odd, or out of place?' The man was certainly persistent.

'Just the invoice I handed over to Sadie.' Kate moved closer to the desk and slumped into her chair.

'Really? She didn't tell me about that!'

'I'm sure it wasn't important.' Kate had given up trying to protect him from passive alcohol consumption.

Charleston was still hovering anxiously, so she added 'You'd better ask Sadie about it. I didn't really see what it was about, I'm afraid.'

'You'll let me know if anything else turns up? Or if there's anything hidden in a computer file, perhaps.'

'It would be easier if I knew what I was looking for.'

'Lists,' said Charleston, vaguely. 'Names, perhaps. Some sheets of analysis paper with figures written on them.'

Kate laughed. 'They make Chris Townsend sound like a blackmailer!'

There was a nasty silence for a few seconds, then Steven Charleston joined in her laughter. 'Oh, very funny,' he said. 'Tell Sadie about it some time.'

'Well, I have to get on with some work now,' said Kate, hoping that he would leave.

'I should try drinking a large cup of black coffee first,' he said, and took his boiled-ham face and ginger tweeds out of her office.

Chapter Seven

> '. . . thou may'st know
> What misery th' inabstinence of Eve
> Shall bring on men.'
> John Milton, *Paradise Lost*, xi

'Would you care to continue with the story of your life?'

Zophiel has reverted to fifteen feet in height and a strong, manly bearing. His wings are a plain, unadorned dark blue.

'Why? Are you still trying to prove that I'm a born victim?'

'I didn't say that victims were born. I think there is evidence to suggest that a man's behaviour throughout his life fits him for his role. He practises it in small, everyday situations. He advances in minuscule steps. And I believe that in your case in particular the status of victim was carefully nurtured and developed.'

'Rubbish!'

'But of course I cannot be sure about that until I hear more.'

'You wish us to learn the meaning of my life?'

'What makes you think that a life has only one meaning? Does a poem have a single reading?'.

'I thought it did. I thought that once you had understood the poem, or the particular piece of life that you were considering, that that was it. Done for all time.'

'Well, now you're starting to learn something new, after all.'

'What do you wish me to tell you now?'

'I think I would like a passage from some period between the departure of Dianne and the appearance of Briony. An interim period, as it were.'

'You are referring to Viola.'

'Am I?'

'The first real love of my life.'

'That sounds an appropriate subject for my notebook.'

'We met at university. Our salad days, as Cleopatra once called it.'

'Oxford?'

'Not quite.'

We met at university. London, not Oxford. A life of bedsitters and tube trains, rather than medieval staircases and punts on the river. Where did we meet? In the queue at the student canteen. Our plastic trays touched, and some spark was lighted. I was eating steak pie and chips, with a side plate of corn and chopped green peppers. She had chosen the vegetarian dish: lasagne made with tofu and rennet-free cheddar, with a green salad and a glass of apple juice. There were only two free places in the whole room, and they happened to be at the same table. Just before she laid her fork down for the last time and picked up her canvas shoulder bag with the Greenpeace logo, I invited her to the late-night show at the film club: *Silent Running*, I remember. I had already seen it twice, but I guessed it was her kind of film and I was right.

After that we were an item. We described ourselves as going out together, but in practice we did a lot of staying in. At the beginning of the next term we found digs in the same building, and spent our nights and most of our days together. It was an enjoyable time: Viola had kept herself fit with hill walking, and supple with yoga, and had a refreshingly open attitude to sex, which was especially welcome after the dull suburban girls I had known previously.

She cooked for me. I got used to seeds and nuts and a lot of raw vegetables, organically grown, while she added fish to her diet. She chopped up pounds of vegetables with her black-handled knives, dribbled in sesame seed oil, sprinkled them with herbs grown in pots on her windowsill. I ate tofu, while she agreed to buy white meat, as long as it had been reared in a free-range environment and was chopped up very small and rendered unrecognizable as dead animal before it reached her plate.

During the summer vacation she bought fruit from the pick-your-own farm and made it into the most delicate preserves, cooking it for the minimum time necessary so that the flavour of the fruit was really quite intense. Delicious! I remember it still, the sight of Viola in her long, flower-sprigged skirt and embroidered white blouse, bending over the strawberry plants or leaning up into the raspberry canes, her fingers and lips stained with scarlet and purple juice. The food cupboard in my room was full of jars of this conserve, in various flavours, and we would eat it, on toast, at tea-time. (At other times we used it as an ingredient in our love-making, but I doubt whether you wish to hear such details.)

Under Viola's regime, my complexion improved. I lost the few pounds of extra flesh that I had gained after I had discovered the joys of drinking beer. I took up jogging and squash, as well as joining her when she tramped the Welsh hills. I laid the foundation of the smooth brown tan which was so much a part of my physical attraction when I was older.

'Is this story going anywhere? Delightfully rewarding as the experience must have been for you at the time, in your account it is not yet an unusual one. It sounds as though one or other of you is about to find a new lover, and leave

the rejected partner feeling unhappy and betrayed. And if so, I feel a yawn coming over me.'

'Be patient. The story is about to take its surprise turn.'

Together, Viola and I joined our college student union, and together we were eventually voted on to its committee. Viola was Secretary, I the Treasurer.

Have you any idea how large the funds of a medium-sized London college union are? What with compulsory subscriptions from students, and additional money from the college, I was in charge of a substantial income. Of course, there were checks and constraints in place to prevent embezzlement of these funds. Any cheque had to be signed by two committee members.

Viola and myself, for example.

It is an observable fact that a woman in a happy sexual relationship will not look too hard to find the faults of the man involved. She wants to believe in him; perhaps she needs to do so. And Viola, so sophisticated in some ways, was quite gullible in others. She came from an unthinkingly comfortable background, and it did not occur to her that some people might need to hustle for the money they wanted. She was not spoiled, or over-indulged, but she did run a small secondhand car. And in her unreflecting affluence, she had never learned to budget effectively. Her parents gave her a moderate allowance, which they paid into her bank account every couple of months. By the end of every first month she was running out of money. I subsidized her, and she paid me back with a cheque when her allowance came in. Her car failed its MOT, and I paid to have it repaired. She was short on her rent money, I gave her the cash. It was always cash that I gave her, and she was too innocent in financial dealings to wonder where I got it from. Or as I mentioned before, perhaps she didn't want to know.

But then, I had quite a neat little scheme going, and

it would have taken a more sophisticated girl than Viola to see through it, even if she had wanted to.

'I think I'll stop there for a moment,' said Christopher.

'Why? I was just getting interested.'

'I like the sense of power that comes from holding back the end of the story. I'll tell you the rest tomorrow. And don't bother to give me the one about time not being a concept with which you are familiar. I'm sure you're getting the hang of it, just as I'm getting the feel of Eternity.'

Kate was in the cubby-hole behind the Bursary, drinking coffee, when she was joined by Annette Paige and John Clay. She had left Sadie alone in the office, busy coaxing money out of people for her latest project, an extension to the library. The cubby-hole was so small that intimacy was forced upon its occupants.

'I see you're taking your proper breaks from the word processor,' John began.

Kate felt herself pushed on to the defensive and so answered brightly: 'Yes, that's right,' and flashed him a brilliantly insincere smile.

'And how are you getting on with the preparations for the descent of the swarm of locusts?' he asked.

'Our students for the study fortnight? Oh, I think it's all going very well,' said Kate, confidently.

'I hope you've phoned the printers. They'll never have those leaflets ready unless you get after them,' said John.

'Funny how everyone knows all about my work,' said Kate.

'I should watch that,' said John. 'It's not a good idea in this place to let anyone else know your business. It's best to keep it to yourself.'

'I doubt whether there's anything very secret about our students,' said Kate.

'Students! Locusts! More like parasites!' muttered Annette, sipping genteelly at her coffee and nibbling at the corner of a fat-free biscuit.

Kate took a large bite out of a chocolate digestive. 'Just think of the money they'll bring into the college,' she said, dropping crumbs on to her black jeans and brushing them away with a careless hand, so that Annette glared at her. 'Two hundred and fourteen students at a hundred and ninety-five pounds a day, for fifteen days, that's . . . well, it's a lot of money, anyhow.'

'Now that's just the sort of detail I should keep to myself if I were you,' said John. 'Money's a tricky subject in this college.'

'Never mind that, what of all the expense and the bother they cause?' grumbled Annette. 'And the extra work for the rest of us. This used to be our quiet time of year in the Bursary. Now it's one of the busiest. And the things we get asked to do!'

Kate managed not to point out that Annette was paid for a year's work, and presumably had a normal holiday entitlement. 'Their registration fee covers all the preparations,' said Kate. 'I'll be looking after their every need while they're in college, so you shouldn't be bothered by them this year.'

'Oh, you talk quite glibly about how easy it is,' said Annette. 'You just wait until they're here, and you'll find out different. And you'd better watch how you behave. They're so pernickety, some of them, and if they complain about you too much you'll find yourself out of a job.' She sounded quite pleased at the prospect.

'I expect I'll manage,' said Kate breezily. 'I'm quite adaptable, really. And I think you'll find that the college has made a hefty profit at the end of the fortnight, so they'll probably give me a big thank-you.'

'It's not as though they really need the money,' said

Annette, changing tack. 'The college is immensely wealthy already.'

'Oh, surely they're struggling to make ends meet like every other college?' protested Kate.

'Well, just look what they've been spending!' put in John.

'You mean that new epergne thing, or whatever it's called, for the Senior Common Room?' said Annette.

'An early nineteenth-century ormolu centrepiece,' corrected John. 'Decorated with cherubs holding a vine.'

'Sounds hideous,' said Kate.

'But expensive,' said John. 'And have you wondered how much they must be paying our lovely Bursar?'

'The usual rate for the job, I suppose,' said Kate, wondering why she was the one who was taking the part of the Establishment, for a change.

'Then how can he afford that car of his?' said John, triumphantly.

'And those expensive holidays,' added Annette. 'I'd like to go to Morocco or New Mexico, but chance would be a fine thing.'

'What are you hinting at?' asked Kate, nosy as ever.

'The Bursar at this college is a member of the academic staff, too,' said John. 'That's why he has an Assistant Bursar. Me,' he added unnecessarily. 'I should be called Bursar, by rights,' he said, obviously airing an old grievance.

'You will be one day,' said Annette soothingly. 'When everything comes to light,' she added cryptically.

'And then there's the Accountant, and the Steward,' said John. 'But it's the Bursar who has overall control of the finances of the college. It gives him a lot of power, you see.'

'You're saying the Bursar – that nice man Robert Grailing – is accepting backhanders?' asked Kate bluntly.

'Oh, we're not exactly saying that,' said John, putting

his cup firmly back in its saucer and placing them on the tray.

'We wouldn't like to accuse anyone,' said Annette, pushing the last of the dry biscuit into her mouth and chewing it very thoroughly.

'But there are some very dubious students registered for higher degrees,' said John, standing up and moving over to the door. 'Students from very wealthy backgrounds, you might say.'

'And rumours about how you land a contract for building work at Bartlemas College,' said Annette, following them out.

'But nobody tells us about it. They all keep their secrets, and whisper in their corners,' said John, from the door.

'They wouldn't want to share any of it with us,' said Annette.

'But then, it's best not to gossip, don't you think?' came back John's voice.

'Committee meeting in ten minutes,' said Annette. 'Please don't be late.'

'Time I was getting back to work,' said Kate, thoughtfully. But since the cubby-hole was empty now, she made herself another cup of coffee and drank it in happy silence.

Kate just had time to pick up her agenda and papers for the committee meeting and find her way to Seminar Room 4. She was actually pleased to see that Annette was already there: at least that would take care of the minutes. If there was one thing she hated, it was taking minutes instead of paying attention to what was being said.

Once it got under way, what was said at this meeting was really quite interesting, she found.

'The anthology,' said Rob Grailing, who was chairing
the meeting. 'Nothing much to discuss there—'

'Yes, there is,' put in Harry Bickerstaff, loudly and
quickly.

Rob looked up with a tolerant but bored expression
on his face. 'What's worrying you about it, Harry? I'm
assured that everything is going well.'

'Nobody has asked me for my contribution,' he said.
Rob looked a little discomfited. 'And I was expecting -
as the most senior author here - to be asked to edit it.'

'No, no, Harry,' Rob started to say.

'But I was told that a young woman called Senta
Norris would be undertaking the work,' continued Harry,
overriding Rob's interruption. 'I haven't even heard of
the woman. Who is she?'

'Yah, well, Henry,' said a young woman in her twenties with scarlet nails and hair to match. 'Senta Norris:
that's me. You'll find my new book, *Passion's Scourge*,
on the bestseller shelf in the bookshops. And, like, I'm
authoring the anthology, if you know what I mean.'

'But surely the whole point of an anthology is that it
is composed of a number of pieces by different people,'
interposed Harry.

'Nah. My agent has signed us a really good deal with
Fergusson's, and since they already publish yours truly,
it felt right to be the name on the title page.' Senta took
a long pack of cigarettes out of her bag and went to light
one, caught Rob's eye on her, thought better of it, and
put the cigarettes away.

Harry opened his mouth to argue, but Rob Grailing
spoke rapidly.

'Fine, Senta. I'm sure that's cleared up the whole
matter. Harry, I'll speak to you about it later if you're
still unhappy, but for the moment I feel we should move
on to the next item on the agenda. Angela?'

'Press and publicity,' said Angela Devitt. Kate had

seen her name on the covers of many brightly coloured paperbacked crime novels. She was a small, grey-haired woman, wearing a beige jersey top and skirt, neither of which appeared to have much shape.

'Ah, Angela dear,' said Harry Bickerstaff. 'I'd heard you were looking after the press and publicity side. But no one has asked me for an interview. Do you think you could check on the arrangements and let me know when I'm wanted, and where?'

'Sorry, Harry. You know how difficult it is to get writers on to national radio and television, unless there's some scandal associated with their name, of course.'

'But I thought you had managed to get us some coverage,' said Rob.

'Well, I myself have been invited on to *Kaleidoscope* during the first week of our fortnight, and I have been commissioned to write a five-part drama which Radio Four is broadcasting, starting this week. Crime seems to be very much the genre of the moment, I find!'

'And what about the press?'

'Yes, I've written a piece for *Guardian* Women, and I'm being interviewed and photographed for the *Oxford Times.*'

'I notice that the Central Library has arranged a display of all your books,' said Harry, thick eyebrows descending aggressively over stony grey eyes. He scratched his broad stomach thoughtfully.

'Yah, well, what about the rest of us, Angela? You know what I mean?' asked Senta.

'Well, I'm doing my best, but really it isn't easy, Senta dear,' replied Angela. She doodled on her notepad: a dagger piercing a heart. She completed a particularly well-formed drop of blood before replying: 'I'm not sure that *Passion's Scourge* belongs to quite the genre that Oxford book-buyers prefer.'

'Thank you very much, Angela,' said Rob, hastily.

'Now, how about liaison with Oxford's bookshops? Harry? You're our bookshops person, aren't you?'

'Will you ring Blackwell's and arrange a signing for me?' Angela put in, quickly.

'They have already arranged one signing session for *me* this week, and of course they don't like doing too many of these things, you know, Angela. It devalues the currency, as you might say,' said Harry.

'Speaking of devaluing the currency, I see that you've also got a signing at Dillons, at that nice bookshop in Summertown, as well as at the Museum of Modern Art. Don't you think that you're being just a little greedy, Harry?' said Angela. Senta looked as though she might attack him with her long scarlet nails at any moment. Harry just beamed back at her and carried on scratching.

'I do seem to be so popular, even after all these years,' he said.

'Well, I've invited the *Oxford Mail* to come and take a photo for their newspaper,' said Angela. 'It'll be a group photograph, with all of us included.'

'That's all two hundred and fourteen students, as well as authors and tutors, is it?' asked Harry.

'I'm doing my best,' said Angela, sounding sincere.

'Yes, well, let's go on to the next item,' said Rob Grailing, looking hunted.

On the way back to her office, Kate wondered whether everyone was on the make. Did no one undertake a job at this study fortnight for the general good? Did they all have selfish motives for everything they did? And could she not add her own name and book titles to the reading list? And how about popping into the Paperback Shop in the lunch hour to make sure they had all her titles in stock?

In the Development Office Sadie was on the phone,

speaking in her most cajoling tones. As she got to her desk, Kate thought she could check on the leaflets, and pulled out the file. The bright blue document wallet was in the top drawer. She paused. Was that really where she had left it? But then, who would want to snoop into the correspondence between a college and a firm of printers? She started to turn over the papers. Sadie, meanwhile, was still on the telephone, apparently speaking to the same person as before, so she stopped to listen.

'I'm sure you remember how hard it was to find a quiet corner in the library while you were studying for Finals, Mr Kent,' she was saying. 'Well, now we're planning to provide a small reading room, which will be silent at all times, where serious students can work, undisturbed by their rowdier friends. No, of course College isn't engaged in turning out people who are interested only in their books.' The telephone quacked back at her. 'Yes, I'm sure that the standard of rowing in your day was considerably higher than it is now, but I can't think it is entirely due to the fact that we now admit women to the college. No, of course there's nothing wrong with a little high-spirited larking around, but . . .' Sadie sat with the receiver away from her ear, pulling faces at it until the quacking sounds stopped. 'And can I put you down for a contribution? I can!' She sounded surprised, and wrote a sum of money down on her notepad which seemed to Kate to contain a string of zeros. 'Yes, that's very generous of you. Your name will be engraved on the brass plaque listing the benefactors, and of course circulated in our *Development Fund News*. No, don't send me a cheque yet. I'll send you our information pack first, and that will give you all the details you need, and tell you which particular fund to make your cheque payable to. Thank you so much for your time, Mr Kent. Goodbye.' She whistled through her teeth as she ticked a name on the list in front of her and started to dial again.

Kate stopped listening and concentrated on her own work. She turned over papers until she reached the letter from the printers, quoting a price and promising a delivery date. She paused, and held her breath for a moment. She looked again.

Someone had fixed a sticky fluorescent note to the sheet, and on it was written in green felt-tipped capital letters:

CURIOSITY KILLED THE KAT

You've spelled cat wrong, she wanted to say. But she knew that whoever had written it had known just what they were spelling.

Who *had* written it? Who had left it there? John? Annette? Sadie? The Bursar? The Master, the Master's Wife, the College Secretary? Any of them could have popped into the office for the minute or two that it took to stick the note to the letter from the printers. And she could add the Accountant, Faith Beeton, even Senta Norris, to her list, if it came to that. But why? And had John Clay made sure that she opened that particular file when he had reminded her about the leaflets? Were he and Annette ganging up against her? And had the man in ginger tweeds been searching for something he had mislaid, or was he adding unwanted materials to her files? She tried to remember whether she had noticed the blue wallet in the top drawer immediately after the visit from Steven Charleston, but failed.

The note itself offered few replies to her questions. The handwriting was unadorned and unrecognizable. The felt-tipped pen might have come from the stationery cupboard, and everyone had pads of fluorescent sticky notes. Various admonitory notices were affixed to the edge of every computer screen and cupboard door, taken from just such a pad. And if the first note had been addressed to Christopher Townsend, what was it that connected the two of them? The thought that she didn't want to face told her that the note was the same as the one that had been stuck to the corner of the invoice with his query in red Biro, apart from the spelling of the word 'cat'. And now Christopher was dead.

Oh, what was she bothered about? It was probably someone who didn't like her face, or voice, or spiky personality. So what? Hadn't Sadie mentioned something about the way she went around making enemies? She remembered how Sadie had snatched the misplaced invoice away from her on her first morning. Yes, Sadie was the most likely suspect. She must make more of an effort to be friendly to people, and forget about spiteful little notes. It was surely coincidence that Chris Townsend had received just such a note and that Chris Townsend was now dead. She took a deep breath to prepare herself to confront Sadie about it right away, but at that moment Sadie replaced her telephone receiver, picked up a manila folder and left the room. She would have to catch her later.

She started to dial the printers' phone number, then heard the door opening, and quickly hid the new note under another letter in the file. Someone came into the room as she was put through to the person she wanted.

'Mrs Norton? Kate Ivory here from Bartlemas College. I just wondered how you were getting on with the leaflets for our study fortnight. Oh, you'll deliver them tomorrow? Yes, of course it's soon enough for us. That would be wonderful. Thanks very much.' So if there was no problem with the printers, what had all the fuss been about? Had people been directing her attention to that file for their own reasons?

'Hello.'

She had forgotten that someone had come into the room while she was on the phone. He had been standing quietly just inside the door, observing her.

'I could go away again and come back when you're in a better frame of mind,' he said.

'Huh?' Kate realized that she had been frowning ferociously, and composed her face into friendlier lines. 'No, no. Do stay. Now is fine.'

'Perhaps you don't remember me. I'm Rob Grailing, the Bursar.'

He sounded quite diffident. And of course Kate remembered him.

Rob Grailing wandered round the room, picking up things at random and putting them down again, in a way that reminded her of another male friend of hers. She wondered what he wanted.

'Getting on all right?' he volunteered at last, sitting down in Sadie's chair. 'Any problems at all?'

'No,' said Kate, sharply. 'Should there be?'

He smiled. He had a pleasant smile, she thought. Attractive, even. This, too, reminded her of her friend Paul Taylor. Her kind, dependable friend, Detective Sergeant Paul Taylor. So Rob Grailing must be all right, mustn't he?

'I'm sure everything's fine,' he said soothingly. 'You came highly recommended.' But he failed to enlarge on the comment. Recommended by whom, Kate wondered, and as what? 'Really, you have no reason to be so nervous about your job. Nobody's going to take it away from you. Now, have you had coffee?' he asked.

Kate wondered about saying no, but thought it would bring another snide remark from John Clay or Annette Paige, so she said 'Yes' instead. She infused the word with regret, however.

'Well, how about joining me for lunch?' he asked. 'It

OXFORD FALL

would give us a chance to talk things over. There's quite
a good pub up the road. They even do vegetarian.'
   'Dead animals are fine by me,' said Kate. 'What time?'
   'Twelve forty-five,' said Rob. 'In the lodge?'
   'Sure.'
   'I'll see you then.'

Chapter Eight

> Oxford, thou art the flower of cities all!
> Gemme of all joy, jasper of jocunditie.
> > Anon.

'Is this tomorrow?'

'It might be.'

'And you will tell me the rest of the story about Viola?'

'You're sure you're not finding it too dull? Too predictable?'

'I'm sure that you are preparing a surprise twist to the story at any moment.' Zophiel is very polite today, very subdued. Christopher is beginning to find that his own ideas of time are getting a little hazy, with the days not easy to tell apart. But this feels long enough away from his previous narrative for him to wish to continue.

Perhaps I had better explain to you what I had been doing in order to create for myself a supplementary income.

I had invented a college society – I forget now its exact field of interest, but it had a name that was convincing enough to fool Viola, and anyone else who might have seen the invoices and letters that I produced when it became necessary. Money went quite happily from college union funds into this fictitious society. The cheques for its equally fictitious outgoings were made out by me and countersigned by Viola, as Secretary. I made sure that the cheques came in a wad of other, genuine ones, and were made out to the invented society. I withdrew the money, in cash, from the society's bank account, by forging the name of its Treasurer on the cheques. This cash, naturally, ended up in my own pocket, and was then laundered by Viola, when she repaid me the money I had advanced for her car, or her rent, or for the new dress she wanted for the college ball. I am afraid that it was Viola's name, rather than mine, that was on this imaginary society's bank account. I could do a fair imitation of her signature, and since it was my imitation that I gave to the bank at the opening of the account, together with another name that I also invented, as second signature, I am afraid that it was Viola who was pursued by the college authorities when the scheme eventually came to light.

She took it very badly. She was, of course, expelled. (This was not Oxford, where students are 'sent down'; our college preferred the blunter term.) I received a certain amount of sympathy for having been taken in by such a little trickster. I am afraid that Viola did not make a good impression when she was questioned. She blushed, and stammered, and contradicted herself, and tried first to exonerate me, then to accuse me, for it was only at that moment that she realized what must have happened, and what a fool I had made of her. Her contradictions and the way she changed her story counted against her, I'm afraid.

'What happened to her?'

'She left without taking her degree. She must have returned home to her parents, but I had no further contact with her. I sat my Finals a few months later and got quite a good degree. I then went to work for a well-known charity, as a fund-raiser. I think they liked the story of honest gullibility that I gave them, the way I promised never again to be taken in by a plausible, pretty face.'

'And is that it? You got away with it, scot-free?'

'No, not quite.'

'I imagine that Viola was very angry when she realized what you had been doing and how she had been used. Did she make an angry scene?'

'She did attack me in the college canteen. I'm afraid that this was a messy business involving spinach and ricotta cannelloni and a bowl of fruit jelly and custard, but one which gained me even more sympathy with my friends. Viola was removed, gently of course, and I thought I had seen the last of her.'

'I hear from your voice that you are going to tell me the final part of this story during our next session.'

'That's right.'

'Have you seen this?' asked John Clay, as Kate walked through the outer office on her way to the lodge. He was holding a copy of the local newspaper.

Reluctantly, Kate went over to see what he was talking about.

'Here,' he said, and thrust the paper towards her. He sat watching her with his spiteful bright eyes as she read it. It was a report of the inquest into the death of Christopher Mark Townsend. She skimmed it quickly, aware of John's eyes on her all the while.

Death from fractured skull and multiple injuries. No history of depression. No worries about his health. No money worries. A happy and stable marriage. He had eaten a light lunch: quiche, ratatouille, coffee. He had drunk only the equivalent of half a pint of beer. No one else present at the time. An accident.

'Thanks,' she said, as she handed it back.

'I was there,' Annette interposed. 'At the coroner's inquest. I was called as a witness, to tell what I knew about events just before it happened.'

'How distressing for you,' said Kate to her excited face.

'Don't you think it's odd?' John asked her retreating back.

'Why should I?' she replied as she went through the door.

But as she went down the stairs and across the quadrangle, she wondered who had started the story that Chris had been drinking and then larking about on top of the tower. You don't usually do much larking on half a pint of beer. She took the short cut through the Fellows' Garden, then noticed that she was a few minutes early for Rob Grailing. She didn't want to look too keen, so she sat down on a wooden bench, admiring the view along a green avenue towards a stone nymph in a darker green glade. Pink lavatera spilled over the path beside her seat, and there was a smell of honeysuckle. The whole experience was quite delightful, so perhaps Honor and Briony knew a thing or two about gardens after all.

But as she sat there, watching the dappled sunlight on the gold and green of the foliage, darker thoughts began to intrude themselves into her mind. She recalled the note with its cryptic message:

CURIOSITY KILLED THE CAT

She had been fooling herself that Christopher Townsend's death was really an accident, and that the notes were merely unpleasant jokes. But the report of the inquest changed everything. The version of Chris's death that said that he spent a jolly lunchtime carousing with his friends, then slipped over the parapet and off the tower while checking the route for the students' tour had always seemed unlikely. Without the alcohol, it was quite impossible. And the notes took on a more sinister aspect. For if Christopher was murdered, what was it that he had been curious about, which had presumably led to his death? And yet the coroner had found that it was an accident. What she needed was a few words with the coroner's officer, and she had her own ideas on who that might be.

She thought again abut the lunch she had had with Faith Beeton at her house. Why had Faith invited her there? She didn't have a very clear recollection of what they had talked about. Perhaps it was about genre fiction, perhaps it was about whodunits, but in spite of her hazy memories of the lunch, she was left with the impression that Faith had been quizzing her for information. And if she remembered anything at all, it was that Faith had been disappointed in what she had learned. Was Faith, too, someone who was not what she seemed? But who could you trust in life if it wasn't a teacher of English literature, she wondered.

She looked at her watch. She was now two minutes late, which was about right, she thought, so she started walking on towards the lodge.

She was striding along by the side of a screen of foliage, her footsteps making no sound on the soft ground, when she heard voices, just a few feet away, but out of sight. She tuned in and listened.

'. . . so it's no use complaining about it now, since we did need someone to take his place. You couldn't expect the Bursary staff to do it all, not as well as their own work.'

'Why did you have to take on someone so bright?'

'Oh, come on! Ivory's no intellectual, is she?'

She'd known it, they were talking about her! She stopped walking and listened properly, her head half in a thick green bush.

'Well, no. But she's the nosiest woman I've ever met. Haven't you ever noticed how she listens in to every conversation going? I wouldn't put it past her to take notes. She's probably putting the whole college into her next book.'

'Don't worry. She writes romantic pseudo-historical slush, not crime novels.'

'But do something about her, will you? We can't let her go on like this.'

The voices were moving away. She couldn't hear any more of the conversation. And she couldn't identify the voices, either. They were both male, certainly, but the thick bushes had muffled the sound enough for her not to be absolutely certain who they were. Though, naturally, she had her suspicions.

For the moment she was glad that she was going to meet a normal, open, friendly man for lunch. She needed normality as an antidote to her suspicious conversations and dark thoughts. And then again, she knew she could get to like Rob Grailing.

Behind her, as she and Rob Grailing walked out into Bartlemas Row, one of the porters was speaking to a late-summer tourist.

'I'm afraid that the college is closed to visitors for the present. But if you would care to come back at one-thirty I can arrange a tour for you. Informally, of course. But it will take you into all the parts of the college that the tourists don't normally see. How much? Only two pounds a head. Yes. I'll see you here at one-thirty, then.'

They sat with their drinks and their large plates piled high with food at a table in the pub garden, beneath the canopy of a tree. Insects dropped from above on to the table and occasionally into their food, but neither of them minded. They were at that pleasant stage in an acquaintanceship where they were discovering how much they had in common, and how easy it was to talk to one another. They ordered more mineral water and sat in the hot sunshine, sipping at the misted glasses and enjoying being in each other's company.

'They have really good puddings,' said Rob Grailing, as the time crept past one-thirty. 'Shall I get us something?'

A little later, Kate thought she really ought to bring the conversation round to her work, since that was the ostensible reason for their meal. 'Is there any special aspect of the job you wanted to speak to me about?' she asked, as they attacked bowls of apple and blackberry pie topped with opulent mounds of whipped cream.

Rob looked surprised. 'No. Should there be?'

'I thought that was why we were lunching,' said Kate. 'Actually, I noticed you at Chris's memorial service and I've been wondering how to ask you out ever since. I thought lunch would be less threatening than dinner. A chance for us to get to know one another.'

The dappled light under the tree warmed his brown hair and intensified the ambiguity of the expression in his eyes.

'Aren't you married?' she asked abruptly, before instantly regretting the question. Life was simpler if you didn't know these things, she found.

'Yes,' he replied. There was a silence while a spider dropped on its silken thread between them and hung there suspended.

'Elaine and I live separate lives,' he said, eventually.

'And now you're going to tell me that she doesn't understand you.'

'Oh, I think we understand one another all too well. We married when we were both very young and there is little that we don't know about the other.'

'So why don't you separate?'

If they were separated, it would be all right to fancy him, wouldn't it?

'Habit, probably. It's hard to disentangle the threads of two lives that have been woven together for so long.'

She wanted to ask him what he wanted from her, how he saw their relationship developing, if indeed a relationship was what he was looking for, but she sat and watched the spider as it swayed in front of her eyes, and for a change found herself silent.

'We can see one another, can't we?' Rob was saying. 'As friends, that is?'

Oh God, how corny could you get?

'Yes, of course,' she heard herself replying. 'And I am in a relationship myself at the moment,' she added. If you could call it a relationship when you met one another only when the demands of your respective jobs allowed you to do so, when you seemed to have nothing much in common, and when you didn't dare invite him round to meet your friends. Some relationship! she thought.

He appeared to relax. 'I can help you at work,' he said.

'Do I need help?'

'No. But sometimes it's good to have someone to discuss your worries with. If you have any, of course. Any little thing that might be troubling you.'

Like the death of Chris Townsend, thought Kate. Do you want me to discuss *that* with you? Is that why you've invited me to lunch? But Rob was looking at her with such transparent interest that she couldn't believe he had any ulterior motive at all. The spider was climbing up its thread again, to disappear into the tree above their heads.

'You do come complete with a certain reputation,' he said.

'You mentioned that once before. Which reputation are you referring to?'

He laughed. 'The one for investigating possible

crimes. Didn't you work with the Computer Security Team and discover some dreadful university-wide system of book thefts?'

'Well, I did help them a little on that,' said Kate, gratified that people knew about it. She had been sworn to secrecy at the time, and had only told her closest friends all the details. She was afraid that they had actually obeyed her instructions to keep the story to themselves. What was the use of doing something clever if no one knew about it?

'And you think there is some equally awful crime going on at Bartlemas, do you?' she asked, made indiscreet by the warm gaze that was directed at her from across the table.

'I do hope not. I'd hate to think that our modest funds were being plundered. But if there were anything, I do hope that you feel you could bring it straight to me.'

He had such an earnest expression, such guileless eyes. What a pity about Elaine, or whatever his wife's name was. Still, if they stayed together through habit, and hardly ever spoke to one another, perhaps it would not be so wicked to meet him occasionally. After all, she didn't mean to be unfaithful to Paul, if it came to that.

'I've noticed what a good listener you are,' he said, still looking into her eyes with his own honest brown ones. 'You must hear a lot, with that gift of yours. I'm sure people must talk to you. Unburden themselves.' He smiled enquiringly at her.

'I'm not sure that I'm that popular at Bartlemas,' she said. 'No one seems eager to press their secrets into my willing ears.'

'Well, if they do, perhaps you'd pass any gossip on to me.'

The time was speeding past two o'clock and she thought of her waiting desk full of work.

'This has been a lovely lunch,' she said, wondering

why he was so insistent about listening to her problems and worries. She picked up her bag.

'In that case, we must certainly do it again,' said Rob. Which was exactly what she had hoped he would say.

When Kate got home that evening, there were two messages waiting for her on her telephone answering machine. The first was a polite enquiry as to her health and wellbeing from Paul Taylor, the other was a voice she didn't know, or anyway couldn't recognize.

'I know you're a nosy parker,' it said. Charming! Kate froze and stared at the machine. 'I've heard stories about you. Death follows you around. You were out there, watching me. Spying on me. But this time, if you've any sense, you'll keep out of it. Or something unpleasant will happen. I mean it.' The message stopped and the machine clicked and whirred as the tape rewound.

She played it through again. First, the soothing, pleasant voice of Paul Taylor. Then the other. She listened carefully this time. Was it male or female? It sounded as though the speaker was talking through some barrier. Not a handkerchief, something that distorted more thoroughly than that. And though the words were not exceptional, the way they were delivered, in those short, explosive sentences, was chilling. She thought about ringing Paul for a comforting talk. But what could she say? Someone put an insulting note in one of my files at work, and then left an unpleasant message on my machine. She couldn't phone him at work over such a trivial worry. The two events were only disturbing in the context of a previous violent death. She kept coming back to the fact that Chris Townsend's death was not an accident, even if the coroner had stated that it was just that.

She was still staring at the phone, as though it could

tell her something. Then she remembered that it could, at that! BT had been advertising their new services in television commercials for months. It was time to give one of them a try. She dialled 1471 and listened.

'Sorry,' said the neutral voice. 'No telephone number is stored.'

Damn! The caller must have dialled the other number, the one she could never remember, that kept their own phone number secret. The telephone repeated the message, as though mocking her: 'Sorry. No telephone number is stored.'

She gave in to her attack of the jitters and rang Paul Taylor at work, but there was no reply so she poured herself a reviving glass of cold white wine and sat down to think carefully about what had happened.

Chris Townsend had fallen off the Tower of Grace, for no good reason, and had died. She had taken over part of his job and had now received two messages warning her to keep her nose out of – what? – or she too would be on the receiving end of another 'accident'. Whoever was behind it all must think that she had found out something that they didn't want to be generally known. She went over the events of the past few days since the first phone call from Emma. Nothing. Except, of course, for that invoice that Sadie had snatched away. And the heavy hints that John and Annette had dropped over coffee that morning. But the main impression she had got from those two was that if there were any dishonest schemes going they wished to be included. If they thought there was money to be made, and they were left out, they would be spiteful about their colleagues. But that didn't mean they were right, or that they knew anything concrete. Think again.

Suppose there were some sort of scam going on in the college, with someone helping themselves to a portion of the large sums that were being collected every day. And suppose Chris Townsend had found out about it and had confronted whoever it was, and had threatened to report it to the Master. And the same who- ever it was had then tipped him over the edge of the tower. And now this person thought that she, Kate Ivory, had stumbled on the same scam, and was warning her off. It made sense, as far as it went, except that if John Clay and Annette Paige suspected what was happening and were searching for evidence, what was the point of silencing her? She was merely the last in a long line of people to learn about it, she assumed. Unless there was something more that she had stumbled over without noticing its significance.

And who was responsible? Her head told her that the most obvious candidate was the Bursar, Rob Grailing. Nice, kind, good-looking Rob Grailing. The one who had asked her out to lunch and then set about charming her into a state of confidence in him. And yet, perhaps she should take notice of what Annette and John had said over coffee. They certainly seemed to be pointing the finger in Rob's direction. But who were they, after all? Just two spiteful gossips who envied him his job. And could that have been Rob's voice on the message? She sidled up to the answering machine and played the messages through again. First, Paul's no-nonsense tones. She felt a little guilty at fancying Rob Grailing with Paul's voice talking to her. Then, the stranger with the threat. She listened closely. She played it through a fourth time. What did the caller mean by 'out there'? Out where? And why 'this time'? Had there been a previous time, and if so, when and where and what was she doing? She had no idea. But she cheered up. Really, hearing it again she was almost positive that the voice couldn't belong to Rob Grailing.

There was one more thing she wanted to check, before she went down to her workroom and tried to concentrate on the plot of her new book. She went to her expenses file, where she had entered the receipt for the new pen and notebook. She found the small piece of paper with pale blue printing. Yes, it was a modern till, which, in addition to thanking her for her custom, had printed out the date and time of the transaction. The date was that of Chris's death. The time was 3.28 p.m. So, she had been right. She was there, just before Chris Townsend was killed. And she was sure now that he had been murdered. She didn't know who by, but she thought she would find out.

Later, when she went to bed, she went round the house checking on the window locks and turning the keys in her door bolts before removing them from the locks. She tried to phone Paul again. Still no reply. Through the wall she could hear the neighbours going about their normal, noisy lives. Usually it irritated her. Tonight it was a comforting sound.

Next day, when she walked through the outer office on her way to coffee, Kate saw that they had a new member of staff: Briony, sitting gingerly at a corner of Annette's desk and dealing out pieces of paper into different heaps. She had surprisingly large hands, with short fingernails, for such a slender woman. Gardener's hands, Kate supposed, not managing more than the occasional stint of lawn-mowing herself. Honor must have persuaded Rob Grailing to take her on after all. And she must have spoken bracingly to Briony for the woman to turn up in the Bursary. She hadn't looked as though she had wanted to do anything at all at the memorial service. It couldn't be easy to come to the college where your husband had worked and take on a job for which, presumably, you had no qualifications. It was kind of Honor to find her something, but it was patronizing, too.

She smiled at Briony. Briony looked at her gravely from her round grey eyes and finally smiled back. She had a small mouth with rather thin lips, and when she smiled they curled up more on one side than the other, giving her a secretive look. What secrets? wondered Kate. Then, don't be silly, she told herself, the woman is merely shy.

Since Briony was there, however, she might as well take advantage of the fact. She would be friendly towards her. She would suggest that they take the occasional coffee break together, or meet for lunch. There was much that Briony could tell her, she felt. Apart from anything else, she could provide her with valuable background information. What did she know about Chris Townsend, after all, except what she had seen that afternoon on the pavement, or heard as gossip from the Bursary staff?

She had set off across the room towards Briony's chair, with a sweet and sympathetic smile on her face, when she was sidetracked from all thoughts of Briony, and of any possibility of questioning her closely on the circumstances of her husband's death, by the sudden appearance of Emma from the Development Office.

'All ready for the invasion?' she cried, sweeping them both into Kate's office and sitting herself on the corner of her desk. In doing so, she dislodged Kate's carefully stacked files and replaced them in the wrong positions.

'I was quite ready,' said Kate, looking at her lopsided files and hoping that Emma had not helped her too enthusiastically in her absence.

'I can only stay for half an hour,' said Emma, to Kate's relief, 'but I thought I'd just check that everything's under control.'

Kate caught another file of correspondence as it cascaded to the ground. 'Oh yes,' she said. 'Absolutely under control.'

* * *

That evening when Kate reached home, she was relieved to see that there were no new messages for her on her answering machine. She rang Paul Taylor immediately.

'What's wrong? You sound upset. What sort of mess have you got yourself into?' he asked. 'Do you want me to come round?'

'None,' she said. 'But yes, I would like you to be here.'

Much later she asked, 'What have you been working on? I haven't been able to get hold of you for ages.'

'I was making inquiries into the death at Bartlemas College for the coroner. I expect you've read about it: the man who fell from the Tower of Grace.'

'I thought that must be you. I recognized your shoulders from Annette's description. I wanted to ask you what you'd found out.'

'I bet you did!'

'Well?'

'Didn't you read the report in the paper?'

'Yes, but I was hoping you'd fill me in on all the background dirt.'

'But you know I can't do that.'

'Spoilsport. And anyway, you must have finished there some time ago.'

'I'm helping with an investigation into a possible fraud.'

'I thought that was very specialized work.'

'It is. But they still need people like me for the routine stuff.'

'And is that at Bartlemas College too? Do you think it's connected with the death of Christopher Townsend?'

'You know I can't answer either of those questions, and anyway, Townsend's death was an accident. That's official, so don't try to make it into something else.'

'No, officer. Quite so, officer.'

'Why don't you shut up and go to sleep now? Haven't you got two hundred and something students turning up tomorrow? I should have thought they'd need all your attention, and loads of energy.'

'I'm feeling relaxed but not sleepy, as a matter of fact.'

'Which means that you want to talk some more, I suppose.' He sounded quite resigned to the fact.

'I was going to tell you about the very agreeable lunch I had at the Turf with the Bursar of Bartlemas.'

'Oh?'

'I thought he wanted to talk about work, but I think he wanted to chat me up.'

'Is this supposed to make me feel jealous?'

'It's obviously failed. But there was something else. Christopher Townsend.'

'Oh no. I've told you, that's all over. Finished.'

'Just listen. Did I tell you that I saw him just before he died? He trod on my foot when I was outside the stationery shop by the traffic lights in the High.'

'Are you sure it was the same day?'

'I bought a few things in the shop that day, and I checked with my receipt. Not only the same day, but less than half an hour before he died.'

'So?'

'He was so normal. Cheerful, pleasant. He didn't have the introspective gloom of someone who is about to hurl themselves from a high place. And he definitely hadn't been drinking.'

'How could you tell?'

'I was close enough to notice a strong smell of beer, or of peppermints, if it comes to that. And there wasn't one.'

'Well, that ties in with the findings of the inquest.'

'But not with the reports of the accident in the paper. Someone must have been putting around that story of the drinking, don't you think?'

'It was probably the most comfortable solution, and

people wanted to believe it. But if you were only yards from the site of the accident, and at about the time of Townsend's fall, didn't you notice anything? I should have thought that you would have come up with ten unlikely suspects for a non-existent murder for me by now.'

'There were lots of people about, certainly, and most of them trod on my feet. Crowds of tourists, a gang of Italian schoolchildren, a few fast-striding locals.'

'But nothing that struck you as odd? No one you recognized?'

'I didn't know any of the people involved at the time, did I? Or only Emma, and there's nothing very odd about her.'

'Hasn't it occurred to you that someone might have recognized you, though? What were you wearing? One of your rude t-shirts?'

'A very tasteful dip-dyed dress, as a matter of fact.'

'Eye-catching, I would have thought. I should leave it in the wardrobe for the next few weeks, in case someone thinks you saw more than you did.'

'You're talking as though you believe Chris Townsend didn't die by accident.'

'I believe it was an accident, but I'm prepared to believe that I could be wrong.'

'And what about my phone calls? They're not very pleasant to come home to, you know.'

'I expect you've made an enemy at work. They sound a pretty weird bunch, you must admit. Have you noticed anyone particularly odd? Anything out of place?'

'So you do think I'm on to something?'

'I seem to remember that, against all likelihood, you've been right in the past. And I also remember that you put yourself in danger.'

'And you care about that, do you?'

'Think of all the paperwork!'

'Oh, very nice, very caring.'

'Put the light out and go to sleep.'

In the early hours of the morning, Paul Taylor found himself awake and thinking.

'Kate?'

'Mm?'

'You awake?'

'No.'

'Have you worn that dip-dyed dress of yours since the afternoon Chris Townsend died?'

'I expect so.'

'Have you worn it at Bartlemas, for example?'

'What? What time is it, for goodness' sake?'

'Early. But I think it may be important.'

'I wore it to Chris Townsend's memorial service. But I was wearing a long jacket over it, and a hat, so it wasn't very noticeable.'

'Did you take the jacket off?'

'Yes, and the hat, before going into the Lamb Room for the reception afterwards.'

'Anything else that might have made you memorable to a . . . to someone who was interested in what you were doing?'

'I was wearing those new ear-rings of mine.'

'The ones that look like a sixties mobile, made out of polished tin?'

'The classy, arty ones, made out of titanium, yes.'

'You'd better give me a list of the people who were present at the reception.'

'*Now?*'

'Tomorrow morning will do. First thing.'

'Can I go to sleep again now?'

'Yes. Goodnight.'

Chapter Nine

> While thus he spake, th' angelic squadron bright
> Turned fiery red, sharp'ning in moonèd horns
> Their phalanx, and began to hem him round
> With ported spears . . .
>
> John Milton, *Paradise Lost, iv*

'You were going to tell me how Fate caught up with you after your treatment of Viola. I have my notebook ready.'

'I'm not sure that Fate had anything to do with it.'

'What, then?'

'Be patient, and I'll tell you about it.'

After her unfortunate interview with the disciplinary committee, Viola returned to her digs and started to pack. She emptied drawers and cupboards into suitcases and plastic bags, ready to load them into her now roadworthy car. And an unworthy, vengeful thought came into her mind. She still had a key to my room. I was out at the pub with some other friends of mine, thinking that Viola would prefer to pack and leave on her own, undisturbed by the sight of me. It wasn't until I got home, late, tired, and a little under the weather, that I discovered what she had done.

'I have to confess that my sympathies are with your friend Viola at this point.'

'They wouldn't be if you had been in my place.'

'Don't you feel at all sorry for her? You ruined her

academic career, after all. What was it she intended to become after taking her degree?'

'I believe she wanted to become a probation officer. At least I saved her from that.'

As I said, there I was, after a celebratory drink or few with my friends, returning to my lonely room. I stumbled to the bathroom, throwing water over my face and making some attempt at cleaning my teeth, then I returned to my room, undressed and threw myself thankfully under the duvet.

Christopher pauses here, as though recalling the exact sensations brought about by the experience.

She had emptied all her jars of fruit conserve, and mine too, into my bed. She had spread them all over the bottom sheet: exquisite raspberry, fragrant apricot, luscious strawberry, all simmered into a light, sugary syrup. Then she had hidden her handiwork by covering it, neatly, with the duvet. As I relaxed down into the bed, so they insinuated themselves even into the most intimate recesses of my body's crevices. Cold, sticky, clinging, runny. Have you ever tried to wash several pounds of fruit conserve off yourself, after midnight, in cold water, in a house where the other occupants object to the slightest noise? And then I had to make up the bed with fresh sheets. Only she'd removed them all, so that I had to lie directly on the mattress, covered with my anorak. I can tell you, I got some very funny looks down at the launderette the next morning when I tried to wash all that lumpy jam off my bedding. And oh, the waste! All that delightful, delicious fruit in its light sugar syrup. I have never managed to find anyone since who could make it as well as Viola. (Nor have I found anyone with as pink and pointed a tongue to lick . . . but enough of that. It is a quite inappropriate thought for this place.)

'I think you have told me a most enlightening story. A

pattern is beginning to emerge, you notice. Soon we shall be able to see exactly how you came here, and why.'

'You're not suggesting that it was Viola who pushed me off that tower?'

'I need one further instalment of your life story before I make any suggestions, let alone come to any firm conclusions. But in your own words, I think we should leave the continuation until tomorrow.'

Kate had found herself an isolated patch of grass in the sun and was enjoying a rare moment of solitude. Since the students had arrived in college, her every minute was accounted for, mostly in the company of uncongenial strangers. One of them, Martha Hawkins, had blue-rinsed hair and crept around in red deck shoes, surprising Kate in what she thought were her off-duty moments. Another, Curtis Skinner, was looking for his life's companion, and had not yet crossed Kate off his list. These are readers, she told herself severely, buyers of books. But her exhortations had no effect.

For the moment, she had escaped from them all. Her eyes were closed, the sun lay hot on her eyelids, and the sound of the traffic was drowned out by the gentle susurration of the breeze in the trees.

'I have so enjoyed your lovely novels.'

Curtis Skinner, creeping up behind her, breathing minty toothpaste fumes into her left ear.

Kate sat up quickly. She did not want Curtis to join her, supine on the grass. 'I'm so glad. My aim is to please.'

'And are you currently working on a further opus?'

'Opus? Oh, book, you mean. Well, I'm turning a few ideas around in my mind at the moment. Considering the possibilities, you might say.'

'It's quite a treadmill that you authors find yourselves on.'

'I seem to remember that when God expelled Adam and Eve from Paradise, he told them that from then on in they had to earn their living and bear children in pain. Well, now we have epidural injections, I believe, but women certainly have to earn their living by the sweat of their brows. But wouldn't you rather earn your bread by writing than by working as a clerk in an insurance office?'

'Insurance can be a very satisfying career choice,' said Curtis, huffily.

'Of course, yes, I'm sure it is,' said Kate hurriedly.

'I hope I'm not annoying you.'

'No, of course not.'

'Because, you see, I don't have many friends of my own. I'm a very lonely person.'

Now Kate remembered the letter in green ink. This must be the one who wrote it.

'I'm sure I can introduce you to a whole new experience in social interaction,' said Kate. 'Let me take another look at the seating plan for tonight's dinner. I'll put you with some really interesting and lovely people.'

She scrambled to her feet and smiled warmly at Curtis. Not too warmly, though. She didn't want him to add her to his list of interesting new social discoveries.

She had stolen this half-hour on her own, but she could see that the students were more adept than she was at finding the quiet corners in the college grounds. Her only escape in future would be to flee the college completely and hide in her own small house.

Registration had gone according to plan, with each student given a goodie bag, printed maps and information about the city, as well as lists of the various workshops and seminars available to them at Bartlemas. Then they had been shown to their rooms. That was when the trouble had started. Within the hour they had turned up by the dozen in Kate's office, asking to be reassigned to more congenial surroundings, and she could see why she was being paid such a respectable salary.

She had tried to point out to them that there was a simple choice, which had been indicated to them on their booking forms, between medieval picturesqueness, sharing one bathroom between three rooms, and living with draughty doors and windows, as against modern concrete-and-glass, with en-suite bathrooms and comfortable beds. The news that fire regulations forbade the smoking of cigarettes or any other recreational substances did not go down well with a small group of nicotine (and other) addicts, either.

In vain had Kate extolled the beauties of the university city and encouraged them to accompany her to the Bodleian, where they could be sworn in as readers. In vain had she offered them a conducted tour of Bartlemas College, including a trip to the top of the Tower of Grace where they would see Oxford spread out beneath them in its leafy glory. She reflected that it might have cheered them up if she had told them about the recent fatal accident. They might have followed her and forgotten their missing hot showers and special diets if she could have shown the precise flagstone where Christopher Townsend spilled out his brains.

And then again, mealtimes had become an ordeal. Kate pointed out that the Bartlemas chef was famed throughout the university. It was just unfortunate that he had a new trainee and took his pedagogic duties very seriously. Young Ian had to practise each dish until it was perfect. Which meant that the first week's menus were repetitious, to put it mildly.

'I thought he was supposed to be such a fantastic dessert chef,' grumbled Sharen Cobb, who had elected herself chief complainer on the food front. 'But all we've had so far is apple pie and rice pudding. My *mother* can cook that, for God's sake.'

'But young Ian is getting very good at it, don't you think?' said Kate. 'I'm sure he'll be moving on to crème brûlée and raspberry bavaroise in a day or two.'

'But what about our cholesterol levels?' put in Martha Hawkins.

'I'm sure that a couple of weeks won't do much damage,' said Kate cheerfully. Martha was a wafer of a woman, no bigger than a size 6, she was sure. Her cholesterol levels, together with her calorie intake and saturated fat percentage, could surely all afford to rise for a fortnight.

'Well, Curtis,' she said now. 'Time to make ourselves beautiful for the reception.'

'No, really, Kate,' he said seriously. 'You have no need to make yourself any more beautiful than you already are.'

And if only Curtis had been a little more prepossessing, she could have enjoyed the compliment.

When she got home to change into something festive yet decorous (a difficult combination to find among the dresses in her wardrobe), Kate saw that there was a telephone message waiting for her. She paused for a moment before daring to press the play button, told herself not to be so stupid, and listened to the message. She let out her pent-up breath. It was Paul, sounding curt and asking her to ring him back as soon as she got home. She looked at her watch: she only just had time to shower, change and get back to Bartlemas for the formal reception of the students, and she would not be popular with the other staff if she was late. She dialled his number anyway.

'Paul Taylor.'

'It's me. You left a message on my machine.'

'Oh yes. You mentioned last night that you'd had lunch at the Turf yesterday. Who was it with?'

'I knew you were jealous, really.'

'Not jealous, merely concerned for your safety.'

'What do you mean?'

'Just tell me who it was.'

'I told you at the time.'

'The name slipped past without my noticing. Run it past me again.'

'Oh, very well. It was Rob Grailing, the Bursar of Bartlemas.'

'Damn.' Which for Paul Taylor was a very strong expression.

'I suppose you disapprove because he's married.'

'I really don't care whether he's married or not, though I think you should, incidentally. But I do care that he . . . Look, Kate, just trust me on this one, will you? I can't tell you what it's about, but I'm warning you off the man.'

Was that a pleading note in Paul's normally prosaic tones? 'It's not jealousy at all, is it?'

'I'm not the jealous type, I'm afraid.'

'No. So it's because you're investigating him for fraud, isn't it? You think he's ripping off the Bartlemas College Development Fund? Have you seen his car? Have you noticed his clothes? Have you asked him where he's been spending his holidays? I knew it!'

'No, you've got it—'

'I think it would be a really good idea if I did stay close to him. I could report back to you, couldn't I? I could find out far more about him than you ever could.'

'Please, Kate, just stay away from him. And don't go jumping to any conclusions. I can't tell you now what it's about, but I will when it is possible. Just trust me on this, all right? And do what you're told without arguing for once.' He was hissing at her down the phone. Perhaps his was the threatening voice on her answering machine. It sounded just as angry. 'I can't speak to you now, I'll see you this evening.'

'No, you won't. I'm going to the reception for the study fortnight students at Bartlemas. I'm not sure when I'll get back.'

The receiver went down at his end without another word.

Kate went upstairs for a rapid shower and to continue her search for a suitable dress.

The reception reminded her of Christopher Townsend's wake. It was held in the same room, with the addition of a further space beyond wooden doors which had been folded back to accommodate the numbers. Apart from the students, who were notable for their leathery suntans and wrinkles, and their lacquered hair, the company was more or less the same as on the previous occasion. The accents were predominantly North American.

Kate thought she was doing rather well, turning several male heads as she made her way through the room. But then she heard a voice behind her.

'Is that the only dress you could find?' asked Emma.

'What's wrong with it?'

'They've forgotten to make it a back. You look naked from behind!'

'Don't exaggerate,' said Kate briskly. 'And my friend Curtis just loves it.' And so did the Master, she noticed, and the Bursar, and several unidentified tutors. She would ignore what Paul had said on the phone. If she could find out more about Rob Grailing and all the other prosperous-looking employees of Bartlemas College, perhaps pierce through to their secret ways of extracting money from the college, then she could present him with the facts and let him reap the glory. It would surely help him in his career if she gave him an inside edge like that. It might, of course, also increase the frequency of unpleasant messages that she was receiving. She just hoped that the unpleasantness stopped there. She didn't like to think about what else might occur if she went on poking her nose into other people's business. She tried not to hear Paul's disapproving voice, but looked beadily round the room, wondering where to start.

For a short while she stood with a glass in one hand and a smoked salmon sandwich in the other and watched the crowd. It isn't just that they're probably getting away with long-term fraud, she thought. One of these people has also been fossicking around inside my files – *and inside Christopher's*, said a voice in her head. One of them has been phoning me and leaving threats on my answering machine. But which one?

Annette had cornered Curtis, and was standing close to him, her face shining red with the wine she had drunk, the strands of her fair hair starting to droop over her face. Over Curtis's shoulder, her pale eyes saw Kate watching her, and she frowned.

'I am a lonely person,' she heard Curtis say to Annette.

'Hello, Curtis!' called Kate, and joined the pair.

'Shouldn't you be circulating?' asked Annette.

'I thought that that was what I was doing,' replied Kate. 'What are you two talking about so animatedly, then?'

'Haven't you found that it's unpopular to quiz people about their conversations?' asked Annette, nastily. 'Perhaps our conversation was private. Had you thought of that?'

'I can take a hint,' said Kate, as Annette continued to outstare her. She noticed that Curtis was looking at her over Annette's shoulder, like a small child at a confectionery display. He would just have to make do with Annette, she thought. And she hadn't learned much there. She looked for her next victim.

John Clay had landed Martha Hawkins and was talking intimately into her ear. Her face brightened at his words. Gossip, thought Kate. Unpleasant gossip, probably. She wished that she could hear what it was. She wriggled round several intervening bodies and stood next to John.

'What's new, then?' she asked brightly.

'Nothing,' said John. 'We were discussing old, old themes,' and he and Martha exchanged an understanding look.

'Talking of which, I must go and find my friend Curtis,' said Martha, and she glided across to where Annette and Curtis were standing, and insinuated her well-conditioned, silver-coated figure between them. Annette's pink face became pinker and shinier, but Curtis took his eyes off Kate, at last. And good luck to them, thought Kate. Perhaps there would be some tiptoeing down corridors, followed by pleasurable activity, at this study fortnight as at so many others. It might keep the two of them happy and stop them nagging her. And perhaps Curtis would be able to drop that line of his about what a lonely person he was. She was growing rather tired of it herself, and she imagined that some of the others were, too.

Annette, giving up on Curtis, came to join John Clay. They both gave Kate such an unwelcoming stare that she moved on to the next group.

The Master had escaped from his wife and was talking to two of the best-looking of the students, his arm brushing their polished golden shoulders, as though by accident. I bet you have trouble with that man, Honor, thought Kate.

Honor herself, encased in pale-blue Crimplene,

managed to look too hot, and rather cross. She still had Briony in tow. Briony was pale of face and was wearing a black cotton dress with small white flowers, which could be taken for mourning. Her slight figure looked fragile, but she was grasping a glass in her capable gardener's hands, their blunt nails ringed with dirt, as if she wished to use it as an offensive weapon. Perhaps she was wishing that Honor would leave her alone.

The Master had been approached by someone who was unknown to Kate: about six foot, she guessed, flat, shiny black hair, the sort of suntan that means you have just got back from holiday, and little narrow dark eyes; pale grey suit, lavender shirt. She made her way between more bodies to get nearer to them.

Behind Kate a figure was standing, unseen, but she recognized the expensive smell.

'Who's that with the Master?' she asked.

'Timothy Happle. Senior English Tutor. This year's Fellow Librarian. My boss, so to speak.'

'And you don't like him?'

'Did I say that?'

They had moved within hearing distance. 'I think you'll be very pleased with what I've arranged,' Happle was saying. 'Such a well-known family in Iskenderun. The boy will need some coaching, of course, but I'm sure we'll get him through Prelims.'

'You mean the lad is thick?' said the Master.

'Not at all. But he isn't necessarily quite up to English educational standards.'

'But I'm sure you'll tell me how it has all been made worth our while.'

'Nothing sordid, Master. Please don't think such a thing.'

The conversation sounded quite dull and Kate turned back to Faith. 'Shall we rescue Briony? She looks as though she's had enough of Honor Flint.' The English tutor moved forwards so that Kate could see her properly: she was wearing a simple dress in vermilion silk jersey and she had painted her eyelids in shining bronze.

'Why?' asked Faith, looking across at Briony with an unfriendly expression on her thin face.

'Oh, I don't know. It seemed a kind thing to do. And it would annoy the Master's wife, don't you think? She behaves as though she owns Briony, complete with all her grief.'

'Annoying Honor has its attractions, but I don't think Briony Townsend is really my sort of person.'

'I thought she was just a harmless gardener. I don't think I've ever heard her speak.'

'No. She doesn't. Hardly ever, I believe. That's probably what I find so tedious about her.'

Faith Beeton wandered off again, making for one of the younger and better-looking tutors. She'll be lucky, thought Kate. All the students are hoping to bag themselves a tutor for the fortnight. Competition is fierce, I would think. She watched as Faith, dull-complexioned and flat of figure, sliced a dark-haired man out of a group of eager matrons, and carried him off to a table where glasses of wine were on offer. Neat, thought Kate, admiringly. But then she thought that she had better go and try to cheer up the disappointed matrons. She would like to go and question the Master, but she had the feeling that she wouldn't get very far with him. She advanced on the matronly group with an encouraging smile on her face. The smile was wiped off, however, when she realized that the group included Martha Hawkins. Why couldn't the woman stick with Curtis Skinner?

'We want a picnic!' Martha was shrieking at her.

'What?'

'We've read through the programme, and there's nothing about an al fresco meal. We want a traditional English picnic. We want punts and a grassy meadow strewn with buttercups, and strawberries and cream in cut-glass dishes, cucumber sandwiches, cold ham and tomato salad.'

'Cowpats,' said Kate. 'Wasps. Flies. A howling gale and driving wind. Sunburn and nettle rash. Angry farmers chasing you off their land. Fornicating couples in the bushes.'

'I beg your pardon!' exclaimed Martha.

'Really,' said Kate. 'Believe me, you'd hate a traditional English picnic. The English loathe them, at least all the sensible ones do.'

'We've read about them,' said Martha, as though this clinched the argument. What you read in books must be more authentic than what happened in real life.

'I'll see what I can organize,' said Kate, recognizing a character stronger than her own. 'How many of you will there be?'

'Twenty-three,' said Martha. Kate wasn't sure whether she was bluffing, but decided to go along with it. First thing in the morning she would telephone punt hire companies. She remembered her own lack of skill with a punt pole, and made a mental note to phone a few young men of her acquaintance and offer them bribes of food and money to come and chauffeur her party on the river. All I have to do now, she thought, is sweet-talk Chef into packing us a traditional English picnic.

'Warm ciabatta,' mused Chef, when she told him about it the next day. 'Earthenware dishes of black olives, goat's milk cheese, sun-dried tomatoes. Chopped basil. Quails' eggs. It's too late for local strawberries, we'll give them apple and blackberry pie and whipped cream. Perhaps some of my crèmes caramel; or flummery, do you think?'

'If we're talking traditional English food, shouldn't it be sliced white bread from the supermarket and pink plastic ham?' asked Kate. 'Rock solid battery eggs and mean little punnets of mustard and cress?'

Chef looked down his nose at her and refused to answer. 'Free-range chickens,' he intoned, 'their breasts anointed with butter and lemon juice, basted every ten minutes to keep them moist, served cold with a lemon-flavoured mayonnaise. A salad of baby spinach and lettuce leaves, with a raspberry vinaigrette, perhaps some rocket if there is any left.'

'OK, I'm convinced,' murmured Kate, and she went to give the good news to Martha.

'I told you so!' crowed Martha, not showing the slightest gratitude. 'This will really be something to tell the family about.'

Kate hoped that nothing too exciting and newsworthy would happen on this outing to enliven Martha's correspondence with her loved ones, and consoled herself with the thought that at least on the picnic they would not be accompanied by some celebrity singing incomprehensible German songs. For, before the outing on the river in punts, she had the concert in Birmingham to get through.

'And what about our tour of Bartlemas?' asked Martha, as Kate was preparing to creep away into the night, back to her own place.

'Now?' exclaimed Kate.

'Tomorrow morning,' compromised Martha.

'But you didn't want to see the college,' argued Kate. 'I did offer, I remember. It was on the programme, but you turned me down.'

'That was then,' said Curtis, at her elbow. 'This,' he added incontrovertibly, 'is now.'

Kate consulted her pocket diary. 'We have a window,' she said, 'between nine and ten-fifteen tomorrow morning. An hour and a quarter. We have a lot of ground to cover, so you'd better wear running shoes. I'll see you here, at nine o'clock precisely.'

And she disappeared out through the lodge in a swirl of thin dark skirt, her hair silver in the street lamps, as she strode home towards Fridesley.

At five to nine, Kate was there at the lodge, waiting for Curtis and Martha, and whichever of their colleagues they had gathered to join them on the tour. I'll give them until nine, she thought. Not a minute past. If they're not here, I shall leave. She watched the minute hand click forwards on the clock above the gothic windows of the hall. Four minutes to go.

At one minute to nine they were there. Just Martha and Curtis, she was pleased to see. Though perhaps any dilution of their combined essence would have been a good thing, she thought, as they set out on her lightning tour.

'The hall,' she stated, leading them in, letting them admire the hammerbeam roof and the candlesticks and the hideous epergne on High Table, but briefly. 'Previous Masters,' she said, indicating the solemn portraits round the walls. 'That one's an Old Boy who made it to Prime Minister. The one in the white wig and the whisky nose was Lord Chancellor.' Then, 'This way!' she shouted, and led them at a gallop through a series of quadrangles. 'Old Quad! New Quad! Founders' Quad!' she called out. 'Chapel!' she cried to the two panting figures behind her. She pushed open the door and stood beside the entrance to the Tower of Grace. 'Very nice seventeenth-century painted windows,' she informed them. 'A lovely whale, and a delicious Eve.' She thought about inviting them to share in the pretty Temptation, but was afraid that Curtis might take her up on it, and then they would both get involved in an Expulsion.

'Isn't that the tower?' asked Martha, ignoring the chapel and staring at the door to Grace.

'The one where the man died,' added Curtis, in case she had missed the allusion.

'I believe so,' said Kate, airily. 'Though I suppose he actually died a couple of seconds later, on the flagstones outside.' That should shut the ghouls up, she thought.

She was wrong. 'Can we go up and look?' they both chorused.

'Have we got time?'

'Yes,' said Martha. 'You haven't lost us yet. You lead the way.'

So Kate had to.

Martha was having a high old time, she realized, revelling in the discomfort as the breeze whipped their hair back from their faces.

'What's that building?' asked Martha. And as soon as Kate answered, she picked out another one for her to identify. Kate could well imagine someone getting tired of the interrogation and pitching Martha off the tower. They might well follow it up by chucking Curtis over to join her. She considered the practical problems. Martha was about her own height but a lot lighter, without much solid muscle, she judged. It wouldn't take much of a shove to get her to clear the top of the wall. What if her attention were distracted? Without thinking, Kate pointed off to their left and exclaimed:

'I say, Martha! Isn't that All Souls over there?'

'What? The one with the twin towers? Are you sure?' Martha leant out over the balustrade.

Definitely possible. You would take her by one shoulder and the opposite foot and pitch her over diagonally. She wouldn't have a chance. And if she were ten or twelve inches taller, and a fair bit broader? Still possible, perhaps. But you would have to be taller and stronger than Kate Ivory. What she found difficult to imagine was

147

Martha overbalancing and falling off the tower accidentally. And what if Martha and Curtis were drunk and 'larking around' as the newspaper account had put it. No, they would bump against the wall. They might stumble about on the floor, but she couldn't see them tipping over. So it had to be—

'No, definitely not,' said Martha. 'That's All Souls over there, just next to the Radcliffe Camera.'

'Of course it is,' said Kate. 'Well, if we're going to complete our tour before ten-fifteen, I suppose we'd better get going.' And she led the way down the stone spiral staircase as fast as she could manage.

'Pesant Quad,' she said, as they stood in the open air again. 'And there's the library over there. We've just got time to look around inside it.' As a matter of fact, Kate had not yet visited the library herself, and thought it was a good opportunity to do so. There was nothing like a college library when she was researching the background for one of her books, and this one could come in handy if she made herself pleasant to the librarian.

'Wow!' she said, when they went in.

This was not the usual shabby college library, hard up for cash, run by one overworked part-time librarian. A lot of money had been spent on this place in the recent past and it had the sleek, well-cared-for look of a place where no financial corners had been cut. On a row of desks stood a dozen new computer terminals and CD-Rom players. A board by the issue desk gave an impressive list of the CD-Roms available. Several thousand pounds' worth, thought Kate, even before they bought all that expensive hardware. In front of her a long bookcase bore the legend 'New Acquisitions' and it was stuffed full of interesting-looking new books.

'Can I help you?' It must be the librarian, thought Kate, but he didn't look like one: much too smart; well-cut hair; shiny shoes, silk tie, plump, well-fed face.

'I'm just showing two of our American visitors around the college,' said Kate. 'I'm Kate Ivory, helping with the administration and doing a little teaching.'

'Really?' said Curtis. 'I haven't noticed any of your classes scheduled just yet.'

'Next week,' said Kate, improvising.

'And I'm the librarian, Brian Renfrew. I'm afraid I can't show you round just at this moment as I've got a meeting to go to at Leicester College, but do make yourselves at home.' And he sauntered out through the swing doors into the autumn sunshine.

'This is nearly as good as the library at my college back home,' said Curtis, admiringly.

'Good,' said Kate. 'Just sign for any books that you borrow, will you? And make sure that you return them before you leave.' And she left them and made for the history shelves.

'What about the Fellows' Garden?' hissed Martha in her ear.

'Oh yes, lovely. Quite beautiful,' said Kate, reaching down a book by Lawrence Stone that she hadn't yet read.

'We want to see it,' said Curtis. 'We still have twenty minutes of our tour left, and we're not allowed into the Fellows' Garden without the presence of a member of our tutorial staff.'

'Just coming,' said Kate, signing the card inside the book and dropping it into the wooden box provided. 'Fellows' Garden, right. Designed by a friend of Gertrude . . . er . . .'

'Jekyll?' asked Curtis.

'Or Hyde,' said Kate. 'Whoever. Some Yorkshire-woman, I believe. But it is much admired, and the gardener is now called Dave,' she added triumphantly. Who cared about a dead gardener when you could meet Dave Evans and have a useful conversation about brightly coloured bedding plants?

The Fellows' Garden was a good idea, thought Kate. For in this hot, muggy September, when the heavy air pressed down like wet cotton wool even at ten in the morning, the garden was a haven of green coolness.

'Now this is more like it,' said Martha. 'What's that called?' She indicated a graceful green shrub.

'I believe it's a *Focaccia pendula*,' said Kate without blushing.

'Are you sure? It doesn't sound familiar to me,' said Martha.

'Of course I'm sure. English people know about gardens,' said Kate.

'What I love about this garden is its privacy,' said Curtis. 'From no one point can you see the whole design displayed before you. You have to explore, to turn corners and find unexpected little arbours and secret places. There could be a dozen people here, and we would never be aware of them.'

As though to underline what Curtis was saying, they heard voices from behind a thick green shrubbery.

'I gather you've been lucky again in your Turkish trip,' said the first. Kate thought she might have heard the voice before somewhere, but she couldn't place it. The voice was male and educated, with no noticeable accent.

'Yes, it was very profitable,' said the second, also male. This one Kate did recognize: It was Timothy Happle, he of the varnished black hair and sarcastic expression. 'We shall soon be welcoming the eldest son of my hosts to Bartlemas College.'

'How lovely for us. And did you have a comfortable holiday?'

'The facilities were all that I could wish for,' said Happle.

'Well, I shall be sending you a memo with my latest list of requirements for the library,' said the first speaker.

'It is so wonderful for us to have such a co-operative
Fellow Librarian.

'Hey,' interrupted Martha. 'Do you always listen in
to other people's conversations like that?'

'Usually,' admitted Kate. 'Unless they're particularly
dull, that is.'

There was the sound of retreating footsteps from the
other side of the shrubbery screen, but Kate had now
placed the other voice: it had to be the Librarian of
Bartlemas, Brian Renfrew. And apart from anything else,
he had been telling a tiny fib about being on his way to
Leicester College for a meeting. It seemed an unneces-
sary untruth, and she wondered why.

'Well,' she said to Curtis and Martha, 'time for the
rose garden and the vegetables. I'm afraid that most of
the roses will be past their best, but the smell is really
quite something.'

A young man crossed their path, pushing a wheelbarrow full of cuttings in small plastic pots.

'Barry,' explained Kate. 'The gardener's assistant. He's
on his way to the greenhouse, no doubt.'

Barry looked up at her, startled, as though he
wondered what on earth she was talking about.

Chapter Ten

> . . . back with speediest sail
> Zophiel, of Cherubim the swiftest wing,
> Came flying . . .
>   John Milton, *Paradise Lost, iv*

'You see, I've always been interested in psychology,' says Zophiel.

'Of men or angels?' asks Christopher.

'Men of course. I don't think that angels have much of what you could properly describe as psychology. And if they had, they haven't a very wide field in which to exercise it.'

Christopher digests this thought in silence for a while before asking, 'So you've studied the psychology of mankind. And what have you observed?'

'I've made a special study of the psychology of the victim. In fact, that's why I agreed to do this tour of duty at the east gate of Eden. It isn't considered much of a job for a cherub, as I am sure you appreciate. And my position is a senior one.'

'Well, no. And not a job for someone as speedy as yourself. What was it you said you were? The swiftest of God's cherubim?'

Zophiel smirks. 'Yes, but I'm not just a pretty pair of wings, you know. I'm the brains of the outfit, too, and, like I say, I've been studying this victim problem. Did you know that eighty per cent of crimes of theft happen to only twenty-five per cent of the population? So just as there is some quirk *of personality that turns a man into a criminal, there must be another that turns someone else into a victim. There is something in his upbringing, in his whole history, that marks him out as a victim of crime. And if this is true of something as common as theft, how much more true must it be of something as comparatively rare, in your city at least, as murder?'*

'Very interesting. So that is why you've been talking to me in this matey way. You were after data. You wanted me to prove, or to disprove, your theory.'

'Of course I appreciate the pleasure of your company, but I have to admit that I have had an ulterior motive in listening to your story. And it does seem to me that a pattern is emerging.'

'What do you mean? We all know the cringing sort of bloke who gets to be a victim. But I can assure you that there is – was – nothing like that about me. I was a self-confident, popular person. No one would have taken advantage of me and lived. I don't see myself as a victim, do you? Viola now, yes. She was quite some victim. She lost a lot as a result of our little adventure, I admit. And it is possible that some of it was my fault. But the silly cow shouldn't have been so trusting. You have to learn not to trust people in life, don't you think? It was a valuable lesson that I taught her.'

'But still,' says Zophiel. 'You cannot ignore the pattern. Tell me, did you repeat your money-making schemes when you went to work for the charity?'

'The odd thing is,' says Christopher, 'that charity workers are really hard-headed people. You wouldn't expect it, would you? But the number of checks and balances they had in place, you couldn't get away with so much as a second-class postage stamp.'

'So you moved on.'

'To Bartlemas College eventually. Yes.'

'I will be interested to hear about it, to see whether the

pattern develops. For it is true that you were, indeed, a victim. Plummeting from a high tower, after being attacked by someone you thought you knew. How do you explain that?'

'You're the psychology expert. You tell me.'

'You'll have to tell me more about the story of your life. When I have it all, I'll be able to explain it to you.'

'You'll do that?'

'It would be better if you could make all the connections for yourself. That is so much more satisfactory than having them pointed out to you by someone else. But please continue with your story.'

'Where had I got to?'

'You had told me about your father. How like him you were. How you divided him from his woman friend and left him to live out his days in a home for the elderly, and how she got her revenge. Then you told me about poor Viola and how you duped her, and how she finally got her own back, although hardly on the same scale as your destruction of her.'

'Are you sure that's what I told you? That isn't how it seemed to me.'

'Tell me the next part, then. Tell me about Bartlemas and Briony.'

'After a period at the charity, learning how to raise money from unwilling punters, I grew tired of the frustrations of the job.'

'You were disillusioned with the bureaucracy of charity?'

'And of the tight rein they kept on their finances. There was no room for manœuvre there at all. No possibility of creatively adding to one's expenses. No perks. No company car. Very dull. So I moved.'

'Oxford?'

'Oh, I moved here and there, perfecting my skills at fundraising in all sorts of ways. I became quite well known in the field. By the time I was into my thirties I was being

head-hunted by one of the Oxford colleges. With the cutbacks in government funding, these colleges were starting to look to their alumni, in the American fashion, to provide money for their current needs. They made me an offer I couldn't refuse.'

'And so you moved for the last time.'

'To Bartlemas College, as Development Officer.'

'And here you found the right field for your endeavours?'

'I found here that cheating was a way of life. It took me a little while to find out all the various schemes that were in operation, so that I could carefully co-ordinate my own small efforts without interfering with theirs – for a fee, or a percentage, of course. And then there was Briony.'

'I don't suppose she would approve of your dishonesty.'

'I don't know about that. I do know that her upbringing had not led her to think that she should live in respectable poverty.'

'Poverty? On an Oxford administrator's salary? Surely not?'

'Not by your standards, or mine. But certainly by hers.'

'I think we're getting closer to the reasons for your demise. I'm all ears.'

'Don't you think this section has already overrun its allotted span? Isn't it long enough? Shouldn't we wait until tomorrow for the next instalment of the story?'

'I've already told you that tomorrow has no meaning for me.'

'Oh, very well, then, it can wait until the next chapter. Will that do for you? Is that a concept with which you are familiar?'

'Perfectly.'

Thursday was a hot, sultry day. Grey clouds hung low over the city, undisturbed by any breeze, trapping the heavy air beneath their leaden surface. As she led her troupe of students out to the coach, Kate was already feeling too hot, and inclined to bad temper. They left Oxford at three o'clock and drove into a countryside where the heat haze lay like blue smoke over the umber fields and dark hedges. In the distance, a flock of inland seagulls perched like a scatter of shining white beads across a brown field.

It was unfortunate for Kate that she got landed with Martha Hawkins as a travelling companion. Martha thought that an hour and a quarter up a motorway was an excellent opportunity to ask Kate all the questions she had been saving up for a lifetime. She started with 'Do you write longhand with a pen, or do you use a word processor?', carried on through 'How do you get published?' and then said, 'I suppose you only write well when you are truly inspired.'

'I'm afraid not,' said Kate. 'If you want to earn a living as a writer, you have to produce a book when it's needed. Inspiration rarely comes into it.'

'Really? I hadn't realized that you earned your living at it,' said Martha. 'Do you write under your own name?'

As the coach sailed past tower blocks and concrete lay all around them, Martha was silent. They were now approaching the centre of Birmingham. 'This isn't the way I thought England was. It's not much like Oxford, is it?' said Martha, doubtfully.

'No gothic buildings built in golden stone, no pinnacled towers, no spires, no meadows by a limpid stream?' said Kate. 'I suppose it isn't. Though there's quite a pretty canal. And, of course, a symphony hall.'

The coach stopped at last and Kate and her charges decanted. Kate cried 'Follow me!' and led the way uphill towards another expanse of concrete. She was making a good job of pretending that she knew where she was and where she was going, but she was helped by neat fingerposts which pointed her in the right direction.

'Symphony Hall!' she announced, as they arrived at a building made of slabs of glass and decorated with strings of fluorescent spaghetti. Across the piazza a giant sculptured figure raised its arm in fraternal greeting. They all entered the foyer of the hall and Kate immediately lost most of her group as they variously made for the loos and the snack bar. The small hardcore group of smokers found themselves some chairs in a corner and lit up.

The place was crowded and buzzing. The celebrity singer, whose name Kate could not remember, was apparently drawing a large crowd of devoted followers. Kate still wasn't looking forward to sitting through a programme of opera gems on an unusually hot September afternoon. But at least the foyer was cool, and Kate fondly hoped that the hall would be air-conditioned. What a relief to be away from the claustrophobic atmosphere of Oxford, she thought. This was a modern, outward-looking city, with a European feel to it. No one here would creep up on you and tip you over the parapet of a gothic tower, or leave obliquely threatening messages on your screen. Emma was right! Birmingham was the place to be on this hot and sticky afternoon. She could relax. She was safe. She could return to her guard duty with the students with a light heart and a willing step.

She hadn't realized just how long, and with how many squabbles, it would take to seat forty-eight uncooperative people in a similar number of apparently identical coral-coloured seats. Three-year-olds would have been easier, she thought. At least you could tuck them under your arm and move them to where they should be, and then stop their mouths with sugar-rich sweeties. When it was finally done, Kate slipped into her own seat, carefully chosen at the end of a row. If she sat there, she would only have the dreary conversation of one, rather than two, of her students, she calculated.

The concert began, and the temperature started to rise. Kate looked for the first time at the white slip of paper inserted into her programme. The celebrity singer had apparently requested that the air-conditioning be switched off in case it disturbed the atmosphere of the music. The combined body heat of the hall full of people was starting to make itself felt in the upper tier where they were sitting, and drops of perspiration trickled down Kate's back. As incomprehensible songs by Alban Berg washed over her, Kate promised herself the new Kirsty MacColl album when she got back to Oxford. At least she would understand the words. The end seat was a smart move: when the audience had given their measure of applause and the house lights went up, she was in an excellent position to sprint for the nearest bar and a long, cold spritzer. If she'd known how hot it was going to be she might have introduced a bottle of spring water into her large shoulderbag. Shouldn't she, a small voice inside her head enquired, be more concerned for the comfort of her charges than for her own? Damn the charges, a more familiar voice retorted, they deserve everything they get. She looked round the crowds of people in search of the nearest bar.

Kate was indeed out ahead of the crowd in the interval, and well near the front of the queue at the bar. As she sipped her drink a few minutes later, she wandered round the balconies, observing the punters and avoiding the members of her group. The place was not ideal for a person who was not keen on heights, or for one wishing to remain out of sight. The walls were of glass and, turning a corner, a broad and unexpected vista presented itself which made her head swim. Take control, she exhorted herself. Be glad this is not the golden stone of Oxford, where dangers lurk around every corner. And as for your fear of heights, get used to small distances, then gradually move on to the larger. She let her eyes move to a transparent wall and focused on the figures that promenaded across the deck, fifty feet away, on the other side of the building. It was like watching fish in an aquarium. Two figures swam past in the swirl of the crowd. One of them she recognized. Perhaps. A man with brown hair and a suntan, his arm protectively around a dark-haired woman.

Forgetting her fear, Kate dashed along a corridor and down a flight of stairs, hoping for a better view of the couple. A flash of bronze and black dress, a familiar hand on an arm. Rob Grailing. And there was something about the way they moved without talking, something very familiar in the way they weren't looking at one another, that made her know that this was his wife. The wife who didn't share his interests, who lived a separate life. They looked pretty together to her, as they made their way round to a door and disappeared back into the auditorium.

Her mind was abruptly removed from the problems of Rob Grailing by the determined advance of Martha Hawkins along the carpeted expanse of corridor. At least all this glass gave her a warning of the approach, and she swallowed the rest of her wine in a single gulp, put her glass down on a convenient table, and sprinted around a corner, up a staircase (resolutely keeping her eyes at her feet as the view spun past her head). She arrived on another level where a different crowd were drinking and chatting at yet another bar. She gingerly approached a blue rail and peered over to see whether she had successfully evaded Martha and the rest of her charges. She couldn't face answering another of Martha's questions for the moment. Below her lay a table covered with a white tablecloth laid with cups and saucers, ready for the coffee-drinkers. She moved a little further round so that she could see more of the crowd of people. The railing here was much lower, but she wanted to reassure herself that she had left Martha behind. Yes, there she was, a scowl on her smooth face, a glass of something red in her hand.

It was at this moment that she felt a prickling sensation between her shoulderblades that had nothing to do with the fact that she was scared of heights, and was leaning over a very low rail. Someone was watching her, she was sure of it. Perhaps she could turn round, very fast, and catch them at it. Perhaps she would see who it was and it would solve the whole rotten mystery of Chris's death and the threatening messages on her telephone in one swift movement.

A strong hand twisted Kate's arm up by her shoulderblade, while a second planted itself in the centre of her back. Kate froze. If the hand pushed any harder, she would be hard put to it to keep her balance.

'Don't move. Don't turn round.' The voice was whispering. Impossible to tell even if it were male or female.

'This is your last warning,' it went on, forcing Kate to bend out over the void. 'Look down there. How do you fancy landing up in the middle of that table?' In her imagination, Kate saw splintered white china, spilled coffee, a body spreadeagled across the snowy tablecloth. It was too vivid an image for comfort. Blood, broken bones. She closed her eyes. She was going the same way as Chris Townsend, she knew it.

Then, suddenly, somewhere a bell rang, and she was allowed to stand up straight again. Behind her she could hear people starting to move. In a minute she would be alone with her attacker.

'Keep out of it! Or you're dead!'

And abruptly she was free, and staggering, turning to see who had threatened her. But all she saw was a sea of backs, streaming into the concert hall, taking their seats for the second half of the concert. She followed them in, slowly.

'Would you like the aisle seat?' she asked Martha, politely. It felt safer to be hemmed in by students of genre fiction than stuck out there at the mercy of every passing murderer.

As singer and accompanist arrived on stage to a storm of applause, she tried to remember in detail everything that had happened.

The hand on her back, was it male or female? It was strong enough for a man, but could equally belong to a fit and healthy woman. The voice had come from a point a few inches above her ear, so it was someone taller than herself. But then, many people were more than her own five feet five. She tried to remember more, as songs by Wagner sounded in the background, but she could dredge up no more details from her terrified memory.

On the way back in the coach, she was only too glad to sit next to the window, pinned in by Martha's loud voice.

'The secret is to make your work more accessible,' she was saying. 'I don't suppose you've found an American publisher yet, have you? No? Well, just remember that people don't want to read about unpleasant things happening to your characters.'

At least no one could get past Martha and attack her. She was safe for at least another hour. And she was quite willing to stop unpleasant things from happening to the characters in her novels; she just wished that someone would do the same for her.

Back in her own house, Kate conceded that she needed help. Was Andrew back from California? Would Paul be at home? Which one of them would she prefer to talk to?

She dialled each number in turn, but neither was at home or answering. There was silence, too, from the neighbours. They must be out for the evening. Who else should she contact? She could hardly ring Rob Grailing, since she no longer trusted what he said. And none of her women friends, she decided, would take her seriously. 'Oh, not again, Kate!' she could hear them exclaim, one after the other. 'Why don't you get your imagination under control?'

She walked around the little house, checking on the window locks and shooting the bolts on the back door. She was as safe now as she could make herself. She sat down on her pink sofa, hugging the marmalade cat, Susannah, for comfort. Susannah, luckily, was accustomed to her erratic affection and made no fuss about it. If she got the television out of the cupboard where it lived for most of the time, and switched it on, and turned the volume up high, she could forget her worries, but then she wouldn't hear an intruder if he, or she, forced his, or her, way in through the back door.

The phone rang. She went, slowly, to answer it, but she had forgotten to switch off her answering machine, and it picked up the call before she could get to it.

First she heard her own voice with its brief message, then the long beep and then, 'Kate Ivory,' the now-familiar voice hissed. 'Don't forget. Keep your nose out of things. Or I'll get you.'

Oh, I will keep it right out, she thought, as she stared at the flashing light and listened as the tape rewound itself. But it would be a lot easier if I knew what your business was and just what I was supposed to keep my nose out of. Paul must be right in thinking that whoever it was who was threatening her assumed that she knew a lot more than she actually did. She must have said or done something to give them that impression. She thought back over the past few weeks, but she couldn't think of anything sufficiently significant to warrant all this intimidation.

Maybe she had seen or heard something important without realizing its significance. She wished she could remember what it was. The paradox was that the only way she could keep her nose out of their business was by finding out more about it.

The trouble had started when she went to work at Bartlemas College, so that was where it must be centred. That much was obvious. She would go in to work tomorrow and really snoop around. People had been very interested in the contents of the drawers of her desk: Steven Charleston, for example, and possibly even Rob Grailing himself. And hadn't Sadie probably looked through them before Kate arrived? Perhaps they had been looking at her computer files, too. The documents weren't protected with a password: they were hardly private and confidential, after all. If anyone had looked there it was unlikely to be Sadie, with her dislike of machines. But any of the others might have come in and rooted around in her hard disk while she was away in Birmingham. They might have thought that there were interesting things to be found there, although all she had come across herself had been perfectly straightforward letters and memos that anyone might have written. Which didn't mean that there was nothing to be found there. Had she looked through every directory and sub-directory? She must find some time to do so. Christopher Townsend had found whatever was to be found, and they suspected that she had followed him in her discoveries. For some reason, they assumed that she was a very inquisitive person, possibly even planted in the Development Office to see what she could find out. They were wrong, of course, at least up to now. But she might as well live up to her reputation. She wouldn't be in any more danger than she was already, wandering around in a cloud of ignorance, liable inadvertently to put her foot in it at any moment. When she thought about it, she had seen the corners of all sorts of money-making schemes, most of them probably illicit, even if not actually criminal. Any of the people involved might be afraid that she was about to blow the whistle on them.

But which of them was important enough to bother about? Certainly she had noticed the entrepreneurial business that was going on in the gardens, and she supposed that the gardeners had seen that she had noticed. But even if Dave Evans was growing and selling cuttings on college time, using college materials, she couldn't think that he would bother to pursue her and persecute her in this way. She hadn't said she'd report him, had she? Why should he get upset about her and threaten her any more than any other member of college? And it was the same with the porter and his informal tours. Who would even care if she went and reported it to someone? She had the impression that everyone, from the Master down, would shrug their shoulders and wish them luck.

The Master's wife, now, was a different proposition. Kate was sure that Honor Flint would take a very stern view of the slightest transgression against strict honesty. Was it worth confronting the old bat and asking her whether she, too, had received nasty threats?

She tucked Susannah under her arm, pulled out the television set, switched on some incomprehensible American cops and robbers series and sat watching it intently for the next hour. Then she rang up a couple of friends and invited them round for a meal later in the week. That should get rid of her nervousness about being at home on her own for one evening at least. She switched the television on again, drank a glass of wine and ate a whole packet of chocolate Hob-Nobs before going to bed.

*

Next morning was still warm, and Kate found it difficult to keep her eyes open and her attention on the subject of the morning's seminar. A slow, lazy bluebottle banged its head against the window, and she found herself watching it and listening to its buzz, until her head drooped on to her chest, and she had to open her eyes and sit up with a jerk. In a moment, she would be asked to contribute to this meaningless jumble of words. She tried to concentrate on what was being said.

Angela Devitt was speaking. 'I feel that when it comes to the genres of crime and detective fiction, then their surreal nature demands a particular, highly coloured vocabulary. It is up to us as women to use our own special language – our *parole*, if you like – to heighten the effect of our writing. We are, after all, writing about death, and so all our language should be emphatic, technicolored – over the top, you could say.'

Death and language, thought Kate. What is she on about? Death is about a young good-looking man flying over the parapet of a tower and falling to the earth. What sort of language do you need to describe something like that? Just plain words, that's all. No heightened effects are going to make it seem any more real, or any more acceptable.

'If we are going to talk about crime fiction, should we not begin by defining our genres?' asked Sharen Cobb. 'And where are we going to start? With Wilkie Collins? Or Poe? Or are we going to move directly to the period between the two world wars, the age that is generally described as golden?'

'A good point,' said Angela, who did not look pleased at having her flow of rhetoric broken off like this. 'Perhaps you would all like to contribute to this definition of the genre? Who would like to start? Curtis?'

If I could define my genre, thought Kate, perhaps I could solve my crime. Or is this subject like so many others: the more you master the theory, the worse you become at the practice, like one of those games that psychologists invent to prove that the more you know, the less effectively you act.

'We should define the duality which lies at the heart of the detective novel, in order to study it more effectively,' Curtis was saying.

Should we? wondered Kate. I think not. I think we should consider the crimes, petty and major, that are being committed in this smug establishment, and think about who is committing them and why they see me, *me*, as a threat to them. Because that must be what it is all about. Somebody, or somebodies more likely, believe that I am about to go outside and blow a very loud whistle.

'Surely we are speaking not so much of a duality, but more of a paradigmatic pluralism,' said Sharen. 'And we should also distinguish the *fable* from the *subject*. Does anybody wish to disagree? I wouldn't want to impose my own interpretation of the genre on everybody else.'

Kate nodded enthusiastically, then realized just in time that she had made an error in semiology, and changed to a vigorous shaking.

'I'm sure we all know,' said Curtis, 'that it is the absent story, the one concerning events in the past, which is the real and significant one; the other story, the story of the detection, although in the present, is, of course, insignificant.'

Oh no, thought Kate. The present story is not at all insignificant. In fact, it is making signs and leaving messages all over the place. And if I don't read them correctly, and race the others, the unseen but significant others, to the solution, I could well be part of the story in the past tense myself.

Chapter Eleven

... nullus daemon suapte natura mas est, vel foe-
mina. Compositorum enim sunt huiusmodi pas-
siones: corpora vero daemonum simplicia sunt
ductu, flexuque; facilia, ad omnemque, configur-
ationem naturaliter apta.

Michael Psellus, *De Daemonibus*

*'You look cold,' says Zophiel. 'Why don't you come over here
by the fire?'*

*Less a fire, more a flaming sword, thinks Christopher,
as he draws near. But it is certainly warmer.*

'Sit down and tell me more of your story.'

I met Briony Shorter during my first few weeks in
Oxford. Her parents lived in a rambling stone house in a
village some ten miles outside Oxford, while Briony herself had digs in a pleasant house in north Oxford during
the week. She was in her early twenties at this time,
and studying office skills at an establishment that was
generally referred to as 'The Ox and Cow'.

She was a quiet, rather nervous girl – and I use the
term 'girl' advisedly – for Briony had never been allowed
to make her own decisions and thus mature from girl to
young woman.

Her parents were both high-powered: her father
a high-flying academic, her mother a successful and

litigious solicitor, well known for espousing feminist causes and fighting for the financial rights of abandoned wives. Much had been demanded of Briony, but she had remained a disappointment to her parents. But then I doubt whether any one child could have lived up to all their ambitions for it. When she was a child, every minute of Briony's day had been filled. There were piano and dancing lessons, ponies and bicycles, swimming and sailing. Briony shone at none of these activities, and was comfortably in the bottom quardrile of her class in all academic subjects. Her parents responded by urging her on to take up yet more pursuits, sporting, academic and recreational. Briony looked for a way to escape.

Since Briony's parents were so fully occupied with their careers, their house was looked after by a competent man who came in to clean and organize them five times week. And the garden was cared for by a woman, a Doris Webster. Miss Webster was an artist. She had trained at one of the good London art colleges and had talent, but she had never managed to earn her living as a painter, especially as she had no ability as a teacher and no wish to become one. So she took to gardening, and expended all her pent-up artistic talents, and perhaps, too, her frustrated maternal yearnings, on producing healthy, vigorous plants and picturesque vistas.

Doris Webster was all that Briony's mother was not. She had greying, untidy hair that she occasionally chopped to ear length using her dressmaking shears. She had weatherbeaten skin and dirt under her fingernails. She wore denim jeans in the summer, corduroy trousers in the winter, a man's shirt in all weathers, and strong boots. She didn't talk much, but when she did, it was in a low and gentle voice, as though she was persuading her garden to grow the way she wanted it to, rather than forcing it into an unnatural pattern.

With Doris Webster, Briony felt comfortable. Nothing

was demanded of her; life was uncompetitive. She started by helping with the weeding, learning what she should and should not pull up. She moved on to digging the vegetable plot, graduated to pruning the climbers, and so to the taking and striking of cuttings. She was introduced to the seed tray, the cold frame, and the greenhouse.

When her A-Level results were not good enough to get her into any university that her parents considered suitable, Briony was despatched on a tour of Europe, staying with various academic friends of theirs.

She studied their gardens.

She came back to England more, rather than less, interested in their cultivation. She was sent to America, where she was supposed to attend classes at the local university. Instead, she spent her time with the gardeners in the beautifully maintained local parks, and learned even more about plants and their habits.

Finally, observing that really it was time that she earned some sort of living, the Shorters sent her to learn shorthand and typing, word processing and the keeping of accounts. Briony spent her mornings in the classroom, learning Pitman short forms and how to cut and paste in WordPerfect; her afternoons she spent illicitly, in touring college gardens, talking to their gardeners.

Which is how I met her.

Have I described Briony? No?

She was quite tall, with a willowy figure that was deceptive, since she did all that digging and wheeling of barrows, not to mention the bricklaying and mixing of concrete. Long, slim arms, with tough workman's hands and grimy nails. A small, round face, which had something wary in its expression, as though she thought you were about to criticize what she was doing and suggest that she did something quite different. A soft-voiced girl, diffident about her opinions. I suppose she was so used to hearing her parents voicing their convictions loudly and confidently on every occasion that she never bothered to develop her own, or think that anyone would be interested in hearing them.

'*You make her sound a poor, dull thing. Not at all an interesting person.*'

'*She had her good points. She was very restful as a companion. She didn't interrupt or press her ideas upon me. She listened carefully, and looked on admiringly as I spoke, and smiled that secretive smile of hers.*'

'*Oh well, if you say so. I was beginning to be bored by her, I'm afraid.*'

Briony had one feature that I found particularly attractive: her long blonde hair. It waved over her shoulders and across her back. With all the time she spent in the open air, it acquired expensive-looking streaks and highlights, rather like pale tortoiseshell. I never tired of seeing it tumbled over the shoulders of her faded blue denim shirt.

And then again, I can't pretend that I hadn't noticed that her parents were very rich. I guessed that their house with its garden and paddocks must be worth close to half a million. And her parents still worked at their lucrative professional careers. They were both so busy that I couldn't see how they could possibly spend all the money they were making. Whoever married Briony would surely be showered with golden guineas.

'*You're going to tell me that it wasn't so?*'

'*I'm going to tell you all sorts of things about Briony, and about our life in Oxford, but in my own way and in my own time.*'

'*In the next chapter?*'

'*Perhaps. You must wait and see.*'

Kate had arranged for the food, the folding tables and chairs, the cutlery, the wine and glasses, to be delivered

by road to their picnic site. As picnics went, this was
going to be quite a grand one, since she had also hired
a couple of the buttery staff from college to serve the
food. Her students would probably think that this was
the way things were always done in England. She had
also agreed with a farmer, who happened to be a tenant
of the college and therefore in no position to argue, that
they could use a meadow by the river for their meal. He
promised that no bulls would be near, though he couldn't
guarantee the absence of cowpats, midges, wasps or
marauding bikers. There was a convenient track that the
college van could use, so that the tables and food would
be transported with reasonable ease.

There had been a brief awkward moment, when
Harry Bickerstaff had said that he wished to be one of
the party, and had looked hurt when Kate told him that
there were no spare places. Yet another conference
goodie from which the poor man was excluded, she
thought. But what could she do? There was no way
they could have lowered his bulk into a punt without a
contraption involving a pulley (and probably a pair of
oxen for power). And the chef had refused point-blank
to allow him to travel in the van with the food. 'There
won't be a single drumstick left if you allow that man
half an hour alone with my picnic!' he exclaimed, probably quite unfairly. But now that they were actually on
the river, she was glad to be without his company.

This was the life, she thought, as she lay back in the
punt and trailed her hand in the water. A young man
with biceps and experience with a punt pole was earning
his five pounds an hour by propelling them smoothly
towards their picnic site. Without the students, it would
have been quite perfect, she thought, watching little
white clouds as they floated artistically across a powder-
blue sky. Birds chirruped in the willow trees, coots and
moorhens paddled up and down the banks, while other

human, water-lovers rowed and paddled their way up and down the river in a variety of craft. Martha Hawkins' voice was far enough ahead, in the leading punt, for Kate to be able to pretend that she wasn't even there.

Groups picnicked on the banks. Families with children lay in the grass or hurled frisbees at each other. Dogs barked and frolicked. The occasional boat with an outboard engine put-putted its way up the river. It was, thought Kate, a marvellous English scene, the trees and riverbanks in shades of green, the river in grey and brown, the women in their pale cotton dresses, with their hair shining in the hot September sun.

'Tell me,' asked one of the students – Sharen Cobb, was she called? – 'how you see the development of the historical novel in the post-modernist age?'

Kate opened her eyes to consider the question. A couple on the riverbank were drinking white wine out of a green bottle, the glass cold and misted with condensation. They looked vaguely familiar, but Kate applied the part of her mind that was still awake and functioning to the question that Sharen had raised. 'I believe that genre fiction in general has by-passed both the modernist and the post-modernist trends in literature, and is continuing the mainstream nineteenth-century realistic movement,' she began, repeating something she had heard Faith Beeton say.

The first punts had already reached the clump of willows near their destination and were being anchored by their punt poles to the riverbank. Arthritic knees cracked as middle-aged students of gender and genre climbed out on to the path and made their way across buttercup-strewn meadows toward trestle tables laid with pristine white cloths. Their steps quickened and their eyes brightened as they saw the ranks of cooled wine bottles on one of the tables.

Kate's attention was on her charges. It had seemed

sensible to place herself in the last punt, so that she could see if any of them should inadvertently fall into the river. Now she saw that they were much more likely to slip down a muddy riverbank and thrash around in the shallows.

'If we think particularly of Wilkie Collins and Charles Dickens,' she continued, hoping to bore Sharen into submission, 'we can see that—'

So anxious was she that there should be no mishap, even to Martha, that she didn't notice the small, swift boat with the powerful outboard motor that came buzzing towards her from upstream.

It all happened so quickly, she told Paul, afterwards. It was over in a flash.

One moment she was pontificating on the subject of genre fiction, while watching Martha scrambling along a punt, hanging on to a willow branch and hauling herself on to the shore, the next, her own punt was being twisted sideways on to the current, and rocked wildly in the wash from the outboard.

Two seconds later she was in the river.

It was surprisingly cold in the water, considering what a warm, sunny day it was. And she had swallowed a mouthful of dilute mud before she realized what was happening to her. She started to tread water, her feet brushing the gravel of the riverbed. Behind her, she heard the buzz of the returning outboard, the loud roar as it came up behind her. Then she felt a strong hand on the top of her head, and a hard downwards push that sent her surging underneath the surface and down towards the murky riverbed. This time she had the presence of mind to hold her breath, so that she soon bobbed up again like a cork. The outboard was disappearing round the next bend in the river, the figure in a navy tracksuit hunched over the tiller, unrecognizable, even as to gender. But then she was swimming, and treading water, and helping her punt-chauffeur to right his craft, and making sure that the three other passengers were out of the water and safe on dry land.

'It can't have been someone who knew me well,' she told Paul. 'I may be scared of heights, but at least I know what to do in the water. Do you think they were just trying to frighten me?'

'Oh, I don't know,' he said. 'There must be hundreds of people in Oxford who are longing for the chance to drown Kate Ivory.'

'Be serious! What do you think it was all about, and who do you think was doing it?'

'I think you probably know the answer better than I do.'

'I suppose it could have been a furious Harry Bicker-staff. I wouldn't let him come to the picnic, so he hired a small boat with a powerful outboard motor and came up the river to mow me down and drown me.'

'Could it have been him?'

'Not unless he had lost about ten stone between breakfast and lunchtime.'

'I think you're right that they were trying to frighten you, or warn you off, perhaps. With all those people around, you're unlikely to have drowned. And they must have frightened your students more than they did you. It can't have been much fun for three middle-aged women, in their party frocks and hats, to be hurled into cold brown water.'

'That's quite a thought, isn't it?'

'How do you mean?'

'I don't think I'm very popular with the students now. And the Bursary staff all smirk when I walk into the room and say things like, "Going swimming again today, Kate?" and "Shouldn't you wear your swimsuit next time?" '

'Just a few feeble jokes. What did you expect?'

'You're probably right. Maybe it was just some incompetent idiot out on the river, who ran us down because he couldn't steer properly, and then didn't stop, or turn round, because he didn't know how, or was too embarrassed to face us.'

'It does sound the most likely explanation to anyone who lacks your colourful imagination.'

'I didn't even get any of the picnic, you know. All that warm ciabatta bread and black olives, the cold white wine.'

'Why not? Were you in disgrace?'

'Martha said that my dress was eye-catching enough when dry, but that when it was wet it was positively indecent. She sent me home in the college van and wouldn't even let me take a sandwich back with me.'

'Here, have another glass of wine. You've already eaten all the olives, so you can stop feeling sorry for yourself.'

Next morning, as Kate walked through the Bursary, John Clay looked up from his desk, where he appeared to be reading a glossy magazine, and smiled slyly at her.

'I hear you had too much to drink yesterday.'

'You heard wrong.'

'Drunk in charge a punt, someone said. I thought it was only students who drank too much and then fell into the river. Aren't you getting a bit old for that sort of antic?'

'Aren't you getting tired of this joke?'

Kate closed herself into her own office. Sadie wasn't there, though the jacket over the back of her chair indicated that she had been in that morning and might soon return.

Kate switched on her computer. She had come in half an hour earlier than her contracted time of nine-thirty, especially so that she could look through Chris Townsend's files again. Perhaps she had missed something before. The screen in front of her gradually brightened. She typed Alt J to see what reminders she had left herself for today. The screen filled with blue index cards, each one showing a job for her to do that morning. But her attention was riveted by the first one.

Was that ducking enough for you? I just hope it cooled you down and gave you time to think. Keep your nose out of our business, or next time it will be more than just a warning. And have you noticed that we are always here, watching what you do? We are not going to go away and there is no way that you can escape from us. Remember that curiosity has killed one cat and it can easily do so again.

She watched the screen for several minutes, thinking hard about who might have placed the message there, as though by watching it, it might dissolve and disappear. Eventually, her screen saver took over, and the words were replaced by fish swimming around, blowing bubbles. She wasn't sure that she wanted to be reminded of water and fish, but it was an improvement on the message, anyway.

She had been right in thinking that people had been searching through her computer files. Or rather, Christopher's computer files, she reminded herself. She pressed a key so that the bright blue message reappeared. She was no expert on such things, but she thought that its style was quite different from the messages on her telephone machine. Those had been short, exclamatory, breathless. This ran to longer sentences, anyway. So, either they were sent to her by different people, or they were written by someone, like

Faith Beeton for example, who understood about these things. Though, come to think of it, that included most of the people at the conference. The message disappeared and was replaced by bubble-blowing fish.

The door sprang open and Sadie came in.

'Hello! You're in early!'

'I thought I'd get a good start to the day, to make up for yesterday's disaster.'

'Falling out of the punt? Oh, I shouldn't worry. It could happen to anyone. Everybody will have forgotten about it in a day or two.'

Not if John Clay keeps on with his snide little jokes, thought Kate.

'By the way,' she said casually. 'You haven't touched my computer, have you?'

'Me? You must be joking! I'm the original computer-terrified klutz.'

'Yes.' Sadie had said as much when they first met. It seemed an age ago, but it can only have been a couple of weeks or so. Was it true, or was she bluffing? 'So you are.'

'What's wrong? Are you having problems with it? I believe John Clay's our PC wizard. He'd love it if you asked him for help, though you'd never hear the last of it, of course.'

'No, don't worry. I think I can work it out for myself. Thanks.' It would be nice to think that that little weasel John Clay had put the message on her information manager. Should she go and confront him about it, or just beat him about the head with her handbag? On the other hand, if it was anybody in the Bursary who had been playing these tricks on her – and that had to be the most likely solution – then she didn't want them to know that she was rattled. She decided to walk around with a calm and serene expression on her face, as though everything in the world was marvellous and quite under control.

That ought to annoy her persecutor – or persecutors – anyway. And if it didn't, it would at least infuriate Annette Paige.

She should really be having dinner in hall with the students, she knew, but she had crept away after the last session of the afternoon. Surely being thrown into the river was enough for any person for one week. She had earned an evening off. She dropped into the Covered Market during the afternoon and picked up the makings of a supper for the friends she had invited in.

She was letting herself into the house when she saw Harley in the next-door garden. He was so subdued these days that it was easy to overlook him.

'Any news on Dave?' she asked.

'Dossa and Darren are still looking after him,' he said. 'But their mum's going to get fed up of him soon, isn't she? I give them the money for his food, but it's ruining me, getting up early to do the paper round every morning.'

'Still, it's got to be worth it,' said Kate.

'He'll forget me if he stays away much longer,' said Harley gloomily.

'Surely not,' said Kate. 'If there's one thing that dog's good at, it's loyalty. He'll remember you for ever.'

'You think so?' Harley looked marginally less unhappy.

'Sure of it,' stated Kate.

''Ere, Kate,' said Harley, as she opened her door and pushed her plastic carriers inside. 'Someone been round your place. You know what I mean?'

'They have?' Prickles of fear ran down her back. 'Who was it?' Should she ask if they were carrying something that looked like a bomb? Or were they bugging her telephone?

'I dunno. I didn't see them.'

'Then how do you know someone was there?'

'I hear them. I was sat out here, minding my own business, and I hear someone walking round by your house, quiet like. Maybe they was sussing it out, looking for a way in. You leave a window open while you out?'

'No.'

'You got a video recorder?'

'No.'

'Your computer got a Pentium chip and multi-media?'

'No.'

'Well, you're safe enough all right. No one's interested in the other stuff you've got, all them books and that.'

'Thanks, Harley.' And Kate went inside her house and closed the door. She wished that she felt as confident as Harley that she was safe in her own house.

As she went through to the kitchen, she cheered up. She only had a couple of hours to spend alone before her friends Camilla and Carey turned up. She unpacked her bags; olive ciabatta, fresh butter, goats' milk cheese. She would have her picnic meal, even if she had to prepare it herself. She unwrapped the free-range chicken and placed it on a wire rack in the roasting tin. She would anoint its breast with lemon juice and butter, and baste it every ten minutes to keep its flesh moist. While the oven heated up, she went to look up a recipe for flummery.

As she set the table, she wondered why she never invited Paul round at the same time as her other friends. Camilla, the headmistress of a polite girls' school, and Carey, a rather dubious permanent student ten years or so her junior, were an odd enough couple. Carey had a habit of juggling in the street when he needed money, which she supposed was preferable to borrowing from Camilla, but she would still feel awkward if she introduced them to Paul, her friend, the policeman. And Paul would disapprove of Carey, and wonder what a sensible woman like Camilla was doing in his company. Kate sometimes wondered herself, but put it down to their rich, shared fantasy life.

Some time later, when the chicken was sizzling gently in the oven, she went out into the front garden again. Harley was still sitting on the wall, staring out into the street.

'Do me a favour?' she asked.

'Yeah?'

'Watch out for strangers round my house. Let me know if you see anyone. A description would be useful.'

'Right.'

'There'll be a small reward.'

'Right.'

'Thanks,' said Kate.

'Listen,' he said.

Kate listened. She could hear the lorries on the by-pass, the cars in the Fridesley Road, the family at number 16 having another row.

'What? I can't hear anything.'

'I reckon that's him.'

'Who?'

'Dave.'

She listened again. In the distance she could hear a dog. Above the spire of the church of King Charles the Martyr, the moon was a pale disc in the opal sky. Perhaps he was right and it was Dave she could hear, baying at the moon.

'If you say so,' she said.

She went back into her house. With Harley on watch outside and the imminent arrival of Millie and Carey, she could relax and feel safe, at least until tomorrow. She washed salad and put it in a bowl, looked out the balsamic vinegar and olive oil to make the dressing. She chopped basil leaves.

The phone rang.

She stood and watched it for half a dozen rings, then she picked up the receiver.

Nothing. Not even heavy breathing. She matched silence with silence. There was a click followed by the dialling tone.

Maybe it was a wrong number. Maybe it was Harry Bickerstaff ringing to ask to be included in another of her little outings, or complaining that his name had been excluded from all the publicity. On the other hand, perhaps it was the madman who had hurled her into the river and tried to drown her. Before going back into the kitchen to baste the chicken, she looked out of the window to check that Harley was still there, keeping watch.

Chapter Twelve

IAGO: Are your doors locked?
BRABANZIO: Why? wherefore ask you this?
William Shakespeare, *Othello*, Act 1, Scene 1

'So, like I said, Briony's thing was gardens and gardening.'

'Very nice,' says Zophiel. 'I'm sure she could design a beautiful garden. But have you not noticed the one behind me here? A flourishing example of every known tree, shrubberies beyond the dreams of Victorian matrons, annuals to delight the heart even of a Dave Evans. You can have enough of it, though. You can get a bit blasé about even the loveliest of gardens, I find.'

'And every one has its serpent, don't you think?'

'Really? Who was yours?'

'I'll just tell the story, more or less as it happened. The analysis, the identifying of archetypes, the drawing of conclusions, is down to you, Zophiel. You're the one, after all, who is trying to prove some theory about the victim.'

'Very well. Tell me the story about Briony. Then I'd like to hear how you made money out of Bartlemas.'

'All in good time.'

The first argument we had was over the house. I insisted that I could buy it, on a mortgage, out of my salary. This was not for any altruistic reason, you understand, but because I did not want my life run for me by the Shorters. Oh, it wouldn't have been anything crass and obvious, but if I had accepted money from them at

182

the beginning of my marriage to Briony they would have subtly affected all areas of our life together, from the colour of our bedroom walls to the location of our rare holidays.

Briony wanted the kind of house that she had been accustomed to living in. I think the place we bought was rather nice, myself: just beyond the ring road, to the west of Oxford, a large old house in an expanding area. Briony called it suburban. The only reason she gave in and agreed to buy it was because it had a large garden, much larger than it would have been if we had lived nearer in to the centre of the city.

And the garden had been left to revert to wilderness by the aged woman who sold us the house. This allowed Briony full rein to her imagination, and kept her happy and occupied for some years after we moved in.

I hadn't realized what an expensive hobby gardening was. Oh, Briony was very good at begging cuttings from her friends, and growing things from seed in her greenhouse. But I was the one who had to pay for that greenhouse, and for the garden shed, and the bricks and slates and stones that had to be imported to form the hard framework of the garden. Then there were the trees and shrubs and pergolas and arbours and the loggia. Many of our plants were the envy of the gardening fraternity for their rarity and value, monetary as well as horticultural.

I am not thinking hundreds of pounds here, you must understand, Zophiel, but thousands. And that on top of the usual carpets and curtains, and fitted cupboards, and the Aga and the quarry tiles that went into the house itself. Personally, I found that the mortgage repayments were already enough of a headache, without adding all these pricey extras.

So, very soon, I needed money. I had no intention of going to my in-laws for help, and Bartlemas would not increase my salary by any amount that would make much impression on all Briony's wants.

Now, the first thing that struck me about Bartlemas, especially when I compared it with the charity, was how sleek and prosperous everyone was. You don't expect it, do you? At a merchant bank, possibly. At a firm of accountants. But not at a college. You'd think they'd all be dressed in tweed jackets and dusty old gowns, buy their shirts at Oxfam, that sort of thing. But not at Bartlemas, I can tell you. And they all had the sort of suntans that you only get from frequent foreign holidays: lying by a pool in the summer, topping up the tan in the Alps during the winter.

So I thought, I want a piece of this.

I had listened, idly, as one does, to the gossip in Hall at lunchtime. I would not have been eating there, with the Bursary and administrative staff, if I had not been practising mean economies to pay for Briony's latest whim, a reproduction Victorian conservatory. But eventually it struck me that what people were talking about were various money-making schemes. The people at Bartlemas had none of the sophistication in financial matters of my friends at the national charity. They believed in the basic honesty of the educated individual. And there were schemes, major and minor, going on in every department of the institution. From the porter who 'borrowed' academic dress from senior college members and hired it out at profit to recent graduates returned for their graduation ceremonies in the Sheldonian, to the tutors who accepted dodgy students in return for expensive holidays in exotic places, or part shares in a race horse, they were all at it.

I'm sure that everyone in the place was up to something, from the Master downwards. No, I tell a lie. There was one person who remained aloof from all this petty dishonesty. Not at all the person you might have expected to be so honest, and it was in misreading this personality that I made one of the major mistakes of my life.

But I'm running ahead of my story. The first thing I did was to observe, and to make notes. At the end of about six weeks I was pretty sure that I had most of the Bartlemas black economy sussed. I was not so naïve as to imagine that anyone in power in that place would be surprised or shocked at my discoveries, though I do believe that no one person had documented their full extent.

I called each of the entrepreneurs, as I privately called them, into my office for a little talk. I made no threats, and issued no warnings. I did point out what the consequences might be if their nefarious little schemes became public – and by public I meant splashed over the national dailies. No, I wasn't interested in cleaning the place up. I wished for a small percentage of the action, that was all.

You would be amazed at what a five per cent cut here and there brought in for me. Briony had her conservatory, and probably a more opulent model than she had ever dreamed of. Perhaps not: I continually underestimated Briony's expectations of me, and her ideas of what was due to her, as of right. Once she had the conservatory, she very soon thought of some other costly luxury that I should provide for her. I realized that five per cents were not enough. I needed to develop my own scheme.

I saw that there was scope for a more ambitious version of the trick I had pulled off at my college. If I could invent a fictitious fund and persuade people to pay money into it, I could solve my financial problems and pay for any amount of garden buildings for Briony. Of course, I needed a partner, and I spent some time in looking around and choosing the right person. Again, building on my experience in London, I decided to go for a woman, and a woman who would find me physically attractive and hence not look too closely into my motives.

'Are you sure that was your only motive for choosing a female partner?'

'You're learning to read me too well. Briony and I had been married some three years by now, and I was beginning to tire of her rather cool personality. Viola, whatever her other drawbacks, had been a warm and sexually exciting woman. Briony seemed to have been emotionally deep-frozen at some point in her development, and it took a lot of time and energy to bring her back to blood heat. I was finding the process tiresome, and I wanted to find someone who would be more immediately responsive to my needs, I admit.'

'So you were ready for a sexual adventure as well as a financial one?'

'The prospect of the combination of the two offered a certain frisson of excitement that I was just about ready for.'

'Oh, yes, even the angelic nature can understand the longing for danger, the wish to live on the edge.'

'I told you I wasn't going to run round after these so-called students of yours!'

Kate had just entered the Bursary and had been set upon by an indignant Annette. She composed herself to be calm and reasonable, assertive but not aggressive. 'What seems to be the trouble?' she asked, patiently.

'The Martha Hawkins woman has set fire to her room.'

Calm and reason started to desert Kate. 'How did she manage that? The woman is a rabid anti-smoker.'

'She had lighted a scented candle to disperse the noxious fumes that she felt were rising to her open window from the traffic in the street outside.'

This sounded like the Martha that Kate knew too well. 'Was there much damage?'

'Yes, and not only to her own room.'

Annette was starting to look excited. Now that she was no longer the one who had to deal with this emergency, she could wallow in the awful details.

'Not to her person? Is she all right?' If she had been a truly lovely person, she would have asked that question earlier. Unfortunately, the thought of Martha disappearing in a column of smoke and flame was not an unwelcome one.

'Oh, she's fine. She left the candle on her windowsill and went for an hour's quiet meditation in the chapel. The candle, naturally enough, blew over in the evening breeze and set fire to the curtains. The bed is ruined, the carpet also. Ms Hawkins has lost all her personal possessions, including her clothes. And of course, the damage from the firemen's hoses was quite extensive, too. The place will need redecorating.'

'I suppose so.'

'And then of course the fire spread to the room next door.'

'Oh dear.'

'Mr Skinner. He's very upset at the loss of his clothes and the destruction of all the books he'd brought with him, and those he's acquired since he arrived.'

'So I'd better deal with them?'

'You'll have to find them new rooms, won't you?'

'Yes. I'll get straight on to it.'

'It's all very well, gallivanting off to some Shakespeare play in a college garden, or off up the motorway to a concert, but some of us have to cope with the real problems here, you know.'

'I said I'll deal with it,' said Kate, through gritted teeth.

The trouble was, of course, that all the rooms in the

modern blocks, the ones with bathrooms and showers, and reasonable numbers of lavatories, had already been allocated. There were empty rooms in college, but these were situated on the old and picturesque, but uncomfortable, staircases. They were quite suitable for fit young undergraduates, but middle-aged persons of uncertain temper might not be so thrilled by them.

Kate left Annette looking triumphant and jotted down a list of things to do. She must see the housekeeper and find which rooms were available before confronting a doubtless irritated Martha, and an equally furious Curtis. And who was going to pay for the damage? She couldn't see Martha holding herself responsible. She would have to compose polite letters to insurance companies, talk to the Bursar. Well, that was her day planned for her, anyway. And it had the great advantage of having no time slot for worrying about people who might be out to murder her.

She'd better get on with it. In the afternoon she had a workshop to run on writing historical fiction, then she had to take off rapidly to accompany her group to a performance of a Shakespeare play in the Fellows' Garden of Leicester College. She wasn't sure which she was dreading most: sitting through a Shakespeare play performed by over-confident amateurs, directed by another amateur who was determined to be original, or a visit to the college where her erstwhile lover was a Fellow. At least the weather was still hot and sultry. Sitting in the open air might be quite pleasant if the midges held off, and in this increasingly unseasonal weather they were unlikely to have to crouch under golf umbrellas, blowing on their fingers for warmth.

By seven-thirty, Kate had sorted out the rooms for Martha and Curtis. It had taken longer than she had planned, because Martha had personally inspected the shower in the nearest bathroom and had instructed Kate in how to clean the shower head so that it supplied the requisite quantity of water.

Curtis had commented adversely on the fibre content of his breakfast, so Kate had asked the kitchens to supply his favoured cereal for the following morning.

Martha had capped it by complaining about the lack of wardrobe space in her new room.

Kate had been tempted to point out that since she had set fire to all her clothes she hardly needed wardrobe space, but she had asked a porter to move in a cupboard with hanging space from an adjoining room. She had nearly suggested that Martha and Curtis move in together: it would have placed her two main grumblers in one location, and would have stopped Curtis's protestations about the loneliness of his life, but she thought the suggestion would not be well received.

Then she had raced away from her housekeeping duties to a seminar room in Pesant Quad and led a lively workshop. Her students had written the exercise she had set, and read their work aloud: they had role-played and talked about research and where to find out the things you needed to know. Several of the class had shyly approached afterwards and asked her to sign copies of her books. A successful afternoon, she had thought.

Now it was evening, and time for her dose of Shakespeare. She had managed to find herself an unobtrusive seat under the huge spreading copper beech tree in a corner of the Fellows' Garden at Leicester College.

This is where Liam and I met, over teacups and strawberries and cream, she thought. From the pool of light on the stage a woman's voice said:

'I am not merry, but I do beguile
The thing I am by seeming otherwise,'

while Kate thought, how true! On that distant June afternoon, the rain fell from a granite sky and we ran for the marquee together. A few hundred people, crammed in with the smell of wet gowns surrounding us.

> '. . Besides, the knave is handsome, young, and hath
> all those requisites in him that folly and green minds
> look after.'

I thought he was so wonderful, and I was so wrong, for all the time he was seeing another woman. That was the trouble with men. They found monogamy a very difficult concept. Perhaps that was what was wrong with Chris Townsend, too, she thought. It seemed to be the trouble with Rob Grailing, certainly.

> 'Perdition catch my soul
> But I do love thee, and when I love thee not,
> Chaos is come again.'

The voice declaiming the verse broke into her reverie for a moment before she fell to dreaming again. Even the Master of Bartlemas had a roving eye, it seemed to her. Did Honor mind? Did she even notice? But then, at some level, every woman noticed, and minded. It was some time later that she was once more awoken by words from the stage.

> 'O, beware, my lord, of jealousy.
> It is the green-eyed monster which doth mock
> The meat it feeds on . . .'

Once more it was a man speaking, she noticed. They were very keen to tell you not to be jealous, she had found, particularly when they were busy two-timing you, and lying about it. She sighed, and tried to concentrate on the action on the stage. Not a very good production, she thought, and hoped that her more obstreperous students would not let her know about the production's shortcomings when she met up with them again. She knew that Martha and Curtis were there, somewhere, in the darkness, and Martha was probably taking notes and would nobble her tomorrow morning and tell her everything that was wrong.

It seemed to be an interval, though only a very short one, the programme warned. A voice from behind her in the darkness said, 'The setting is a common motif of romance, you notice. The place of trial surrounded by the turbulent sea.' It was Faith Beeton, leaning forward to speak to her.

'Really?' But Kate wasn't interested in hearing what Faith had to say about Shakespeare's play. She was too busy reliving the scenes of her own love story of the past couple of years, and trying to fit her own experience into the shape of the mystery that surrounded her at Bartlemas.

'And interesting to compare Shakespeare's hero with his predecessor in Sidney's *Arcadia*, Amphialus. Another man who meant well but always managed to hurt those whom he loved.' A man's voice. In spite of herself, Kate twisted round to see who it was. Flat black hair, eyes dark and shining as basalt, an amused, sardonic voice: Timothy Happle.

'I've met men like your Amphialus,' muttered Kate.

'What was that?'

'Nothing. Just thinking out loud.'

'Of course,' Happle was saying, 'you feminists have taken against our poor heroine: the virtuous woman who is not allowed to speak her mind. And yet how were the

Jacobeans supposed to demonstrate virtue on their stage to the audience of the time?'

'I'm glad we've outgrown the idea that the only good woman is a silent woman,' said Faith. 'The time is past when a life of significant action, of female rebellion, was a life that had to be silenced, figuratively, on the whole, but in our present heroine's case, literally as well.'

'Well, no one could accuse you of overdoing the virtue of silence, Faith dear,' said Happle.

'Although those of us who stand up and speak out for what we know to be right are still castigated as viragos and harridans.' Faith continued as though he had not spoken.

'Surely you're exaggerating,' came Happle's silky voice. 'I'm sure we all listen to what you have to say with the greatest attention, Faith, on each and every occasion that you have graced us with your forthright opinions.'

Kate wouldn't have been surprised to hear him laugh at the end of that speech.

'Don't push me too far,' said Faith, very quietly.

What were they talking about? This didn't sound much like a discussion of Jacobean drama to Kate.

'Kate Ivory, with her historical perspective on these matters, will surely take my side,' said Happle. 'Don't you think that it ill befits a woman to stand and preach at her elders and betters, even if she has had a strongly religious upbringing and is earnestly convinced that she is in the right?'

On the stage the actors were reassembling and the lights were going up. Somewhere in the background someone played a lute, but not very well.

'I'd like to watch the play now, if you don't mind,' said Kate rudely and inaccurately. Anything rather than get involved in other people's wrangles.

'Really? I thought you looked as though you were

remembering certain unhappy events in your own life,' said Faith. 'You had that expression on your face, soft and yet reserved, that means that someone has done you wrong.'

Kate turned away and feigned interest in the stage. Some time later she heard an actor say,

> *'I kissed thee ere I killed thee. No way but this,*
> *Killing myself, to die upon a kiss.'*

Trust a man to justify murder and suicide in such a poetic way, thought Kate viciously. But she brightened as she realized that with the main characters lying dead upon the stage, the evening's entertainment must be all but over.

Leicester College was little more than five minutes' walk from Bartlemas, and Kate felt that even students as accident-prone as Curtis and Martha could find their way back without her help. Surely they would not set fire to themselves or one another if she left them to their own devices for such a short time? She sat on under the copper beech tree, with the air cooling and a light breeze blowing through the dry leaves, as the crowd drifted back through an archway, and the darkened stage was cleared of its furniture and properties.

One of the good things about Oxford was that everything started again in the autumn. In October, every October, a whole new generation turned up, ready to learn, and live, and even to fall in love. In most places the time of hope was the spring, but here it was the autumn. Fall. A time to let go of the unprosperous past and look forward to remaking your life in a shape that pleased you better. Someone had expressed that thought in verse, she thought.

> *Ah Love! could thou and I with Fate conspire*

To grasp this sorry Scheme of Things entire,
          Would not we shatter it to bits – and then
Re-mould it nearer to the Heart's Desire!

This habit of quoting chunks of poetry was getting to her. She might end up quite an intellectual if she continued for long enough in her present company. Yes, that's what she wanted to do: re-mould the past nearer to her heart's desire. But then, didn't everyone?

No one noticed her sitting there in the shadows in her dark blue dress, and she closed her eyes and let the cool evening air play over her face.

But there was someone else. Someone who slipped a twisted silk scarf around her neck and pulled it tight, so that her head was jerked back and the sky and stars whirled about her.

'You haven't been listening to what I've said.' It was the same hissing voice, genderless and threatening. 'I said stay away. I said keep off. You need a lesson.'

And the scarf was pulled tighter still, until the starry sky dimmed before her eyes, blotted out by scarlet sunbursts, and pain invaded her throat and head. She scrabbled at the scarf, she tried to stand, so that she could kick and defend herself, but she was at too much of a disadvantage, sitting there on the leafmould. She couldn't make enough noise to summon help across the expanse of the garden, and through the thickness of those medieval walls.

The pain was unbearable. Her head was being forced down on to the ground. A boot rested with the weight of a body behind it on her cheek.

Then, as consciousness ebbed, the pressure was released. She could still see nothing, feel nothing, while hearing, that last of the senses to depart, told her that someone was running, across the grass and out of the garden.

She struggled to sit up, her hands to her neck. She still couldn't speak. It felt as though her throat was on fire, and would never be of any use in speaking again. She brushed off leaves and twigs and got to her feet. Her head swam. She leant against the solid, reassuring trunk of the tree.

Who was it? There was no way now that she could follow her attacker and catch up with him or her. They must be long gone, along the Broad, or down through Radcliffe Square and into the High. Perhaps the porter in the lodge noticed something, but she doubted it. He was probably sitting snugly, reading his evening paper or watching an illicit portable television in the room behind the lodge.

She tried a few steps and found that she could walk, if slowly. She tried to call out, but all she could manage was a croak. In the High Street she did something that she would never normally do. She hailed a taxi and had herself driven back to her house in Fridesley.

At home, doors locked, windows closed, she went upstairs to look at herself in the mirror. There was a red mark on her neck, but nothing too obvious; a smear of dust along her cheek; a dead leaf or two in her hair. Nothing that she could take down to the police station and report.

She made herself a pot of tea. Her head was aching and she couldn't face alcohol, though she longed for the oblivion it might bring. A thought was coming to her. This was like some children's game, dimly remembered from childhood parties. Hunt the slipper, or thimble, or some such. As you got nearer to finding the hidden object, the adults had all chanted, 'You're getting warmer!' and when you moved away from it again, they called out, 'Colder, colder!' That's what was happening to her. As she got closer to solving the mystery – or mysteries, as she was now convinced they were – so she was attacked with increasing violence.

When her head had cleared and stopped hurting, she would think over the events of the day. Whatever it was that she had done or seen or heard, her unseen assailants thought that it was very dangerous to them. She only wished she knew what it was that worried them so much. For the moment, with her painful head and the constriction that still remained in her throat, she couldn't think of anything suspicious. Martha? Curtis? They were both there in the audience this evening, but surely they had nothing to do with it. Perhaps, though, she should find out how long they had been in England before they came to Bartlemas.

She was on the right track, she thought jubilantly. Though goodness only knew what the baddies would do to her when she got really close. They were unlikely to shout, 'Well done!' and hand her a fluffy toy wrapped in gaily patterned paper and tied with gold ribbons, and send her home clutching a helium balloon. How close would she need to get – and how would she know when she had reached that point – before someone threw her over the balustrade on the roof of a fifteenth-century tower?

She thought about it. She knew that Chris Townsend had received the Post-It note with **CURIOSITY KILLED THE CAT** on it. Had he been buzzed by the outboard, threatened with spreadeagling the coffee cups at Birmingham's Symphony Hall, or half strangled with a silk scarf before he was finally dealt with? How many warnings did these people give?

Silk scarf. Something tugged at her memory at the thought of the silk scarf. Where had she seen someone wearing one? Faith Beeton's face came into her mind. Faith, with a vermilion scarf tied round her neck, lighting up her sallow skin. Faith, with an emerald scarf twisted through her black hair, underlining the darkness of her eyes. But then again, her assailant at Leicester had not been wearing Faith's distinctive scent. What she couldn't quite recall was whether Faith herself had been wearing it when she spoke to her earlier in the evening.

She looked at the clock. So much had happened that she thought it must be at least midnight, but in fact it wasn't yet eleven o'clock. So it wasn't too late to telephone a friend. She needed a voice she knew and trusted. She dialled.

'Paul Taylor.'

She tried to say, 'Hello, it's Kate,' but still the best she could manage was a croak.

'Hello. Who is it?'

She cleared her throat and tried again, and this time her words were just about comprehensible.

'It's me. Kate.'

'Are you all right? You sound a bit odd.'

'I'm fine. I've just got a bit of a sore throat.' For once she was telling the truth, but she didn't think Paul would be very pleased about the manner in which she had acquired it, so she kept quiet about the earlier events of the evening.

'I was just wondering whether you'd like to come round for a meal tomorrow evening,' she said. 'If you're free, that is.'

'I should be. Would half past seven be all right?'

'Fine. Lovely. Wonderful. I look forward to seeing you then.'

She replaced the receiver. She could imagine that Paul was still looking at his in amazement. She hadn't meant to sound quite so enthusiastic about his acceptance, but she was just so pleased that she wouldn't be on her own, and at the mercy of her unknown attacker.

She went over to the window, drew the curtain aside

and looked out into the street. She could just make out the form of Harley Venn, sitting on the wall, presumably listening out for Dave. She could go to bed sure that no strangers would get past him and into her house.

There remained the telephone, so she pulled the jack out of the wall plug, and went to bed with a copy of *Jude the Obscure*. She felt like a good, depressing read before she went to sleep. Even after she had turned out the light, she thought she could hear footsteps on her garden path, then someone trying to open the back door. She just hoped that she was mistaken.

Chapter Thirteen

For Spirits when they please
Can either Sex assume, or both: so soft
And uncompounded is their Essence pure,
Not ti'd or manacl'd with joynt or limb,
Nor founded on the brittle strength of bones,
Like cumbrous flesh; but in what shape they choose
Dilated and condens't, bright or obscure,
Can execute their aerie purposes,
  And works of love or enmity fulfil.

John Milton, *Paradise Lost, i*

'Where were we in your story?' asks Zophiel. 'I want to hear what happens next.'

'Before I tell you,' says Christopher, 'could we settle something even more pressing? Do you think you could decide which sex you are?'

'We of the cherubim don't go in for sex. Not often, anyway.'

'Perhaps I meant to say gender.'

'You decide on the genre, and I'll pick the gender accordingly.'

'You mean that we are about to embark on a fortnight's study of the effect of genre on gender?'

'You've caught on. Well done.'

Have I told you about Briony's garden?

I expect you are imagining something neat, with a square of lawn surrounded by conventional herbaceous borders, perhaps sporting a bird bath or a stone sundial. Well, Briony's garden was nothing like that. She had been studying the works of the great Edwardian designers. She visited Sissinghurst and Stourhead. She drew careful plans on squared paper. She consulted with expensive garden architects.

Of course, in our west Oxford property, large as it was by city standards, she really didn't have enough room to work out all her ideas. She had to compress them, bring them down in scale. She planted a succession of interlocking rooms, as it were, so that as you passed from one to the next the atmosphere, the ambience changed. But, unfortunately, the difference in scale meant that our garden, although magnificent and the envy of the neighbourhood, had something – how shall I say? – claustrophobic about it. I felt that I was being hemmed in, imprisoned in a cage of greenery. No sooner had I emerged from one thriving green cell than I walked into the next. There was no escape. As the months and years went by I felt as though I had to fight my way out of that exquisite jungle with spear and lance, like some fairytale prince. Or perhaps it was a machete that I needed. I'm sure you notice how my images are becoming more violent by the minute, with a sexual dimension to them.

'You are once more seeking my sympathy with your extra-marital affair?'

'I thought you might be able to see my point of view.'

'You forget that I am employed as a guard by the giver of the original book of rules. You can hardly expect me to condone their transgression.'

'Oh, very well. Don't sympathize if you don't want to. But I shan't tell you the rest until we reach the next chapter.'

'But you still haven't told me anything much about Bartlemas and the people you met there. It sounds so very much like my own dear Garden.'

'Tomorrow. At the start of the next chapter.'
'Ainsi soit-il.'

'Well, that was really great,' said Martha.

'Oh yes,' agreed Curtis. 'It was. Certainly. Quite wonderful.'

'Well, I'm glad to hear it,' said Kate, mystified. What could possibly have pleased her two most difficult students like this? Had they found the city abattoir? Or the chapel of some cult which went in for human sacrifice?

'So much more interesting than the tour you took us on,' said Martha.

'I'm sure,' said Kate. 'Well, it would be, wouldn't it? But where did you go?'

'The Bodleian,' said Curtis.

'Ah,' said Kate, understanding at last. 'You've been looking at the university's library.'

'Such a charming man!' said Martha. 'So knowledgeable, so cultivated!'

'You must be referring to the Library's Assistant Secretary,' guessed Kate.

'Indeed I am,' said Martha, a foolish smile on her blade-like face. Martha was wearing the most flattering of the new outfits she had bought since the unfortunate incendiary accident. 'But now I must go and relax before dinner. I shall take off my shoes and rest my aching feet.'

'So you got the five-star tour? The one that lasts three hours and takes you into every nook and cranny?'

'Your Lord Humfrey's library,' said Curtis, reverently. 'The underground book stack, the historic motorized conveyance of books from one library to another, Radcliffe's Camera.'

'Duke Humfrey, the Radcliffe Camera,' corrected Kate without thinking. 'Did you go out on the roof?'

'But of course,' said Martha. 'And you should take lessons from the Assistant Secretary in how to conduct such a tour. So different from that lightning dash around Bartlemas to which we were subjected on our arrival. And the vistas from the roof! The way he could name every building!'

'It is easier to recognize them if you are capable of opening your eyes, I admit. And I'm sorry you found my own tour lacking in enthusiasm,' said Kate. 'But any time you would like a re-run of our visit to the Tower of Grace, just let me know. I'll happily take you up there again.'

'I think we'll wait until you've had a lesson in presentation from that lovely Assistant Secretary,' said Martha.

'I'll work on it,' said Kate. 'But don't let me keep you from your cooling shower and your well-deserved rest. I'll see you at dinner, no doubt.'

'I was going to show you the photographs we took,' said Martha. 'I had hoped that you would be interested in them.'

'But of course I am,' said Kate, peering at the bundle Martha took from her large canvas bag. There was a green Post-It note attached to the top of the packet, with writing in dark blue felt-tipped pen. It looked familiar, she thought. *What!* No, it wasn't possible that Martha, or even Curtis, had been responsible for the nasty notes she had found in her papers. And anyway, they hadn't known Chris Townsend, surely.

'Here,' said Martha. 'You can see our lovely group standing by the Sheldonian Theatre.'

Kate leant across, trying to see what Martha's green note said. Martha took the folder, with the attached note, from the top of the pile and transferred it to the bottom so that the message was no longer in sight. Bother.

'And here is one of you,' said Martha. 'You were wearing that blue dress of yours, as you see.'

Yes, she could see. The dress was a very bright blue, shading from pale aqua at the scooped neck down to brilliant peacock at the rather short hem. Her ear-rings caught the sun and flashed into the camera lens. And her hair, too, shone in gleaming shades of silver and gold in the brilliant light. Very striking, she thought. And if anyone had seen her wearing just that outfit, on the afternoon of Chris's death, they would very likely remember exactly what she looked like. Perhaps in future she should have her hair dyed in mouse-grey and rat-brown, and wrap herself in unflattering beige from neck to ankle.

She thought back to the time she spent on that pavement, looking into the shop window. But she still couldn't remember any details of the people who had milled around her in the street, or pushed past between her and the window. It was all a blur. She had a vague memory of Italian students, the odd gowned academic figure, one or two middle-aged housewives, but their faces were a blank. They could have been anybody. Any of the people she had met at Bartlemas since she came to work there could have been present, and she wouldn't recognize them. But anyone would remember the figure in the blue dress, she had to admit. Probably every person who was there that afternoon carried an image as precise as this photograph back with them.

'Yes, of course I'll make you a present of the photo, if you like it that much,' Martha was saying, as she tried to prise it from Kate's fingers. 'But I was hoping to take a complete record of our England trip back to North Carolina with me.'

'No, really, I don't need it,' said Kate. 'Do take it back with you. But thank you so much for showing it to me.'

Martha put the photos back in her bag and Kate craned over her, hoping for another glimpse of the green note, but she was disappointed.

'By the way, how long have the two of you been in England this time?' she asked.

'I don't know about Curtis,' said Martha, 'but I've been here nearly three weeks now. I shall have spent a whole month in England before I return to the States.'

Kate raised her eyebrows at Curtis, hoping for a statement from him, too, but he ignored her. She couldn't help thinking that they had both been there in Leicester Fellows' Garden when she had been half strangled. She tried to remember any details she could about the phantom strangler. A boot, heavy on her face. Martha was unlikely to wear boots on her tiny, narrow feet, Kate admitted. But what about Curtis?

As Curtis and Martha retreated towards the outpost where she had relocated them after their unscheduled fire, she could hear Martha saying, 'I hope she wears a dress with a front as well as a back tonight.' She didn't hear Curtis's reply, but she didn't think he sounded as disapproving of her evening apparel as Martha.

How could she possibly suspect a couple like that? What motive could they have? If they were scaring her, and leaving odd notes for her to find in her desk, then they must have left them for Chris, too. And why would they want to kill Chris? Well, she thought, just suppose that Martha (rich, widowed Martha, after all) or Curtis had written a large cheque for Bartlemas Development Fund, and then had discovered that the money had been purloined by someone – Chris, for instance – and not used to build the tasteful student accommodation that they had intended it for.

Unlikely? Yes, but not impossible. She would keep the thought in the back of her mind. It was as well to be on her guard in case anyone else wished to strangle her, or merely throw her into the river.

'Off home again already?'

It was Timothy Happle, the evening sun glinting on his oiled black hair and bringing out the rich red tones of his silk shirt.

'Not yet,' said Kate. 'I'm spending a virtuous evening with my students, sharing their evening meal in Hall, and engaging in intellectual conversation.'

'And how do you manage to get any writing done? It must be very difficult for you.' Timothy Happle seemed in no hurry to get off to his own evening meal.

Why was the man showing such concern? She didn't trust him. 'I'm in between books at the moment,' she answered. 'So, when I get home, I can curl up with my cat on the sofa and spend the rest of the evening watching mindless television programmes.'

'Doesn't your computer beckon? I thought you authors had to write your measured stint every day.'

'It doesn't get a chance to beckon. It's shut up in my workroom and will not be disturbed until I'm ready to start on the next Chapter One. In the meantime, it can enjoy the limited view over the back garden and recharge its batteries.'

'What a fascinating insight into the creative mind,' said Happle. 'Thank you so much.' He walked off towards the College offices, his right hand smoothing down his hair across his scalp.

It was only right that she should eat in Hall with the students tonight. Last night she had escaped, and had cooked dinner for her friend Paul Taylor. The evening had proved very satisfactory, though there had been a few awkward moments while he had wondered aloud what it was that she was hiding underneath the chiffon scarf around her throat. Kate had muttered something about her sore throat – he remembered that she had a sore throat when she phoned him last night, didn't he? But Paul had given her his straight look and said that he thought she was probably hiding something from him. He hoped that it wasn't something to do with a criminal case, as he was tired of rescuing her from potentially fatal situations. And wasn't it about time she found herself a proper job and settled down?

Kate failed to rise to this bait, since she was too aware that dusk was falling on Fridesley, and she really couldn't expect a child who was not yet twelve years old to stand guard outside her house all night and every night, even if she had offered to take Dave for the weekend. Just the one weekend, you understand, Harley. This did not establish a precedent, she had explained. It had occurred to her, if not to Harley, that a dog, even one as stupid as Dave, would afford some sort of protection against intruders. She knew he wouldn't attack or bite anyone, but he might bark and scare them off. Well, he might, if the moon was full and he was in the mood for baying at it. She only wished she could train the animal to answer the telephone as well.

She looked at Paul, sitting comfortably on her pink velvet sofa, reading a newspaper, and thought of telling him all about it. But what would she tell him? A story of silly notes on her computer screen and messages on her telephone answering machine. Gossip about people who were on the take. Suspicions about a death that had already been labelled as accidental by a perfectly competent coroner.

'What do you do if you think something odd is happening inside a private institution?' There, that was too vague to raise his suspicions.

'Hmm? What are you talking about? What sort of institution?'

'Well, a school, or a department store, say.'

'Or a college, I suppose.'

'Not necessarily.'

'And what sort of something funny? Do you mean some child has been stealing from its friends' lunch packs, or a shop assistant has his fingers in the till?'

'I don't think you're being very helpful.'

'Well, in the first case, we wouldn't know anything about it unless the school contacted us, and in such a case that would be unlikely. In the second case, the store would call us in and we would investigate in the usual way.'

'But suppose nobody called you in. Suppose you just suspected some monumental fraud in the institution, what would you do?'

'Why should we suspect any such thing? I mean, you can't just stand on the pavement and point to some building and say, "I think that something funny's going on in there," can you? You have to have a very good reason to put your riot boots on, break the door down and charge inside looking for villains.'

He was not taking her seriously. No one, if it came to that, had taken Chris Townsend's death very seriously. Would they have done so if it had been more widely known just how many dishonest schemes were going on in Bartlemas? And suppose Paul did take her seriously, what would he do? Presumably, as he'd hinted, he'd walk into Bartlemas College with a bunch of his booted colleagues and they would frighten the students, interrupt the conference, alienate the staff and lose her her job. No, she couldn't afford that. She would have to carry on the way she had, trying to find out what it was all about, then present him with a folder full of evidence. Unlikely, she had to admit, but definitely better than getting the sack.

Meanwhile she smiled at Paul and offered him the choice of two puddings, and brandy with his coffee.

'Do you mind if I watch the cricket?' he asked, and pulled the television set out of its cubby-hole. Kate would rather have had gentle music on the CD player, but at least the television stopped any more conversation about suspicious happenings in Oxford colleges.

While Paul was watching television, the phone rang. Kate half-hoped it was her threatening caller. It would be nice to have a witness, and a policeman at that, to the way she was being harassed. But it was Faith Beeton.

'I need to talk to you,' she said, without preamble. 'Can I come round now?'

'I don't think that this is a good time, especially if you want my undivided attention.'

'You mean you've got someone there.'

'Right.'

'Are you doing anything tomorrow evening?' she asked. 'No, forget that, I'm accompanying a group of students to Stratford. I'll be away all day, probably until midnight. How about Saturday?'

'It might be all right,' said Kate cautiously. It was as well to find out what you were letting yourself in for before committing your time, she had found. 'But aren't we supposed to be eating in Hall with the students?'

'I suppose we should turn up and amuse the punters for an hour or so before they eat in Hall, but we don't have to join them, do we? I happen to know that it's Chef's night off, and his trainee is still practising steak and kidney pies and rice pudding.'

'In this weather? I can't believe it.'

'It's true.'

'Enough! Come to supper with me instead,' said Kate. 'Sevenish?'

'Fine. Thanks.'

'By the way, what do you want to talk about?'

'Some odd things that are happening, and remarks that I've overheard, and which seem to involve you.' She disconnected and left Kate feeling thoughtful. She was glad that she had company for the evening, and possibly beyond.

'Who was that?' asked Paul. 'One of your other men friends?'

'Why do you think that'

'The way you wouldn't talk with me present, and the fact that you've invited them, not me, to supper on Saturday.'

'How perceptive of you,' said Kate. And that just showed how wrong policemen could be in reading a situation, she thought. It was just as well that she hadn't discussed her problems with Paul, after all.

Later, they put the television away and sat companionably together on the pink sofa. She would have removed his tie, but he managed to do that for himself.

Chapter Fourteen

High on a Throne of Royal State, which far
Outshon the wealth of *Ormus* and of *Ind*,
Or where the gorgeous East with richest hand
Showers on her Kings *Barbaric* Pearl and Gold,
Satan exalted sat.

> John Milton, *Paradise Lost*, ii

'So, today we are to compare Edens,' says Christopher.

'I think I've heard enough about Briony and her garden for the moment. Seen one Garden of Eden, seen them all, I've always said. But you broke off your account of what was happening at Bartlemas College, and I really did want to hear more about your dishonest dealings. It seemed that it had more to do with my paper on The Victim than your minor spats with Briony.'

'What title have you given it? "The Effect of Gender on the Victim"? "Victim and Genre"? "Victim on the Page", perhaps?'

'Stop being facetious and tell me more about Bartlemas. You did promise me a full account, after all. So far it seemed as though you had dropped your little round peg into an exactly matching round hole.'

'Oh, in many ways I had.'

'But?'

I had reached the point where I needed a partner. And my first thought was to choose a woman. Women, as perhaps you have noticed, find me attractive. It

210

worked with Viola, it worked with Briony herself. In fact, I believe that I won over Briony's mother with a combination of my cheekbones and the boyish lock of hair that fell over my forehead.

There were two candidates at Bartlemas for the position. The first, and most obvious, was Sadie James.

I really went for that abundant, shining chestnut hair. She tossed it around a lot and looked up at you with those black eyes, through long eyelashes. And what about the glistening red lipsticked mouth? She knew just the effect she was having, I can tell you. I would see the corner of her mouth twitch, and lift a fraction of a centimetre when she caught me looking at her. She had an air of knowing something very exciting that the rest of us didn't: something that she could demonstrate to you in your bedroom, or on your staircase, on top of your dining table or on the rug in front of your fire. Even when she was wearing jeans and a t-shirt she gave the impression that her underwear was of silk, and I imagined I could hear the whisper of the material as she moved.

Sorry, I got carried away there.

Yes, I thought that she was setting her traps and that I was the prey she wished to catch. So I asked her out to lunch. A friendly, we're-just-colleagues kind of an invitation. I took her to a very nice small restaurant not far from the centre of Oxford, where we were most unlikely to meet anyone we knew.

The bill, not including the tip, reached three figures. And when I hinted at my proposition, my financial proposition, that is – I didn't get as far as introducing any other kind – she laughed at me. Didn't I realize that she was heavily involved in a project already? And as for sex, she was nicely provided for, thank you very much.

'Why did you encourage me?' I asked, hurt.

'Such good camouflage,' she replied. 'Everyone thinks that we're at it like knives, all over the Development

Office carpet, and so the spotlight is off my partner and myself.'

'What partner?' I asked, as I reached for the bill, swallowed a gasp, and hoped that my credit card wasn't too close to its limit.

'Find out!' she said, her red lips pushed towards me. And she got up from her chair, definitely with the whisper of silk underwear this time, and led the way out of the restaurant.

'And did you?'

'Yes. But by that time I had been made to look even more of a fool.'

'And you still maintain that your status of victim was a pure accident?'

'What happened was hardly my fault, was it?'

''Ere, Kate!' It was Harley, welcoming her as she arrived home.

'Hello, Harley,' she said, then wondered whether ''Ere, 'Arley!' wouldn't be an easier greeting to deliver.

'You all ready then?'

'Ah.' Light was dawning. This was Friday, and she had just remembered her rash promise to take on Dave for the weekend. She had been hoping that the weekend started on a Saturday afternoon, but looking at Harley's face she realized that this one was due to start in about five minutes' time. 'Dave,' she said.

'Yeah.' Harley's face was mostly mouth and teeth, forming into a huge smile.

'Right. I've got him some food. I've prepared a bed for him under the table in the kitchen. I've warned Susannah to expect a dog, but I'm not sure that she understood the concept.'

'What?'

'I'm sure they'll settle down together, eventually. Have you got his lead?'

'Yeah.'

'I assume that you'll be taking care of his walks, and so on.'

'Yeah.'

'So we'd better go and fetch him, hadn't we?'

'Yeah.' This last was delivered with enthusiasm.

Kate needn't have worried. She hardly saw Dave that evening. The poor animal was walked from one end of Fridesley to the other, and then back again, until his paws were quite sore. He was not a very athletic dog at the best of times, and he looked as though he'd been vegging out at Darren and Dossa's house. He swallowed down the meal that Kate chopped up for him as though he was starving, and then retired to his bed under the kitchen table, where he spent the rest of the evening snoring. Susannah tried to terrorize him, but he was too tired to react to her spitting and swearing.

'You won't let that cat of yours get him, will you?' Harley asked Kate.

'Don't worry about him, Harley,' said Kate. 'He'll be fine tonight. And in the morning you can come round and give him his breakfast and take him out for whatever dogs need to do first thing in the morning.'

'Right,' said Harley. 'Cheers. See ya.'

'See you, Harley,' replied Kate.

'Oh, and by the way,' he added, when he was nearly out of the door. 'There was someone round your place, nosing around again today.'

'There was? Why didn't you tell me about it?'

'Well, I didn't really see them. I couldn't tell you what they look like.'

'Bother.' She did try hard not to use strong language

in front of the young, though she was afraid that Harley was already familiar with her complete repertoire of swearwords, plus a few.

'Don't worry. Dave'll keep you safe tonight. He's an ace guard dog. He's half German shepherd, you know. A killer.'

Dave's snores came back to them through the open door. 'Yes, but the other half of Dave is Welsh sheep as I remember it. Goodnight, Harley.'

''Night, Kate.'

She went back into the kitchen and glared at Dave. 'Guard dog!' she jeered. 'Huh! Susannah would do a better job of savaging an intruder than you would.'

'Hello, Kate!'

Kate was immensely pleased to hear Andrew's voice. For one thing, he wasn't hissing threats into her ear, and for another he sounded wonderfully normal. And happy.

'What's been happening in your life?' she asked. 'You sound much more cheerful than usual.'

'Oh, I had a lovely time at the conference. Very productive.'

Well, thought Kate, since no one could possibly get cheerful over schemes for the co-operative cataloguing of theology books, there must have been some successful tiptoeing down corridors in between the sessions.

'So are you coming round for a meal to tell me all about it?' she asked.

'I thought I'd take you out and treat you instead.'

My goodness, he was in a good mood. 'That's a lovely idea, Andrew. But not this weekend, I fear. I'm baby-sitting.'

Andrew made a noise that expressed extreme disbelief.

'Not actually a baby, you understand.'

'Oh, thank goodness for that. I can imagine the awful things you could do to a poor defenceless baby.'

'I might have a highly developed maternal sense, for all you know.'

'I don't believe it.'

'Anyway, there's no baby, but there is a dog. That barrel of red fur that used to live next door at the Toad-face house.'

'The one that was terrified of your kitten?'

'That's the one.'

'Right. I understand that you can't possibly leave the poor defenceless animal on its own, it would be panic-stricken. I'll come round on Monday night, and I'll bring a bottle of wine and the rather nice single malt whisky that I picked up at the duty-free shop.'

'Warm ciabatta, cold chicken, green salad do you?' asked Kate.

'And new potatoes with lemon mayonnaise. Is it too late in the season for a summer pudding?'

'Probably, but I'll think of something else. Do you still eat whipped cream?'

'Yes, and lots of it. I'll see you at seven-thirty. Oh, and Kate . . .'

'Yes?'

'I'm so glad you're doing a really sensible job at a college, instead of getting mixed up with all that criminal riff-raff you usually collect.'

'And whose fault was it that I got mixed up with such unsavoury characters?'

'Certainly not mine. *A lundi!*'

Good, she thought, as she put the phone down. That's another evening I won't have to spend alone. And before she went to bed, she again checked windows and doors. She checked on Dave, too, but he was out to the world, and snoring loudly. Susannah came and joined her on her bed in disgust. But Kate didn't turn her out tonight. She was glad of the company.

Harley was at Kate's front door at an amazingly early hour the next morning. A rather weary Dave allowed himself to be taken for a walk round the streets of Fridesley and through the churchyard before they both came back to Kate's kitchen for breakfast.

'You used to get up and do that jogging, didn't you?' said Harley. 'Don't you do that no more?'

'Sometimes. I'll get going again when I've finished this job at Bartlemas.'

'You could take Dave with you.'

'He's just here for the weekend, remember.'

'Yeah, well, I expect you'll get used to him.'

'I have to go out and work, you know. I have to go into Bartlemas this morning, for example.'

'That's all right. I'll look after him while you're out.'

'Fine. Don't tire the poor animal out too much. He's lethargic enough as it is.'

She looked in the drawer of the kitchen table. 'Here, Harley, you'd better have this.' And she gave him the spare keys to her front door. 'You can help yourself to as many Cokes as you like, but don't eat all the white Magnums. There are times when I really need some comfort, and that's the only thing that will do.'

'Yeah. All right,' said Harley. And that, Kate knew, was a term of approval. 'You should get yourself a dog,' he added.

Thanks to Harley's early-morning call, Kate was in her office at Bartlemas at a good hour that morning. Which was just as well, since she had a deputation from her two favourite students just ten minutes after she arrived.

'Do sit down,' she said. 'What can I do to help?' That ought to disarm them, anyway.

'There's something very funny going on,' said Martha.

'There is?' Well, she knew that there was, in fact she knew of several very funny things going on, but she was interested to find out what Martha and Curtis had turned up.

'First of all,' said Martha, 'there are people here who really do not like you, Kate Ivory.'

Kate tried to look surprised.

'Now, to begin with, we understood why that might be, as regards the students,' said Curtis. 'I mean, you can be very sharp, and a little dismissive when you want. And we've seen you run and hide in the Fellows' Garden when Sharen Cobb wishes to discuss a point of genre theory with you. And then there's the way you miss out on dinner in Hall when the rest of us have to eat steak and kidney pie and rice pudding.'

'Sorry about that,' said Kate. 'I'll try harder next time.'

'And then there are people who work for the college, other members of staff. There are some of them who don't like you, either. There are people who have been saying really unkind things about you, and some of them aren't even true. Now that was more surprising, because to us you don't seem any more unlikeable than the rest of the staff.'

'Thanks,' said Kate, trying to work out whether this was a compliment or not.

'But there are people here who've really got it in for you,' said Martha.

'They want you *out*,' said Curtis.

'You've noticed that, too,' said Kate.

'Now, I think that incident on the river the other day was kind of foolish on your part,' said Martha. 'Especially when you wanted to sit in the field in your wet dress and eat your way through the picnic food. But someone, back at college, was putting it about that you had been drinking, and that was why you fell in. Now, we were watching you, and the wine was all lined up on the tables, and I'm sure that you were ready to dash across that field to get to it, but there was no drinking being done in the boats.'

'We call them punts. No, you're right,' said Kate. 'That would be drinking on duty, as it were. It wouldn't do at all.'

'So who put the story around, and why?' said Curtis.

'Good question,' said Kate. 'But I don't know the answer, I'm afraid.'

'Then there was something about our trip to Birmingham that didn't seem quite right, either,' said Martha. 'I wouldn't have remembered it if it hadn't been for the other things happening. But when you came back after the interval you looked pale and shaken, and I did think that it was you I saw being hassled by someone just before the interval bell went. Tell me, Kate, did someone attack you?'

'Did you see them?' asked Kate.

'So it was true! They did!' said Curtis.

'Yes,' admitted Kate. 'I don't think they really wanted to injure me, but they wanted to create a disturbance and cause me a lot of embarrassment. Rather like the punting incident, come to think of it. I think I fooled them by not being quite where they expected me to be.' She didn't explain that she was escaping from Martha herself at the time; it seemed particularly ungracious since the woman was taking so much interest in her and her problems.

'So there's a conspiracy!' said Curtis. 'I thought that I was a lonely person, without too many friends, but you're a lot worse off than I am.'

'Someone's after your job!' said Martha.

'I shouldn't think so,' said Kate. 'It isn't a very good

one, or very well paid, and it only lasts another ten days or so. What would be the point?'

'We'll have to think again, Martha,' said Curtis.

'There's one more thing,' said Kate to Martha. 'When you so kindly showed me your photographs, you had a green Post-It note with a message written on it in green felt-tipped pen in your bag. Do you think you could show it to me?'

Martha went pink. 'No, I don't think I could.'

'Why not? What have you got to hide?'

'It's private,' said Martha. 'And why do you want to see it, anyway?'

'Because I, and Chris Townsend before me, received threatening messages on slips of paper just like it.'

'Oh, show it to her, Martha,' said Curtis. 'She'll suspect that we've been attacking her if you don't.'

'Very well,' said Martha, tight-lipped, and she drew a bright green note from her bag and showed it to Kate.

Last night was a dream, Princess. Shall I see you again tonight?
Your Curtis

'She wants to see the reply you sent me, I expect,' said Curtis.

'But you are not going to show it to her,' said Martha in a voice that would not be contradicted.

'No, really, that's fine. I believe you. I wouldn't dream of intruding on your privacy,' said Kate.

'And now would you care to explain to us what's happening?' asked Martha.

'Gladly,' replied Kate. 'If only I knew. There seem to be two or perhaps three separate things happening here, any one of which could be down to the person who is getting at me.'

'And what did you mean about Chris Townsend

getting threatening notes as well? Why would this Chris Townsend be involved?' asked Martha. 'We corresponded with him, of course, before coming over here. I thought he died in some sort of accident, falling off the tower.'

'There was a rumour there, too, that he was drunk,' said Kate. 'And there are too many loose ends for me to believe that his death was really an accident.'

'And you believe that his death is connected with these things that are happening to you?' asked Curtis.

'It seems unlikely that there is more than one major mystery in this place, don't you think? And by the way, did you notice anything odd happening at the Shakespeare performance at Leicester?'

'Hey!' exclaimed Curtis. 'Look at the time, Martha! We have to get going, Kate. But we'll talk with you again about this.'

'Come to supper at my place. Tuesday. Seven-thirty. And it won't be steak and kidney pie, I promise.'

'Well, thank you,' said Martha. 'We'd be delighted, wouldn't we, Curtis?'

As they walked away, Kate heard Martha say, 'Maybe she's not so bad after all, Curtis. She has an attitude problem, I know, but maybe she can learn to do something about it, in time, with help.'

Attitude? What attitude problem? wondered Kate, pushing her hands through her hair, and striding through Pesant Quad towards the seminar room where she was to run a creative writing workshop. What made these people think they could write, anyway? It took more than a little talent, it took courage, and perseverance. It took *attitude*.

Chapter Fifteen

And he that sat was to look upon like a jasper and a sardine stone: and there was a rainbow round about the throne, in sight like unto an emerald.

Revelation, 4, 3

'It seems to me that we are entering upon the final phase of our story,' says Zophiel. 'In terms of time, as far as I understand the concept, we must be approaching the point where someone hurled you from the Tower of Grace and sent you to wait at the gate to the Garden of Eden.'

'The trouble is that the longer I spend here in your company, the less I remember what time was like. But I suppose it must be as you say. There is not much more that I need to tell you.'

'And who was your second choice of partner, both romantic and financial?'

'I should have thought that that was obvious by now.'

Faith Beeton. She had just joined the college on a three-year fellowship. She was older than you might have expected, only a year younger than I, in fact. And she had an ignorance of the ways of the world, combined with a very sharp intelligence, which I thought I could use. She also, I could see, was just starting to discover the good things of life. I imagine that they had not figured very largely in her experience up until then.

First of all there were clothes. She liked to wear silk

in deep jewel colours: a red dress; a collection of brilliant scarves; several deep-dyed shirts. Or leather: long conker-brown boots; a purple kid jacket; capacious handbags. These lifted her rather uninteresting features and sallow skin and made them glow, could almost convince you that she was a beautiful woman. If you had seen her wearing ordinary clothes, without her jewel-coloured silks, her brilliant leather, you would not have looked at her twice, unless you noticed the intelligence in her eyes. She was a monkey-faced woman, with dark, wavy hair growing low on her forehead. A thin, wiry figure that you would not have thought of as being so full of sexual tension that it seemed to crackle, giving off silver sparks in the darkness of the night. Oh, am I talking nonsense? Faith made me think, talk, live nonsense. I was outside myself. In love, I think, for the first time. For the first time I cared about someone other than myself. I thought about her all the time. When I smelled that scent she wore, I was on fire. I've never met anyone else who wore it. I don't know what it's called, but if I caught a whiff of it now, I would recognize it immediately. I would shout 'Faith', and I would see her, exactly as she was on that last day of my life, and I would come running.

But clothes like that cost money, and she enjoyed buying them. She would take the coach early in the morning to London, then the tube down to Knightsbridge, and she would start shopping as soon as the stores opened. In the evening she would return to Oxford, her carrier bags filling and overflowing the compartment above her seat, so that no one else could stow their luggage.

I wondered how to approach her. This was no Sadie. If I got it wrong I would be treated to her caustic tongue. I might even become the laughing stock of the college, and I certainly didn't want that. I thought about taking

her for an expensive lunch, but I had been caught like
that once, and I didn't intend to be taken again.

We were at one of those drinks parties given by the
Master at the beginning of term to let staff and students
alike know that they are part of a warm, caring com-
munity. Briony wasn't there, and I don't suppose Faith
even knew that I was married. Perhaps she did, though,
and perhaps she didn't care. After talking for a while, and
drinking three or four glasses of the Master's Australian
Chardonnay, we were feeling happy enough to wander
off by ourselves along Bartlemas Row and into the High
Street.

It was a warm, balmy evening, the last of the light
just fading from the sky behind Carfax Tower. I thought
about what we were to do next. I could hardly ask her
back to my own house, with Briony waiting there. I was
about to suggest a pub or wine bar, though the atmosphere of neither was quite what I wanted for us. A
restaurant? We were not far from the one to which I had
taken Sadie, and the image of my humiliation was too
close for my comfort. Perhaps we could go to one of
the Thai restaurants that had recently opened in the
neighbourhood.

On reaching the end of Bartlemas Row I had automatically turned left, towards Carfax, but Faith took my
hand and pulled me gently in the other direction.

'My place,' she said, simply. 'It's only five minutes
away.'

'What about your scheme for making money?'

'Oh, that. What about it? It didn't matter then. Nothing
mattered except Faith.'

'But you didn't forget about it?'

'Oh no. I did bring the subject up.'

'So tell me about it.'

'Have I told you about Faith's background?'

'To hell with Faith's background. Tell me what happened.'

'Time, as I say, has no meaning now. Be patient.'

'Be brief. I want to hear what happened. I want to know who killed you. And why.'

'Very well. I'll be as concise as I know how. But if you are going to understand what happened, and if you are going to fill up that little black notebook of yours with useful data, you are going to have to listen to her story, or a small part of it, anyway.'

'Oh, very well. But keep it short.'

Her parents were religious. She was not entirely sure what their religion was. It seemed to consist only of duty. Duty towards God, towards Church and State, and towards all authority figures. Duty above all towards parents. No duty, of course, of parents towards children. I believe she worked for them rather like a maidservant. She washed and cleaned and did the shopping. I doubt, myself, that they often asked her to do the cooking. If they did, it can only be because they had no sense of taste. Such a clever girl, dear Faith, and they cared for her brains not at all. They were a sign of intellectual pride and therefore to be denigrated. She sailed through O-Levels. Struggled with A-Levels while being told by her parents what a selfish girl she was to concentrate like this on her own wishes and desires.

Her father I think you would describe as a professional invalid, her mother a martyr to his cause. It was of course her mother who died first, quietly slipping away. And it was Faith who took over her father's care. She gave up all hopes of going to university, although these hopes were so pale and evanescent as to have no reality for her.

It was on her father's death that Faith at last could realize what she wanted out of life. College, university. Degrees, more degrees. And at last the Oxford Fellowship.

The house came to her, and the meagre savings. It

was a small legacy for someone with such expensive tastes.

I put it to her that she could have all the books and pictures, the furniture, the clothes, the CDs, that she wanted. All she had to do was join with me and together we could fool the world. Or, if not the world, at least Bartlemas College. With my schemes and her intelligence put to their refinement, we would be invincible. And rich. There was thirty or forty thousand pounds coming into the Development Office every morning. If we sidetracked only one day's takings every week, we would soon be very well off. And there was no reason why we should be found out for a very long time. I thought she would jump at the opportunity.

You know what she said to me?

Nothing. She laughed at me.

'Don't you know me?' she asked. 'Don't you understand me? See who I am! I am my father's daughter. My mother's daughter. I may earn money. I may spend it on myself. But to steal it?'

'Steal it? How can you say that?'

'But that is the difference between us, dear Christopher. I at least know the meaning of stealing, of dishonesty. I was brought up to know that there were such things as right and wrong, and that the difference between them was unbridgeable.'

'But everyone is doing it.'

'Honesty, you should understand, is indivisible. You cannot be just a little bit dishonest, Chris.'

'So what is your answer?'

'No. You must know that.'

'But wasn't adultery also a form of dishonesty?'

'Oh yes. She knew that. She knew the difference between right and wrong. But in that instance, she chose the wrong. But she didn't try to convince herself that she wasn't doing wrong, that it didn't matter. She was capable of making

*moral choices, but they were not always quite what you
would expect.'*

'An unusual woman.'

'A woman to love.'

'And did she kill you?'

'Don't you know the answer to that?'

'Not yet.'

'I believe that next time is our last.'

'What time do you want to go back to Darren and Dossa's
place?' asked Kate.

'How long can you keep him?' responded Harley.

'Till this evening, I suppose. I've got a friend coming
round for supper.'

'One of your men?'

'No! I have only the one man in my life. Didn't you
know that?'

'If you say so.'

'I was going to suggest that Dave spend the evening
here, and then you, Faith and I could walk him back
after supper. Would half past ten be too late?'

'Nah,' said Harley. 'Term's only just started. This is
like the holidays still. Mum don't mind what time I go
to bed.'

Actually, Trace didn't mind what time her children
went to bed during term time, either, it seemed to Kate.

Harley hadn't moved, so Kate said, 'You can sit and
talk to Dave in the kitchen. Only don't get in my way,
all right?'

'Yeah.'

'Are you hungry?'

'Nah. Had me tea.'

'Well, if you get hungry you can have some of the
pud when we get that far in the meal.'

'Yeah.'

'And you'll have to keep out of the way when my friend turns up, because we want to talk, in private.'

'I could do the washing-up for you.'

'This is an all-new side to your personality, Harley.'

'You what?'

'I mean, thank you.'

'You see,' said Faith an hour or so later, as she tucked into moist, delicate chicken flesh, potatoes cooked with applemint and glazed with fresh butter, and green salad, 'it all goes back to the way I was brought up. Although my father dictated the way we lived, or indeed failed to live in any true sense of the word, he was an absent figure. He was never there, with us, in our daily lives. He lay in bed upstairs, giving orders, manipulating us by the state of his nerves. But anything important, anything real, was accomplished by women. As far as I was concerned, women ran the world. My mother, my aunts, even myself. I *did*, I achieved. I shopped, and cooked, and cleaned and did the washing. All that was real. But my father just lay in bed. He appeared downstairs only on special occasions, like Christmas or on his birthday. So I have always, I think, regarded men as being the icing on the cake, as it were. Something that you bring out on a dull day, rather like the television set, to amuse you when you have nothing better to do.' She paused for a moment and looked at the food on her plate. 'Did you say that there's a dressing for the salad?'

'Yes, sure,' said Kate. 'There's a raspberry vinaigrette if you'd like some.'

'Thanks.' Faith shovelled more food into her mouth. 'I don't suppose you have bottled salad cream? No?' She was apparently one of those skinny people who needed large quantities of food at regular intervals, but who never put on any weight. 'Now don't get me wrong,' she said, reverting to the previous subject, 'I don't dislike men, but they are an amusement, not something to be taken seriously. No, that isn't quite true. You have to take them seriously so that they don't mess your life up and stop you from doing the real things that you want to do. If you let them they'll fill your life with trivia, like children, housework and cooking. And you'll spend your time endlessly listening to their half-baked ideas.'

Kate raised a hand to stop Faith from speaking.

'Did you hear that?'

'What? No. You're imagining things. Thanks, I'd like some more wine. Have you ever noticed just how often men assume that they can speak with authority on subjects about which they know nothing? Women are much more reticent in those circumstances.'

'Very interesting, but how is it relevant to your story? Oh, and pass the mayonnaise, would you?'

'Chris expected me to take him seriously. He expected to be the centre of my life, to be my main, indeed my only, interest. But how could he be? He was married to someone else. I quite liked the man, although I couldn't admire much about him. As far as I was concerned he was an amusement for empty afternoons. I like sex. I enjoy it. But I don't want to get deeply involved with my partner.'

'Chris? You mean your were involved with him? But I thought he had something going with Sadie.'

'So did everyone, but they were wrong. Is there someone in your kitchen, by the way?'

'Yes, a young friend of mine called Harley. Take no notice of him, he's going to wash up for us.'

'Oh, good. I hate washing up. Where was I?'

'On the subject of men.'

'I don't want to pick someone up at a pub or on the street and take them home. I need to have continuity, and something in common with my partner. But essentially, Chris was as important to me as my hairdresser, or the pictures I put on my wall. Enjoyable, good at his job, but not in the centre of my life.'

'I wish I could be like that, but I always seem to let men right into the middle of my life so that they can destroy all that is most important to me. I'll go and fetch in the puds.'

'Yes, lovely. But you're making a great mistake. If you want to be a writer you have to learn to be on your own, not dependent on others for your emotional needs.'

'But I *am* a writer. I've written eight books now. Doesn't that qualify me to call myself a writer?'

'But think how much better you'd be at it if you were free from all that emotional mess.'

'I'm not sure about that. I think that emotional mess is what I write about best.'

'If you say so.'

'And I want to know what happened next. Did you fall out with Chris? *Did you kill him?*' Oh, why did she ask stupid questions like that while sitting at her dining table cutting slices of chocolate and almond cake, alone with a possible murderer? Was it the emotional mess at the centre of her life, perhaps? Should she practise being more rational? She spooned cream over Faith's portion and handed it across the table.

Faith was laughing at her. Did murderers laugh? More important, did murderers laugh at their victims before pushing them over a parapet? Luckily they were at ground level at this moment.

'Of course I didn't kill him! Is that what you've been thinking all this time?'

'It was a possibility, after all.'

'Chris was at my place for lunch that day. He brought a quiche from the Italian shop with him and put it in the oven to heat through. He made some sort of fried-up mixture of funny vegetables—'

'Ratatouille?'

'I think so.'

'I found a couple of courgettes in the fridge when I was cooking at your place a few days ago. They were left over from his meal, I suppose. I didn't think of ratatouille at the time.'

'I rarely do think of ratatouille, myself.'

'Go on with the story.'

'There isn't much to it. The poor man was feeling hounded by Briony. She was spending more and more of his money on expensive knick-knacks for her garden. Very expensive knick-knacks, like a Victorian conservatory, I suppose. I don't think Chris would have taken to crime if she hadn't been so demanding. I don't think it ever occurred to her to ask how he was supposed to get the money for all her extravagant schemes.'

'I'm not so sure about that. I can't imagine that there wasn't something in his past life that put him on the road to dishonesty.'

'How hard you are! Well, anyway, he was with me that lunchtime. We had rather a lot of fun in the room upstairs. I don't suppose you really want to hear the details, do you? No, I thought not. We ate our quiche and our veggie stew, both prepared by Chris, and Chris drank a half of lager. Then we kissed one another fondly on the doorstep, I told him that all was over between us, lovely as it had been, and he went striding off towards Magdalen Bridge. That's the last I saw of him.'

'What?'

'Oh, didn't I tell you? I'd had enough. He was becoming too demanding, emotionally. I'd been warning him that it was over. Men never believe these things, don't you find?'

'What did he say?'

'He made a bit of a fuss, but he had to accept it eventually.'

'What did you do when he'd left?'

'I spent about five minutes clearing up, left the dishes for later, then I followed him back to Bartlemas. We didn't like appearing together, you see, especially in the circumstances.'

'I might have seen you, I suppose. Or then again, I was probably inside the shop.'

'I expect you were inside. I think I would remember you if I'd seen you. You've got one of those faces that people don't easily forget.'

'I thought it was my brilliant blue dress and bleached hair that stayed in their memories.'

'Those too.'

'So, that was it. That sight of him, striding away towards Bartlemas, was the last I ever had.'

'You didn't see him in college, later?'

'No, I went straight to my rooms. I wasn't avoiding him, I wanted to draft some notes for next year's undergraduate teaching. Do you know the *Arcadia*?'

'No, I'm afraid not. And did you see anyone else who might have—'

'Might have killed him do you mean? But I thought it was an accident.'

'Is that what you think?'

'No. No, I don't.'

'Well, then?'

'I'm sorry. I can't think of anyone suspicious, or even of anyone at all. It's all over three weeks ago now, and the days do tend to run into each other.'

'If you think of something, will you let me know?'

'Why? Who are you? The Famous Amateur Detective?'

'Perhaps we're in the wrong genre, and I'm just the historical novelist, but still, if you do remember something, please tell me about it.'

'Is there any wine left?'

'I'll open the other bottle. Neither of us has to drive tonight.'

'I'm afraid I've got rather a long way from what I came here to tell you.'

'I thought you came to tell me all that stuff about Chris, and how he cooked you lunch, and how you were having an affair, and how it was all over.'

'I actually came to tell you that I overheard a most peculiar conversation.'

'When? Where?'

'A couple of days ago. Just before I rang you about it. I wanted to tell you straight away, but you said that you had someone here with you.'

'My friend, Paul.' My friend, Paul, the policeman. But she couldn't say that, even to Faith Beeton. 'What happened?'

'I was walking through the Fellows' Garden. You know what that place is like. You can hear all sorts of things going on behind leafy screens. You can't see who the people are, but you can hear what they're saying. Well, I suppose you could peer round hedges and find out who people are, but then they'd know that you'd been listening, wouldn't they?'

'That would certainly take a lot of the fun out of it. What were they saying?'

'They were being most indiscreet. Did I ever tell you, by the way, that that was how Chris and—'

'Quiet a moment!'

'What?' Faith was whispering in response to Kate's warning.

'Listen! Can you hear something?'

'What?'

'That!'

They could both hear them now: footsteps coming up the garden path, going through the side gate, making their way round to the back door.

'How many of them do you think there are?' hissed Kate.

'One, possibly two,' whispered Faith. 'Maybe it's someone delivering the parish magazine.'

'Is it hell!'

'I would normally assume an innocent explanation for their presence, myself, but I suppose you know best. What do you want us to do?'

'Let's make our way very quietly into the kitchen.'

Harley looked up but didn't speak as they crept into the kitchen and sat opposite him at the table. Dave stayed in his place underneath the table. Susannah was out on her own affairs.

'It's him, the prowler, he's come back,' said Harley.

'Great,' said Kate. 'What do we do now?'

'Kill him?' queried Harley, hopefully.

'I think not,' said Kate. 'Let's put the light out.'

'Why?' asked Faith.

'Because it might encourage him to break in, and then we can catch him.'

'That sounds like a really bad idea,' said Faith.

But Kate had switched off the light and was saying in a loud voice, 'Let's leave the washing-up until tomorrow, shall we? I hate coming back into the kitchen after I've cooked a meal!'

'No one who knows you is going to believe that,' whispered Faith.

'Shh,' said Kate.

They sat for a few minutes in the dark, then they heard the grating noise of someone trying the back door knob.

It turned.

Did I really leave the back door open? wondered Kate. I must have left it open because Harley was here. Could she galvanize Dave, protect Harley, use Faith as a battering ram?

Someone came in through the back door. A solid shadow against the darkness of the garden. A second shadow followed the first.

At this moment Dave, seeing the moon through the open back door, lumbered to his feet and started padding across the kitchen towards it. He was a very solid dog, over-fed and under-exercised, especially since he had been living at Darren and Dossa's.

The first intruder, who had apparently not yet got his night sight, moved towards the middle of the room, and in so doing fell over Dave. There was some shouting, and swearing, and a little minor barking from Dave.

Faith switched on the light. Harley was standing with his back to the door, ready to protect his dog. It was left to Kate to confront the two intruders. One of them was on the floor, holding his foot, and still swearing. The other was standing, looking down at Dave, who was planted in the middle of the floor, wagging his stupid tail. Kate grabbed the heavy rubber torch from the shelf behind her and raised it above her head.

Then, 'Dr Happle,' she said, disgusted. 'And Mr Charleston. I might have guessed. What are you two doing here?'

'Hello, Timothy,' said Faith. 'Why don't you sit down at the table and explain yourself. And Steven. How exciting to meet you here like this. Why didn't you just ring the doorbell if you wanted to come in?'

'Shut up, Faith,' said Timothy Happle, rudely. He and Steven Charleston were wearing dark tracksuits and trainers, in Happle's case looking as though they were borrowed from a larger man. He flattened his black hair back into position over his scalp, then sat down on a chair and rubbed his shin. 'I've had enough of your facetiousness, thank you very much.'

'And I've had enough of people breaking into my house, and leaving messages on my answering machine, and writing nasty notes and putting them in my desk drawer,' retorted Kate.

'And don't forget the threat on your computer screen,' added Faith.

'I've no idea what you're talking about,' said Happle. 'And we didn't break in. The door was open.'

'But you didn't knock or ring,' said Faith. 'I think Kate should telephone that nice police sergeant she knows.'

'How did you know about him?'

'Oh, everybody knows.'

'Well, I'm not sure that's a good idea,' said Kate. 'He might come rushing round with a gang of his friends and we'd all have some explaining to do.'

'Well, ring up the *Oxford Times*,' said Faith. 'Ask for the news desk. They're always interested in human interest stories like this one. And they do love tales of sleaze in the university, of course.'

'All right, Faith,' said Timothy Happle. 'We get the message.'

'We were going to ring the bell,' said Charleston. 'If the back door hadn't been open, we would have done.' He looked quite ridiculous in his tracksuit, with his round red face bulging out under his navy blue bobble hat.

'Dressed like that? Just the thing for an evening call!' said Faith.

'What do you want from us? If it's something reasonable, we'll give you what you want and then go quietly, all right?' said Happle.

'I think we should tie them up,' said Harley. 'And gag them, and—'

'No, Harley,' said Kate. 'Let's just settle for hearing what they're doing here and why I've been persecuted ever since I went to work at Bartlemas.'

'Which of you is going to begin?' asked Faith. 'Timothy?'

'What are you doing in my house and what are you looking for?' asked Kate.

'We're looking for Christopher's notebook,' said Happle.

'It should have been on his desk,' said Charleston. 'I looked for it there, but that woman' – he gestured towards Kate – 'interrupted me. He must have taken it away.'

'You must try to be more polite, Steven,' said Faith. 'I'm sure you've already been introduced to Kate Ivory, so you should use her name, like a good boy.'

Charleston looked as though he could happily strangle her, but she just shook her head and then smiled her bright monkey smile at him.

'Did you expect to find this notebook in my kitchen?' asked Kate, who had had enough of Bartlemas politics and power games.

'We expected you to be here alone and watching television,' said Charleston. 'It is, after all, what you said you were going to do this evening.' He seemed irritated that Kate hadn't given him an accurate forecast of her movements.

'And we all know that you have a workroom in the basement looking out on your back garden,' said Happle. 'That's where we expected to find the notebook, if you'd got it.'

'Why not wait until I was out?' asked Kate. 'I'm at college all day. Why didn't you come round then?'

'I tried,' said Charleston. 'A few days ago. I came to look around, see how easy it was to get in. But there was some kid hanging around the place—'

'That was me!' put in Harley.

'It seems to me that it would be interesting to find out what was in this notebook that Timothy and Steven are so keen to discover,' said Faith.

'I think this is our chance to clear up a lot of our

queries,' said Kate. 'Let's come to an agreement, shall we? Dr Happle and Mr Charleston will answer all our questions as fully as they know how, and in return we'll keep quiet about the fact that they turned up at my house, late at night, dressed as burglars, and entered my kitchen without an invitation.'

'You couldn't say that!' said Steven Charleston.

'Oh, yes, I could,' said Kate. 'And I have two witnesses. In fact,' she said, opening a drawer and taking out a camera. 'I shall have photographs to prove it. Have you any idea how foolish you both look at this moment?' Their eyes opened wide as the flash went off. 'Let's just have another one for the front page of the *Gazette*, shall we?' And the flash went off again.

'Very well,' said Timothy Happle. 'We agree. Let's get on with it, and then we can all go home.'

'Did we finish the second bottle of wine, Faith? No? Well, let's offer our guests a glass. No, not you, Harley. You wouldn't like it, anyway. Help yourself to a Coke. Ring Darren and Dossa and tell them that Dave will not be returning there this evening. Then you can go home and leave Dave here. He'll be perfectly safe now that we've caught our burglars. And thanks for your help, by the way.'

After a brief interval during which Harley said his goodbyes to Dave, they all settled themselves round the table and Kate poured the wine. Happle still looked sulky, but Charleston had the air of a man who would tell her everything he knew about any subject in the world if it would prevent his photograph from appearing in a newspaper.

'Now that we've established that it was the two of you who have been creeping round my house by night and day, I want to know what else you've been responsible for,' said Kate.

'I only came here once before,' said Charleston. 'It

was during the daytime, while you were busy with your students.'

'I'm sure Harley mentioned prowlers more than once,' said Kate. 'I'll have to check that with him tomorrow.'

'What about the notes in the correspondence files?' asked Kate. 'The one that said *CURIOSITY KILLED THE KAT.* And the previous one, if it comes to that, the one that was put there for Christopher: *CURIOSITY KILLED THE CAT.*' She spelled the difference for them.

'That was Brian Renfrew,' said Charleston. 'He told me all about it with great enthusiasm. He didn't like you for some reason. Didn't you do some work for the University Libraries' Security Team a year or so ago?'

'Yes, but I don't remember that Brian Renfrew came into it.'

'I believe that you inadvertently stopped some little money-making wheeze of his. Anyway, he put those notes in the drawer. He wanted to scare you off, I think.'

'But why was it stuck to that duff invoice? Sadie grabbed it away from me, so I'm sure it had to do with stealing money.'

'Please don't use that word,' said Charleston. 'I don't believe Renfrew knew what the invoice was. He heard everyone talking about trouble with deliveries from the printer, so he just stuck it in that file because he knew you would soon be looking at it.'

'And did he put the message on my computer screen?'

'I don't think so. Do you know anything about it, Timothy?'

'I think that was Rob Grailing. He and Sadie were involved in syphoning off sections of the Development Fund and were afraid that you had noticed. They didn't want you to know that they were having an affair, either, that's why Sadie always pretended she was keen on

Chris. They wanted to keep you worrying about Chris's death and wondering whether you were in danger yourself. It seems pretty childish now, but they were very pleased with themselves at the time.'

'I was attacked in Birmingham. What about that? And the punting accident? *And* I was half strangled in Leicester College garden. Who the hell did that?'

'Brian consulted us about getting rid of you. You must have really worried him for some reason. Of course he's got it made there in the library. He strolls in and out when he thinks he will. He takes days off when he wants them. His lunch hours are notorious. He wouldn't find another job like that anywhere, so he's very concerned to keep this one.'

'And he talked to you about killing me!'

'Not killing, just getting rid of you. We thought that if we made you look a fool in front of the students often enough we could get you the sack.'

'Thanks a lot. I suppose I should be grateful that you weren't planning to drop me off the top of the Tower of Grace.'

'Didn't you notice Brian at the Birmingham concert?'

'I don't think I knew him at the time. And my attention was on the other members of Bartlemas staff that I'd just seen.'

'He certainly knew you.'

'Yes, everybody seems to.'

'You are quite easy to describe and recognize, Kate,' put in Faith.

'But I don't know anything about an attack in Leicester College garden. What happened?'

'I was watching some Shakespeare play, and when it was over someone tried to strangle me.'

'The play was *Othello*,' said Faith.

'How appropriate,' said Happle.

'What do you know about it?' insisted Kate.

'Not our style. Too crude,' said Happle. 'Really, you weren't important enough to kill, and I have to tell you that we are not violent people. And we had found that if we distracted your attention with something you saw as a clue you would go running off in all directions and miss seeing us at all.'

'So why didn't you leave it at that?'

'Because we had to have the notebook back.'

'And you haven't mentioned the telephone messages.'

'What telephone messages?' Happle and Charleston both looked blank, and Kate had to believe that neither of them was responsible.

'How about you, Faith? Did you leave messages on my answerphone?'

'Of course not!'

'So although you've explained quite a lot, I'm left with threatening phone calls, a possible second prowler around my house, an unpleasant attempt on my life, and the mystery of Chris Townsend's death. I think that his death was connected with the dishonesty at Bartlemas, so you'd better tell me more about it.'

'How much do you know already?' asked Happle.

'Quite a lot,' said Kate. 'In the past couple of weeks I've tripped over the fact that most of the staff of Bartlemas College, at all levels, are on the take.'

'What an unpleasant expression, but I suppose it covers it,' said Happle.

'I also think that Christopher Townsend may have discovered what was going on and been killed because he threatened to talk about it.'

Happle laughed, the first genuine laugh Kate had heard from him. 'Did you meet the man?'

'Briefly.'

'Then you were taken in by him the way most women were, apart from our dear Faith, of course.'

'How do you mean?' She didn't believe him.

Happle had taken on the role of spokesman for both of them, apparently, so he said: 'Chris Townsend was the worst of all of us. He, like you, noticed what was happening at Bartlemas soon after he got here. He said nothing about it, however, until he was ready to do so. Meanwhile, he observed and he took notes. Then he approached us, one at a time, told us what he knew, and informed us that he wanted his percentage. Then he refined some of the schemes, initiated others for us to carry out, and set about putting one or two of his own into effect. We were just amateurs compared to him; he was the professional.'

'Are you sure?'

'He's quite right,' said Faith. 'Chris approached me as well. He couldn't understand that someone might not want to be part of it.'

'So what you are looking for,' said Kate, 'is the note-book where Chris Townsend wrote down the details of all the scams going on in the college.'

'And the sums involved,' said Charleston.

'Well,' said Kate. 'I haven't got it. I've never even seen it. I wouldn't have known of its existence if you hadn't asked me about it.'

'So who has it now?' asked Charleston.

'That is a very interesting question,' said Faith. 'I imagine that you will find the answer to it when you get a phone call with an invitation to a meeting, followed closely by a demand, with menaces, for a percentage of your turnover.'

'Either that or a visit from the police,' said Charleston, gloomily. 'You will destroy those photographs you've just taken, won't you? They won't help us if they appear in the newspapers.'

'Very well,' said Kate. 'Since you've been co-operative I'll tear them up.' Though she privately thought she would keep a single copy for her own collection.

'That's why we wanted the notebook back. We thought Kate here would pass it on to her policeman friend.'

'I think that if some honest citizen had come across it you would have heard about it by now,' said Faith. 'If someone is hanging on to it, it is because they are calculating the best way to profit from it. No, you can expect the phone call and the demand for cash: in a couple of weeks, I should think.'

'Is that it?' asked Happle. 'I believe we've told you everything we know.'

'The thing we still don't know is who killed Chris Townsend, and why,' said Kate. 'I thought it had everything to do with the dishonesty in the college, but now I'm not so sure.'

'Perhaps you should accept the fact that it was an accident,' said Happle.

'Then why did someone tell the press that he was drunk when it happened?'

'Malice, I should think. He was not popular, remember.'

Happle and Charleston got to their feet. They had recovered their usual confidence and were unaware of how ridiculous they looked in their burglars' outfits.

'We'll be on our way, then,' said Charleston.

'I'll be going too,' said Faith.

Kate stood at the door and watched them leave, on foot, towards the centre of Oxford. But who had been telephoning her? Who had attacked her at Leicester College?

And, if it came to that, who had killed Chris Townsend?

Chapter Sixteen

Think'st thou Heaven is such a glorious thing?
I tell thee 'tis not half so fair as thou,
Or any man that breathes on earth.
Christopher Marlowe, *Doctor Faustus*

'The woman was like that, too,' says Zophiel.

'What woman?'

'The first one. You call her Eve. I heard her speaking as she and Adam came through the gate and walked down the hill. He was unwilling to go, kept stopping and looking back at Eden as though he would remember every last detail of it for ever.'

'And Eve?'

'She said to him that it was for the best. It was time to move on. I know what I shall do with my life, but you've got some decisions to make.'

'I thought, though, that early woman was meek and submissive. And silent.'

'That's what the stories say. But the stories were written by men, you must remember.'

'I thought you were male. But you sound as though you sympathize with the woman.'

'Angels may take whichever form they please: male or female. And equally, they may take whichever point of view appeals to them. Fluid is the term that best describes us.'

'But, returning to our gardens, I was going to tell you how it all started to fall apart.'

'What did gardens have to do with it?'
'Everything.'

Briony had become a great friend of Honor Flint's. I don't think she actually liked her – it was difficult to think of anyone being fond of Honor, though I suppose the Master must have been, once. No, what the two of them had in common was a passion for gardens and gardening.

Honor had taken over the planning and supervision of Bartlemas College gardens, and the Fellows' Garden in particular. I don't think that Dave Evans enjoyed her interference, but he was fully occupied in exploiting all the resources of the place in other ways, so I don't suppose he cared. Honor was too much of a snob to believe that anyone like Dave or Barry, his assistant, could be hoodwinking her, so they got away with a lot.

Anyway, Briony was spending a lot of her time at Bartlemas, talking gardens with Honor. They exchanged cuttings, and ideas, I suppose, and visited exhibitions and garden centres and so forth. They also talked.

Do you know the Fellows' Garden at Bartlemas? The most irritating thing about it is the way that several people can be there at the same time, without ever seeing each other. This means that just when you think you are having a private conversation, out on your own, communing only with your companion and with Nature, there may be anything up to ten other people listening in.

And that's what happened to the three of us. I was hailed by Honor as I took a short cut to Pesant Quad. She was hauling me over the coals because it had just come to her notice that Sadie and I were carrying on together, as she put it. Sadie! The unfairness of it! I denied it, of course, but she had times and dates and, apparently, Sadie's own admission on the subject. The cunning girl wanted to hide her own relationship with

Grailing, I suppose, and it amused her to land me in the shit with the Master's wife. I told Honor it was none of her business, and she was not to mention any of it to Briony. She trumpeted that she had no intention of hurting poor dear Briony's feelings by telling her anything of so sordid a tale, but what neither of us realized was that poor dear Briony was just behind some adjacent piece of greenery, listening to our every word.

She was furious. Have you noticed that about people like Briony? They go along for years, apparently sweet and contented, but suddenly they come out with all this stuff that they've been bottling up. She hadn't forgotten a single one of my peccadilloes. Every last one of them was taken out of the closet, looked at, measured and counted. What do you do with a woman like that?

'I've been trying to tell you about this ever since you got here. This is how you came to be a victim.'

'How do you mean?'

'The gradual building up of resentment over the years: Dianne, Mark, Viola, Faith, Briony, and most of the staff at Bartlemas College. Eventually there was bound to be the sudden explosion. I have to tell you that you had it coming.'

'Oh, thank you. Very understanding, very caring, I'm sure.'

'Well, you did ask me. But now, go on with your story.'

'I can't. I can't remember any more. At least, I can get as far as that day, the last day. I went to see Faith at lunchtime. She's a hopeless cook, so I made us both lunch. Something simple, so that we had plenty of time for our mutual enjoyment. No, I know that you don't want to hear about that.

After it was all over, she told me she never wanted to see me again. Or words to that effect. I tried to argue with her, but she was adamant. But you know women, she would have come around in a day or two. It wasn't over. We both knew it. It was just a game she was playing to keep me keen on her. Anyway, I waved her goodbye and walked back to Bartlemas.

From then on I have only fragmented memories. The High Street was crowded with tourists. There were gangs of foreign students, and groups of Japanese, hung about with cameras. Then, by the traffic lights, on the narrow pavement, I saw a woman. She was wearing a vivid blue dress, and shining metallic ear-rings, and her hair was a bright silver-gilt. Someone stepped on her foot and I pretended it was me, just so that I could speak to her.

I saw Brian Renfrew walk past, I remember. And Timothy Happle. But I took no notice of them. I was trying to think up some excuse to see this woman again. Well, I could have taken Faith at her word, couldn't I? It would have been her own fault. Funny, isn't it? If I'd succeeded with the woman in the blue dress I'd still be down there, instead of sitting by this gate talking about gardens to one of God's cherubim.

And then it grows cloudy. I know I saw another couple of people I knew, walking up towards Bartlemas Row. But I can't remember who they were, or even if it was important. But then I saw somebody who hissed at me and told me to follow them. This person was wearing boots, and strode up towards college. I remember anger. This is it, I thought. I'd better go.

Then the tower. I had my back to the parapet. I was arguing. I thought I was winning, but then I was attacked, suddenly and violently. I was pushed back against the stonework. I think it was sheer surprise that made me fall. I just wasn't expecting it, you see.'

'*And that's all that you can remember?*'

'*Yes, at the moment.*'

The heat of this September weather is unnatural and oppressive. It hangs over the city, pressing down on the buildings and the people, till they long for a whisper of breeze to move it on. The months of heat, with scant rain, brought forward the harvest, so that August looked like September. Flowers have bloomed, seeded and died as though in a hurry to spend themselves. The leaves dried on the trees in August, and now that September is here they are turning to yellow and gold, weeks before their usual time.

Still there is no rain. The air is sultry and a storm threatens, but fails to arrive. It is as though the clock has stopped at the moment of Chris Townsend's death, and time is stuck in late August, unable to move on until he has been avenged. The seasons are waiting for a solution. Only when his murderer is found will the storm break and the rain come pounding down. Then the year will be able to move towards winter.

Kate feels that the time of resolution is approaching, nevertheless. Hot drops of rain fall from the sky. Not the storm that they are all hoping for, but single messengers, here with a warning of the battalions to come. The round drops hit the pavement and spread into dark circles, but within minutes have evaporated and disappeared again. People walk the streets holding golf umbrellas, huge canopies of black and white, or emerald green. Sometimes they are raised, as the hot drops fall again, as though their very presence will bring about the rainstorm that everyone is waiting for. They render all the inhabitants anonymous, thinks Kate. Anyone could be hiding under their hemispheres, as they cover hair, face and shoulders.

As she crossed Cornmarket, splashes of water dropped out of the sky from the dun clouds, and again the umbrellas were raised over heads and shoulders.

She walked, herself, with bright head uncovered, wearing a short, sleeveless dress, legs bare in leather sandals. Iridescent ear-rings flashed and glittered from earlobe to shoulder. This is how I looked that Monday afternoon, she thought. This is where I was walking, she thought again as she turned into Market Street. Once more, she stopped at a stall and bought apples, slipping them into the canvas bag she had slung over her shoulder. She felt like an actor taking part in one of those reconstructions they did on television when they wanted to prompt the memories of witnesses. Enough, she thought, and turned towards Golden Cross and the bright, noisy thoroughfare that was Cornmarket.

She was being followed. She could feel it, like a finger touching her spine. She increased her pace, dodging back down Ship Street, turning right. Just as she had come to re-enact the performance of that Monday afternoon, so had the murderer. The difference was that this time it was she who was the intended victim. She looked behind her, but all she could see were umbrellas. But her pursuer was still there, she knew it. She turned right again, then left. She was running through the narrow alleys of the Covered Market.

Perhaps it would be best to stop and confront whoever it was, here, where there were people around who could protect her. But there was a deeper fear than reason that forced her to flee onwards.

She turned right past the butcher's, then a quick left up the next alley. She glanced behind her. Here in the market, under the domed roof, umbrellas had been taken down. She caught a glimpse of a pair of jeans, of conker-brown boots, a head hidden in a big tweed cap. It could be anyone. She went straight past the florist's. She kept on running.

She was back in the High Street and moving towards Magdalen Bridge. She cross the High and she stopped outside the stationery shop, just as she had on that other afternoon, and waited. The display had changed, and she noted the new patterns on the covers, the new pens on their velvet background. She could hear her heart pounding in her chest, and the shallow breaths that she was taking. The other difference from that Monday was that Chris Townsend would not fall over her feet.

'Come on!' a voice hissed in her ear. 'Follow me!'

So she followed the figure in jeans, boots and cap, up the road towards Bartlemas College.

'Where are we going?' she called. There was no reply.

They entered through the lodge, crossed the main quadrangle, they passed through an archway, turned right. In front of them stood the gate into the Fellows' Garden.

'Are you coming?'

Kate followed, through the green corridors of the garden, past the trees with their pendant creepers, and out through the gate at the other end, until they stood in front of the Tower of Grace.

'You don't want me to climb to the top, do you?' asked Kate. 'I really wouldn't want to do that.'

'No. But it's cool inside here. And we'll be sheltered from the storm when it starts. And it's unlikely that anyone else will be here.'

They sat on a bench facing the Temptation scene.

'I thought you'd have a gun and force me to go up to the top of the tower,' said Kate.

'Where on earth would I get a gun from?'

'People in crime novels have guns.'

'You've been taking your seminars too seriously.'

'I always thought that Eve looked just like you,' said Kate. 'The long, waving blonde hair, the small, heart-shaped face, even something about the expression on her face.'

'And you've guessed?'

'I think I've worked most of it out.'

'Aren't you frightened to be here alone with me?'

'You've already said that you haven't a gun. And when you had a chance to strangle me you stopped and ran away. I think you'd been working up to your explosion of rage with Christopher for years. I hardly think you've had time to work up such a head of steam against me in the short time since we've met.'

'He was so surprised,' said Briony. 'He thought he knew me. He thought I would always be the doormat he had taken from my parents and married. All over the years it built up, the little put-downs, the infidelities. Faith Beeton was the final straw.'

'Why Faith, particularly?'

'She was so plain, so ordinary. She wasn't glamorous, or the sort of woman that you could forgive any man for falling for. If it had been Sadie, I might have understood. I really couldn't compete with someone like her. But Faith. *Why her*? I asked myself. I knew I was better looking, more attractive, possibly more fun to be with. Certainly a better cook and housekeeper.'

'You're right there,' said Kate. 'Mind you, anybody would be.'

'I got so tired of the transparent lies. And when I overheard Honor in the Fellows' Garden tearing him off a strip about Sadie, I flipped. I knew about Faith, of course. That woman was too arrogant to try to hide her feelings about Chris. It radiated from her every time I saw them speaking together at one of Honor's little get-togethers. But I couldn't take the fact that Honor thought he was screwing Sadie as well, even though I knew he wasn't. Everyone believes it, I thought. They'll all look at me with pity in their eyes. Poor old Briony! Married to such an attractive man, he has any woman he wants, and she doesn't know how to keep him.'

'Why didn't you just leave him?'

'It would mean leaving my garden.'

'You could have made another one, somewhere else. There are people all over England who would pay you to make beautiful gardens for them.'

'No, you don't understand. That's not what I mean. I couldn't leave it because it was a prison. I couldn't get away from it. The hedges grew higher each year, the plants multiplied and took over my life. I felt as though I had to arm myself with a machete just to go down to Sainsbury's.'

They sat and stared at the picture in front of them: another couple, another garden, another tempter.

'She probably did it on purpose,' said Briony.

'Did what?'

'Took the apple. Well, it gave her knowledge, and the possibility of having children, and the wonderful freedom of leaving that garden behind and getting away from it. That was the real temptation: the pull of the garden. If Eve had spent much more time there, sowing, planting, taking cuttings, pruning, building a greenhouse, laying down a path, she would never have escaped. She had to take the apple and run. It was her passport to real life: pain, love, death. Better than that fantasy they were living before, with God always on the premises, looking over their shoulders, telling them what to think.'

'I thought that's what marriage was supposed to be about,' said Kate. 'Didn't you find it so?'

'I thought it was all going to be so wonderful,' said Briony. 'I had it planned: the house, the garden, the warm, enfolding security blanket of our relationship. I thought that was what Chris wanted. If it comes to that, I thought it was what I wanted, too.'

'Why didn't you get a job?' asked Kate. 'You seem so good at things: haven't you a career of your own?'

'Career?' mused Briony. 'You make me sound so assertive, so ambitious. Two things that I'm not. I suppose I would have got a job, eventually, if I hadn't been able to have children. Husband, house, garden, children. Can't you see them with their blonde heads above the blue of the delphiniums?'

'I can see them picking off the heads of the daffodils, digging for worms in the seedbeds, riding their bicycles through the azalea bushes and demanding a sandpit and swings. All your intricate leafy rooms would have to go to make way for jungle gyms and sand play.'

'I don't think I would have the sort of children who demanded jungle gyms,' said Briony.

'Don't be too sure. It would start with Lego in the flower beds and Power Rangers all over your sitting room floor. Lurid plastic animals in the bathroom. You'd have to put My Little Pony wallpaper in the girls' bedroom; pink frills on their dressing table.'

'I don't believe it. If you bring children up to appreciate good taste then they naturally choose what's best.'

'Oh, *good taste*,' said Kate. 'Bring them up with good taste and they'll yearn for Disneyworld, believe me. Give them books to read and they'll howl for Donkey Kong.'

'Well, what do you know about it? Have you been married, have you had children?'

'Not in person,' said Kate. 'But I'm a keen observer of the human predicament. And have *you* ever been over to Emma Dolby's place?'

'No.'

'Well, try it. It will provide a crash course for you in what the average child can do to a civilized living space in minimal time.'

'And do you know what he saw in her?'

'Sorry?'

'Faith. I expect you wonder what he saw in her.'

'Well, she's quite amusing, if you like that sharp sense of humour.'

'It wasn't that. It was because she'd done it, you see. Like Eve. She had got away. She was born into this inward-looking, claustrophobic family. They told her that she had to be like them, that she had to conform to their view of life. And she did, for a time. But she planned in secret and when she had the chance, the very first chance she had, she took it with both hands. And she was away, out of the cold suburban house with its Old Testament texts and its Boots prints on the wall, off and away to university. It can't have been easy for her, can it?'

'No,' said Kate, who had failed to take the same escape route herself and had never ceased to regret it. 'But I don't see why that makes her so attractive to a man like Christopher.'

'That's why I hate her,' said Briony. 'She took her chances. I didn't take mine. And I can never forgive him for preferring her to me. I gave everything up for him, so why couldn't he love me in return?'

Life, Kate wanted to say, doesn't work that way. But she sat and nodded and looked sympathetic, and looked up at the picture, and at Eve with her sly little face.

'And why did you come after me?' asked Kate.

'Because you were there. Just before I killed him. He was talking to you on the pavement. You were looking at him, and being taken in by him, the way we all were. And I could see that he was thinking of some reason to get your name and phone number so that he could look you up. You must have seen me, too.'

'No, I'm afraid not. I was too busy trying to choose between a Parker and a Sheaffer pen.'

'And a week or so later I saw you at Bartlemas. You didn't see me, but you were walking through the Fellows' Garden with Emma Dolby. And there you were at the memorial service, and at the reception afterwards, wearing the same dress, the same ear-rings.'

'I suppose it would have to be a woman,' mused Kate. 'Men never really notice what you're wearing. Was it you who left messages on my answering machine?'

'Emma wouldn't give me your number and address, but she told me your name and she suggested that I'd find them in the phone book. I just wanted you to go away and stop pestering me.'

'But I didn't pester you. I'd probably have forgotten all about you if you hadn't come to work in the Bursary.'

'I know that now, but that's not the way it seemed at the time. Wherever I turned, there you were. So I tried to scare you off.'

'You nearly succeeded. But I needed the money.'

'I understand that now. I should have come to talk to you before this, but I was in a bit of a state, really.'

'I bet.'

'And I'm sorry about the unpleasantness at the performance of *Othello*. Honor suggested that I might like to go "to take my mind off things". I don't think she realized which play they were putting on. And everything in it seemed to speak to me and make it all worse. When I saw you there, I couldn't bear it. I thought of Chris, just twenty minutes before his death, chatting you up on the pavement, and I wanted to kill you.'

'You nearly succeeded, as I remember it. But you changed your mind at the last moment.'

'Oh, no. I couldn't do it. It wasn't like with Chris, years of frustration and humiliation. I'm sorry, though. I hope I didn't hurt you.'

'It didn't last long.'

'Good. And I'm glad we've had this chance to talk. I wanted to clear things up between us.'

'What are you going to do now?' Kate asked, eventually.

'I'm no good at doing the unexpected, or the courageous, so I shall do the sensible,' said Briony. 'I've made an appointment to see my solicitor this afternoon, and I'll tell him what happened, and what I've done. Then I'll take his advice.'

'You're right. That sounds very sensible.'

'I expect that Honor will stand by me.'

'Very probably.' Kate had an idea that Honor knew only too well what it was to be married to an unreliable man.

They were still sitting, staring at the picture on the wall, when Curtis and Martha joined them.

'Are you all right, Kate?' called Martha.

'Yes, of course.'

'We were worried for you,' said Curtis.

'We saw you walking through Oxford, in that blue dress of yours. No one could miss you, wearing that dress,' said Martha.

'And then we noticed that someone was following you, shadowing you,' said Curtis. 'We couldn't quite see who it was, but Martha said—'

'I said, that looks like the person who attacked Kate in Leicester College garden, the night we watched *Othello*.'

'Why didn't you do something that night? Why didn't you help me?'

'Whoever it was ran off when they saw us approaching, and we chased after them.'

'One of us should have stayed with her,' said Martha.

'I wasn't going to let you go after a mugger on your own,' said Curtis.

'We lost her in Radcliffe Square,' said Martha.

'And when we got back to Leicester, you weren't there.'

'We've been worried about you. Are you all right now?' asked Martha.

'I'm fine,' said Kate.

'This is a friend of yours, is it?' asked Curtis suspiciously, looking at Briony.

'Yes,' said Briony. 'But I have an appointment with my solicitor and I have to leave you now.'

'Yes, well, goodbye, Briony.' Kate watched her as she marched out of the tower door. Should she go with her, make sure she got to her solicitor's office? But then it was too late, she was gone.

'Now, how about coming out for tea with me, Martha and Curtis? I know a very nice place where they have marvellous home-made cakes. Very English. Very traditional. And I should like it to be my treat for you both.'

They went out of the tower door together. The rain was streaming down out of the sky, and somewhere over Headington the thunder was rolling about above the hill.

That evening, when she got home, Kate remembered belatedly that she had invited Andrew round for a meal. She checked her refrigerator. There were still the remains of two different puddings, as well as the less interesting portions of a chicken. She had garlic and oil, and half a dozen different vegetables. She could manage something. She set to work.

There was a knock on the back door. It was Harley.

'Come in,' she said. She had seen him that morning when he had called to collect Dave. He quite understood that she couldn't take a dog to the college with her. Dave was once more at Harley's heels, his pointed nose sniffing appreciatively at Kate's cooking preparations.

'I thought you'd like him to guard you again tonight,' said Harley.

Kate was about to say, 'That's not necessary,' but she thought again and said, 'That's a kind thought, Harley. Have you got something for him to eat? I'm rather low on dog food, I'm afraid.'

Harley's face fell.

'Oh, here you are,' she said, going to her purse and getting out her last remaining fiver. 'Mrs Clack will still be open if you run, and she keeps a few tins of dog food.'

Harley disappeared. Dave stayed, and removed himself to his favourite position underneath the kitchen table.

'You'll have to argue your pecking order with Susannah,' Kate told him. 'And Harley will have to look after you during the day, while I'm still working at Bartlemas. But then I'm only there for another week, so that's not serious.'

She looked out an odd blue bowl from the cupboard. That can be his, she thought. Then, What am I doing? she asked herself. A cat, a dog. Occasionally even an eleven-year-old child. On the other hand, cats were independent creatures, everybody knew, and Trace was bound to fall out with her boyfriend before Christmas, and Dave would be able to go back to Harley's place. And Harley was so ancient in many ways that he hardly counted as a child.

It was, as Faith had suggested, about two weeks later that Timothy Happle, Brian Renfrew, Steven Charleston, Rob Grailing and Sadie James received the telephone calls they had been dreading. In each case, the caller gave approximately the same message, the gist of which was as follows:

'I have come across a most interesting notebook, together with some sheets of paper with various figures printed out on them. These seem to refer to business activities taking place in the college, of which, until now, I had very little knowledge. Would you be kind enough to come and see me to discuss the matter? I would not wish to inhibit your entrepreneurial spirit in any way, you understand, but I do believe it is time that we varied the financial arrangements – in my own favour.'

The Head Porter, Dave Evans and various other members of staff at Bartlemas also received messages from the same caller, but their terms of contract were not varied to quite the same degree, and neither did he think it necessary to see them in person.

Annette Paige and John Clay were also invited to join the syndicate, although they, too, did not find out until later who their employer was.

'Just think of me as the Tax Collector,' he said, fingering the black leather notebook, when they had all gathered in his office. 'You will pay me ten per cent of gross receipts, and in return I will help you to expand your businesses.'

There was a small stir at his words.

'Ten per cent? We used to pay five.'

'But now you are under new management.'

'What sort of expansion had you in mind?' someone asked.

'Dr Happle. Timothy, if I may. I think the college will start a fund which will benefit those who wish to travel to bring in business for the college. Generous expenses will be paid for entertainment of all kinds, if it leads to substantial donations to the college. I know that you have good contacts in Turkey; perhaps you would extend your travels to North Africa: I believe that Morocco and Tunisia might well prove fruitful. So many wealthy families wishing to send their sons to Oxford for first, and even further degrees.'

Timothy Happle could do nothing but nod.

'Mr Renfrew. Brian. I believe that you have profited from Dr Happle's efforts in the past, as has our lovely library. Well, in future you are going to have to initiate your own projects. Please think about financial opportunities and let me have your written proposals by the end of the week. Thank you.'

He looked around. 'Robert Grailing and Sadie James. Very good work so far, I think we can say. But have you been truly imaginative? When you let off our student accommodation during the vacations to tourists, haven't you thought what extra value you could offer them? Theatre tickets, concerts. Membership of certain clubs. Video hire. Even, for those who are spending a lonely holiday in an empty room, *companionship*. I'm sure you could organize something, Sadie. And Robert. Rob. I want something in writing from you to generate at least fifty per cent more income for the unofficial Development Fund during the next year.'

There was a silence while Steven Charleston sat looking at his toecaps.

'Steven. Such a talented accountant. I want you to look through every other scheme, as it is proposed, and make sure that it is watertight. I believe it may be necessary to form one or two more companies in order to transfer money from one part of our enterprise to another without leaving any footprints. Come and see me in eight days' time and we'll go over the preliminary proposals.'

He looked from one to the other, round the semi-circle of faces.

'Good,' he said. 'I think that's everything for today. I'll see you all individually in due course to work out the details of your tax payments to the Collector.' He smiled at his own little joke.

When Timothy Happle and Steve Charleston met a couple of days later in the Fellows' Garden they compared the terms they had been given by the new Collector.

'Even nastier than Chris,' said Charleston.

'He would be. Look what he's been up against all these years.'

'Honor Flint? I suppose you'd have to get tough or disintegrate if you were married to her for long.'

'Yes, and he is the Master, after all.'

One evening towards the end of October, Kate telephoned Paul Taylor.

'Isn't it time I cooked you a meal?' she asked. 'It seems like ages since we saw one another.'

'That fraud case I told you about is about to come to the boil,' he said. 'Can we make it Saturday? It should all be over by then.'

'I'll see you then.'

'Well?' she asked. 'Are you going to tell me about it?'

'About what?'

'You know perfectly well what I'm talking about. Was your fraud case to do with Bartlemas?'

'Let's put it this way: if you get the newspapers tomorrow morning you can read all about it. Shock, horror, scandal, the lot.'

'But was I right?'

'I think the only person in that place who wasn't on the fiddle was your friend Faith Beeton. She'll probably end up as Master, since she's the only one who won't have her name in the papers.'

'I expect most of them will wriggle free.'

'Probably.'

He put the cat down from his knee and went into the kitchen for Dave's lead.

'I'll take the dog round the block while you finish getting the meal ready,' he said.

Kate watched his back disappear through the door, accompanied by a happy Dave. What have I got myself into? she wondered. Am I ready for this degree of domesticity?

'So which one of them did it? Was it my father or Dianne, or Viola, Sadie or Faith? Or even one of the men at Bartlemas?' asked Chris, anxiously.

'What about your wife? Don't you suspect her?'

'You can't tell me that it was Briony. She can't have been the murderer. She would never have pushed me over the parapet. I know that she was a strong girl, what with all that digging and brick-laying, but she just didn't have it in her to be so aggressive.'

'Of course, I never knew the woman,' says Zophiel.

'And she was a lovely little housewife,' says Chris. 'I could ask anyone back to the house, at ten minutes' notice, and know that everything would be sparkling clean.'

'True, but still—'

'Briony was a thoroughly good person. Not very bright, not very ambitious, but still good.'

'I have yet to meet a thoroughly good angel,' says Zophiel. 'Let alone a thoroughly good human being. But tell me, do you really still not remember what happened?'

'It's coming back, in odd flashes, like picking old photographs out of a box. The feeling of disbelief is the last thing I remember, and that is the feeling that remains with me.'

'And are you prepared to believe my theory of the victim yet? Can you see how your behaviour over the years led up to this one, inevitable meeting?'

'I'm damned if I know.'

'No, your problem is that you are damned if you don't. Condemned, if you like, to sit here for the rest of eternity, working out the reason why.'

Christopher sits, gloomily contemplating the view, for the rest of the day.

'How do you suggest we spend the rest of the time?' he asks, eventually.

'I'm afraid it's your problem, not mine. My tour of duty is over. You will have a different cherub on guard soon. I was going to say "tomorrow", but that is a habit I picked up from you that I must now discard. It is time that I remembered that "today" and "tomorrow" are meaningless concepts.'

Some meaningless length of time later Zophiel shakes out his wings, tests they are still working, then flies off over the Garden, disappearing into the shining copper sky. Another cherub takes his place on guard duty, but this one is a surly fellow who doesn't even offer to give his name and whose wings are plain, everyday affairs. He has no interest in victims, or in their psychology.

Christopher Townsend sits on his patch of rock, his head resting on his hands. Sometimes he looks up towards the ornate gates and the lush foliage beyond.

'It can't have been Briony. I don't believe it. Which one of you was it? I try to visualize your face as you came towards me that afternoon, screaming, furious, wanting me dead. Which pair of hands did the pushing? Was it Dianne with her plump white, carefully manicured ones? Or were they Viola's, slightly sticky and smelling of strawberries? Were the fingernails polished? Or did they have soil in thin black crescents under their tips?

'What did I do wrong? If I can't work it out I shall have to stay here, outside this garden, throughout Eternity. Give me a pruning saw, secateurs, even a machete, so that I can fight my way out, please.

'Tell me. I want to understand. What did I do wrong? Why did you have to kill me?'

Now you can buy any of these other books by **Veronica Stallwood** from your bookshop or *direct from her publisher*.

FREE P&P AND UK DELIVERY
(Overseas and Ireland £3.50 per book)

Kate Ivory series

Death and the Oxford Box	£5.99
Oxford Exit	£6.99
Oxford Mourning	£6.99
Oxford Fall	£5.99
Oxford Knot	£6.99
Oxford Blue	£5.99
Oxford Shift	£6.99
Oxford Shadows	£5.99
Oxford Double	£5.99
Oxford Proof	£6.99

Other novels

Deathspell	£5.99
The Rainbow Sign	£5.99

TO ORDER SIMPLY CALL THIS NUMBER

01235 400 414

or visit our website: www.madaboutbooks.com

Prices and availability subject to change without notice.